a haunted half-life at JULES MAES SALOON

Funi Daniels

Sabellapress USA

www.sabellapress.com

Library of Congress Control Number: 2009934290

ISBN: 978-0-9727039-8-7

Chapters of the Half-Life

a haunted half-life at JULES MAES SALOON

Dead Tender

"Fuck!" Colby allowed her frustration to echo across the empty bar. The garbled fan tinged rhythmically pushing dead air around with its semi-circular motion. Rusty hinges bespoke the fan's age, older than Colby yet younger than the bar. The speaker's crackled, having only just finished playing the last songs of the evening: a medley of The Clash. She yelled across the bar as if the bar were a person asking her the price of seven drinks. Did she look like the kind of broad who could do math quickly?

"If god had intended me to do math well, he would have made me Asian." It made perfect sense to her, despite the racist implications. Long stringy black hair hung along her face like a frame that didn't quite fit. She didn't bother washing it often. Though her body told the world she was in fact female; Colby was never very good at doing the things other women prided themselves on, like hair and makeup and shopping for shoes. It made her feel awkward really. Her entire body made her feel awkward. Maybe that's what started her love affair with the booze to begin with, she couldn't be exactly sure. She was a bit too wasted to harbor on her own downfalls right then. Glancing toward the mirror she sat in front of, she took a long look at herself and frowned. Milky white skin that looked more Vampira than Snow White housed her chunky body. She wore a tight shirt; not because she wanted more tips but because that's how all her shirts fit now. At least her boobs were big.

She often wondered why bar businesses put gigantic mirrors in front of the booze. The reason, of course, lay in keeping an eye on what was happening while your back was turned. But Colby found it all rather pathetic. Every bar she'd ever worked at, people used that mirror to primp and prune. The very worst were those patrons who caught sight of themselves like Narcissus and spoke to their own image instead of the bartender or their friends; they'd just stare at themselves while they spoke, captivated by their own beauty. Vanity, it seemed, was the true mark of the modern day drunk.

She threw the register's closing report down on the bar and stood to refill her beer. It was exactly her third time closing the bar and she still struggled with the bookkeeping procedures at the end. She stretched her arms above her head and rolled her giant noggin around imagining the confusing jumble of numbers tumbling out of her ears and onto the floor. Grabbing her empty beer mug, she danced it over to the pile of dirty glassware on the dishwasher. There, she dumped it unceremoniously.

"I'll take care of you later." She winked at the inanimate objects. She giggled when her fuzzy thoughts made the glasses wink back, as if Pixar responded for them. She swirled her whole body around in graceless circles toward the cooler and opened it, still smiling. Sure, she'd never win a dance competition with her clumsy equilibrium; she might never win a spot on the Mathletes to prove her mathematical prowess; hell, she'd probably never even win a spelling bee; but, so what? She had all this. She grabbed a fresh, cold glass and poured herself another beer. The stacks of dirty green money sprinkled the bar like coasters but she averted her eyes and pretended instead to be dancing in the arms of her Prince Charming. This job wouldn't get the best of her tonight.

"If it weren't for the beer, I might have left here long ago," she said to her imaginary Prince and gulped down another swill. The label from the Jack Daniels bottle rustled in the still wind.

"And you!" A broad smile bedazzled her face like 90's pants. A shot sounded like the best idea yet. She didn't need to lift the bottle, it dove into her hands the moment she neared it and knocked itself over to pour a healthy shot. One thing about being an alcoholic that didn't suck was the gracious way the booze danced down Colby's throat. She danced more during heightened moments of booze-soak than any other time she lived. At least she thought she did; in truth, she couldn't actually remember the last time she wasn't even a little bit inebriated. Jack burned her throat as he danced on down; but she forgave him, again.

When she looked up, she noticed a set of eyes staring through the window. She flushed and turned away quickly.

"Why do I always get caught doing weird things?" She muttered to herself. She took another swig of her drink and watched the figure just stand there watching her.

"Creepy." She stated aloud. Snarky sarcasm, usually a redeeming quality in a bartender, lost its luster in the wee hours, especially after her fourth shot. Undeterred, he walked right up to the door. Right then, she realized she forgot to lock it. Colby tried hard to recall her Olympic training. She envisioned herself hurdle the bar and sprinting to the door, thus setting a new world record for "Keeping Scary Dudes Out of the Bar," the Olympic sport of the future. Reality pierced through her fantasy pretty quick. No short, slightly overweight chick in a tight skirt with a bit of a buzz ever won a gold medal. She did not make it to the door before it opened and filled the bar with the stink of a homeless bum. She did; however, pull her groin muscle.

"We're closed," she said, a bit too shrilly. She needed to keep her injury quiet; letting a stinky guy get the upper hand in a situation like this never went well. She eyed the bottle of Jack again, but thought it best to wait for the next shot.

Maintain your cool, she thought. In an attempt to convince her body to stay calm, she took a hold of her mug of beer and stood as casually as possible.

He stared her down and stood like stone. Waves of obscene odor flowed off him each time the rickety fan made its rotation; it was the only indication of life. They stood in silence for a minute; Colby tried to control the beating of her heart as she felt certain it could be seen beating roughly through her skin. The constant creak of the fan only served to further intensify the creepiness of the scene.

"I need your toilet." He broke the silence, snapping to with resolve.

"Can't have it – it's closed, just like the bar." Colby didn't like the guy's resolve. Eager to slam down another shot; she did what she could to shuffle the degenerate out.

"You alone here?" He raised a dirty eyebrow.

The reality of her own vulnerability struck her in the head like a lightning bolt. While experiencing extreme irritation at herself for forgetting the simplest part of the evening's side work, lock the stupid door, she realized she still had a bit of an upper hand. She had the mug of beer. If she needed to, she could just smash the guy in the face with it.

Why did I take a job in such a sketchy neighborhood? She tried to keep dumb thoughts from entering her mind. It seemed an inappropriate time to create an inner dialogue about job dissatisfaction.

"Manager's upstairs. Now get out." She moved to the door and opened it.

"Yer lyin'. I can see it in yer eyes." He laughed at her.

"Get out!!!" She screamed. If she yelled loud enough maybe some of the neighbors might hear her and come to check it out. Though loud noises didn't always work to bring help around; it certainly couldn't hurt to try.

The money on the bar ruffled in the stagnant fan wind and the dirty man caught sight of it. Trouble boiled over in the expression of the stinky man's face. The fear overtook her, making her smell almost as bad as the bum, but she pushed past it and looked the man square in the eye. With such a close proximity to the front door, Colby allowed her hand to rise and grab the handle; she motioned for him to leave again. He just shook his head at her and pulled something out of his pocket. He pointed it right at her.

"If it's all the same to you, I think I'll stay for a spell. Why don't you close that door a' for you catch yer death?" He smiled.

Her heart raced. Adrenaline made everything around her bright and focused, but she didn't know what to do. Should she just run out the door? She didn't know if her legs would actually move, or if they might betray her as they had only moments before when she tried to lock this maniac out the first time. Unconsciously, she took a long drag off the beer in her hand.

"Hey!"

"What? Being held at gunpoint makes a girl thirsty."

"Give me that." He motioned toward her drink.

Somehow Colby managed to keep the words *out of my cold dead hands* from passing her lips; for a moment she allowed herself to muse over how adult she acted just then. Her Mother would have been proud. To distract the robber from her beer, which she decided was in fact worth dying over, she focused her attention on closing the door for real. She pulled on it and found it met with some resistance. She continued to pull with all the strength that her empty hand possessed.

"Why don't you try using both hands?"

"There's a beverage here, man." Bartender and thief exchanged incredulous looks, both wondering at the blatant audacity of the other.

"Let's go, let's go."

"I'm trying. Damn thing's stuck." She grunted, finally swinging the door shut and spilling some beer in the process.

"Why don't you lock it this time?" he scoffed.

She faced the window of the door and made a face at him.

"I can see that, you dumb broad. Just lock the door will ya?" His manner angered.

With both of the robber's eyes full of the gleaming sight of liquor and money, Colby sensed she had little time to get the situation under control. She tried to turn the lock and found it just as stubborn to move as the door had been. After several tries, she couldn't get it to budge.

"What are you - some kind of moron?" He shouted.

"It's stuck." With nothing more than a helpless manner, she went ahead and took another sip of her beer.

"You have a problem." He eyeballed her firm hold on the mug wondering if it were worth the effort to try to take it from her. Already he both admired and hated this ridiculous woman. He tried not to dwell on the fact that if he were a bit more of a responsible man with a job and prospects, he might not just hang out in this joint, but he might just ask this gal out. Party girls knew how to have a good time.

"Hey, listen. I don't need your judgmental vibe here; I get enough of that at home. Besides, you smell." All the pride she felt only moments earlier on her ability to keep her stupid mouth shut disappeared.

He sniffed the air around himself and realizing the drunk tender was actually right, stomped to the door and shoved her aside and turned the lock easily.

"That was hard." He snubbed, scowled and rolled eyeballs. But Colby took no notice. She'd chosen that moment to hone in on her inner warrior; she swung as hard as she could with the mug. Aiming for his head, she only managed to brush his ear instead.

Wasted. She thought to herself with an internal giggle.

The blow to the ear must have hurt a little because he did yelp. She thought back on all those movies where they show the desperate lonely women facing serious situations, but somehow overcoming their attackers and kicking massive ass in the meantime, and wondered why Hollywood would lie like that. In real life, you miss, or trip, or aren't strong enough, no matter how focused you become with the adrenaline rush. She felt her first sense of real disappointment and wanted to ponder on it for a minute, but there was no time really because the bastard shot her.

The strength in her arms ebbed away and she watched her delicious beer fall to the ground and shatter, spraying her with hoppy goodness which mingled with the drip of her own blood.

"Fuck," she said for about the hundredth time that night.

She fell to the ground clutching the wound. Energy drained from her body like the floor housed an oil pan. Her head felt light. She looked in disbelief at the blood pumping through her hands and her only thought was: *Crap! I don't want to mop this mess up!* Stink breath hurried around the bar, stuffing money and bottles of booze into his pockets.

"You ass!" Colby shouted; anger didn't begin to express the intensity of her irritation.

"You still alive?" A quick turn and fascinated stare confirmed his question, but it didn't stop him from continuing to stuff his pockets.

She formulated a plan. He'd have to step over her to exit the building, so she would preserve her energy as best she could and make one last attempt to stop this idiot before he left. She spent her few moments of reprieve convincing herself how easy it could be. She tested her strength by attempting to lift her arm. It moved; almost a whole inch in fact. Not allowing any negativity to cloud her judgment; she did something she hadn't done in years. She prayed. The prayer was clumsy and though she couldn't recall the actual words to the Hail Mary; she was pretty sure it included something about kicking the crap out of bad guys. She couldn't have been too far off the mark because that's when the miracle happened. Just as the bum made his way past Colby, she felt light and free.

"HAH!!! Gotcha!!!!" She jumped up with an amazing display of super human strength and grabbed the guy. Finally the adrenaline worked in her favor, just as all those cop shows told her it would; but it wasn't enough. Somehow he slipped right by and out the door into the night.

"Whoo Whew!! That was great!" An older man dressed like a cowboy came out of no where to give his opinion.

"AAAAHHHHHHHHHHHHHHHH!!!!" She screamed so loud that the noise drove the man across the room.

"Jeez little lady, you got a heck of a set of pipes on ya there." He peeked around the corner, checking to see if the coast was clear.

"How did you get in here?"

"That ain't the right question. The question is: how do I get out?"

"Well the door's right there, but a hell of a lot of good that information did me tonight. Are you gonna shoot me too?"

"Nah, I ain't had no bullets since aught 8."

"Duh, this is aught 8." She rolled her eyes. Old people can be so infuriating.

"I suppose that guy was a friend of yours?" Colby mumbled.

"Nah, that dead beat ain't someone we'd associate with, I'll tell ya that much. You know we tried to help ya, but you didn't pay no mind."

Colby looked around to confirm what she already knew: the bar was empty.

"Who is this 'we' you're referring to?"

"The other's like me." The old guy's cowboy hat slipped down his head when he nodded in agreement with himself. He gestured around the bar as if it were full of people. Colby's patience wore thin.

"Listen weirdo, I don't know what you're talking about, but you better get out of here before I fucking lose it."

"You sure do cuss a lot."

"And you don't seem to understand what it means to take a hint."

"Now what's that mean?" He came a little closer. She looked him up and down. He looked a lot better than the smelly guy. His clothes looked strange, but in Georgetown, anything unusual wasn't so out of place. People liked to paint themselves with astral signs and ride reconstructed bikes naked down the street at three in the morning. Progressively frightening behavior ruled the town.

"It means go away. Saddle up and get on out." She pointed to the door.

"Now that's just cruel. I sure do miss my horse."

She laughed at him. "Are you for real?"

"Well, I guess that depends on what you think real is."

"Patience... wearing thin." A deep sigh exhaled from the depths of Colby's chest.

"I'll tell ya what, little filly, the next time ya have trouble closin' a door; jest run on out of it instead of spending time wrestling' with it with a mad man pointing a gun right at ya."

"Were you on the other side of the door or something? I didn't see you."

"Boy howdy, you're thick-headed." The cowboy whooped.

"What are you from? A farm or something... just in town for the cattle show?" she joked.

"Well I'll tell ya, it's an interesting story after all..." He lumbered down then and she could tell that he was a man who liked to stitch a tall tale.

His manner soothed Colby and she instantly liked him. If he'd come in during business hours, she might have not only listened to him but maybe even retained some of the information. Since her day already took on a pretty heavy tone with the robbery and the shooting, she had no desire to elongate it further. She raised a hand to silence the man.

In so doing, something caught her eye in front of the door. It looked oddly familiar. Silence nestled the room like a baby might nestle its Momma's booby. Colby recalled silences in the past that lasted a while, but never one that literally stung her insides. She fluttered. The old man followed her gaze and felt a flutter also.

"It's weird ain't it?" He spoke first, breaking the enduring silence.

"What is it?" Her voice caught in her throat because she knew what it was, but boy, she didn't want to face it right then. She looked around waiting for the guys with the cameras and the studio audience to come and tell her it was all a big joke. Where was Ashton Kutcher when you needed him?

"That there is a dead body. It's funny how you can tell they're dead 'cause they look so dead."

"Whose dead body is that?"

"Well, it's you, ain't it?"

"But how?"

"You dumb or something? The man just shot you."

"I know what happened!" Her anger surfaced hot and fast. "I mean, why doesn't it feel like I'm dead, or whatever? Isn't there supposed to be some kind of light or pain or something?"

"More likely the fire and brimstone'd be comin' fer you, little lady."

"Now Tex, that's rude." A soft voice sounded from the back room. A gorgeous buxom blonde emerged through the doorway. "And besides he said the same thing about me when I first died into this God forsaken family."

"You're the one that was forsaken by God, you Jezebel."

"Well, all those satisfied customers couldn't have been wrong. I'd say the Lord did not forsake me but left me with a glorious gift." She smiled and shook her breasts in a suggestive manner, they threatened to pop out with the strain against the bustier that barely contained them. The corset, spun from thick red satin, pulled her waist to alarming slimness and the bustle attached to the back of her gown made her hourglass shape almost irresistible. The girl watched the old man turn bright red at her comments, and though he spent a great deal of time staring at the voluptuous upper half of her gown, it did not deter him from his ranting.

Colby felt oddly aroused. Knowing herself well enough to understand her intense fascination with the opposite sex didn't stop her from gazing with the same intensity at the beautiful woman. Something inside Colby told her that this woman had the gift to convince anyone of anything at anytime if she were so inclined. Alluring didn't express it; but whatever it was, Colby wanted to learn the secret.

"You dare talk about the Lord, our Father like that." The old man got his cockles up and the lady just laughed at him.

"You're a walking, talking, hypocritical, lily-livered ass," she said as delicately as her crass nature allowed. She turned her attention to Colby. "Now my dear, how do you do? My name is Matilda and I am ever so pleased to meet you."

"Hey, I'm Colby."

"That there is Cowboy Sourpuss." She stuck her tongue out at him and he scowled back.

"It's Jerry, thanks very much."

"Sorry Cowboy Sourpuss – I mean Jerry." She winked at Colby and suppressed a giggle. The woman made Coby giggle.

"This is tiny Tommy." Matilda continued, undeterred by her obvious effect upon Colby. A tiny head popped up out of the floor and smiled shyly at her. He disappeared just as quickly. "He's a bit shy - also the youngest person ever to be murdered at Jules Maes in its history."

"Who would murder a little boy?"

"It was his Mamma; it's kind of a touchy subject," she said softly.

"Oh," Colby replied, mostly because she couldn't think of anything better. She tore her eyes away from the beautiful vixen and scanned the room, really seeing all that had occurred over the past hour. Reality set in suddenly: she was dead. A real fear passed through her and she began hyperventilating.

"Ya alright?" Cowboy Jerry asked.

"No! I'm dead. I'm pretty far from alright," she declared in between gasps for air. Tiny Tommy poked his head back up through the floor to watch the show. He'd never seen a dead person have a panic attack before. Colby waved her hands in front of her face to try and find her breath, but it didn't come.

"How is it that she's not breathing? She is dead, right?" Matilda whispered to Cowboy Jerry as Colby's breath became more ragged.

"Yep."

The three ghosts could do little else but stand by and watch. Colby labored, wheezed and finally when she could take no more of the self-aggrandized anguish; passed out.

"Well, I'll be. I ain't never seen that before," Cowboy Jerry removed his hat and scratched his balding head in confusion.

Matilda, Tiny Tommy and Cowboy Jerry edged closer to the fallen ghost without a clue as to what to do for her. She'd fallen precariously close to her own body. Seeing two versions of the same person lying unconscious beside each other felt spooky - even for a ghost. Without warning, Colby sat up and looked at the three.

"That was kind of pointless." She looked at her dead self with contempt.

"Um hm." Cowboy Jerry agreed.

"Feel better?" Matilda gently prodded. She hadn't a clue of what to make of the strange girl at that moment.

Colby looked at the woman and shook her head to indicate a no. She wound up her hand and smacked herself as hard as she could in the face. Ghostly contact occurred, yet no pain followed. Tiny Tommy burst out laughing. But Colby saw no humor in the situation, which was unusual since she enjoyed laughing at the expense of others. A thought crossed her mind.

"Not to change the subject or anything, but shouldn't we call someone and tell them what's happened here?"

"And just who exactly are you gonna call?" Cowboy Jerry hooted.

"I don't know, maybe the cops or something." Colby frowned, wondering why everything she said sounded so ridiculous to these people.

"Sure you go ahead and call yer cops, I'm sure they'll come right to the rescue." He made a gesture to Matilda to demonstrate Colby's obvious lack of sanity.

"Come on now CJ, she's new, she doesn't understand the rules yet."

"Rules? What do you mean rules? I thought you said I was dead?"

"Jest cause yer dead don't mean you ain't gotta keep followin' the rules."

“This is fucked.” Colby turned back to the bar and tried to grab a bottle of whiskey from the shelf, a shot sounded like a great idea. The stone cold sobriety of death consumed her; she needed to purge it out like a preacher would a demon. To her utter disappointment, her hand passed right through the bottle. She tried several times with the same effect. Then she drew her whole arm down the shelf trying to knock down every single bottle and still nothing happened. If her tear ducts worked, she’d be soaked with her own salty discharge. Her terror over the thought of never having a drink again felt quite agonizing not only to her but to everyone in the room. And the demon-like scream that followed might have shaken the windows and doors of the bar if they too operated on the same alternate plane of existence that she now did.

“This ones gonna take some time to adjust.” Cowboy Jerry whispered to Matilda momentarily forgetting his sincere dislike for the slutty woman.

They watched as Colby stuck her mouth on the beer taps and tried to suck out any beer residue that might be clinging to the tips. She did the same thing to the Jagermeister machine and even tried to lick the bar top. After countless attempts with the same result, she stopped, but she’d backed herself against a whiskey bottle so that her chest looked like a shelving unit for it.

“What in tar nation are you doing?” The Cowboy inquired.

“Maybe if I stand here long enough some of it will permeate into my dead soul.” Colby never felt such defeat in life. Death sucked. She felt a strange desire to write bad poetry.

“Well that’s one I ain’t never heard afore.”

Colby stopped listening to her new friend’s deathlike banter and lost herself in the creative process momentarily. She came forward with this gem:

Roses are red
Violets are blue,
Death without Jack Daniels
Is really hard to handle - es

"That's really bad." Tiny Tommy shook his head.

"How can you stand it? All this booze and you can't have a swallow?"

Colby turned to Tiny Tommy first with a quizzical expression, then thought better of directing her question toward the boy. With equally imploring eyes, she turned her attention to Cowboy Jerry and Matilda.

"Booze? Hell that's the least of yer problems," CJ chuckled.

An inconsolable Colby rocked back and forth over the whiskey bottle. This new world offered only images of horror. Colby was a drinker. She knew this about herself. Others knew this about her. One of the local bars dubbed her "Whiskey Tits" because of her sincere love of the spirit. She couldn't just stop being that drunk because of a little thing like Death.

"Let's let her be for a while." Matilda said.

Her companions disappeared and left Colby alone crying wet-less tears into a shelf of liquor with only her own dead body for company.

Discovery of Dead Tender

It took until dawn for someone to discover her body, though the outside light still blazed brightly illuminating her bloody form for anyone to see. The bum left the door ajar when he exited and the stink of her body began to permeate the surrounding air. But in industrial Georgetown, many smells go unnoticed by most everyone, except the stray dogs. One dog in particular sought the scent out as if Sherlock Holmes set him to the task. Once the little guy found the body, he sniffed curiously and with no ill intention began to lap at the puddle around Colby. When Colby saw this horrendous display of real animal behavior, she freaked. She rushed the dog and tried desperately to shoo him away; but her hands passed through him as it had earlier along the bar.

"Your name must be Jack," She stated flatly.

Normally a dog, sensing the presence of something other worldly high tailed it out, but the feast proved too tasty to give up. He looked right at Colby and gave her a smile in thanks for the meal.

"Jerk," she replied knowingly.

Bam. Crash. Smash. Boom. A loud clatter brought the dog back to his senses and he fled. Spying through the front windows of the bar; Colby saw a guy pick himself up from on top of the trash can he spilled over. The sound of loud drunken laughter filtered down Airport Way, followed by a trash can lid that continued to meander down the street long after it should have stopped. The drunk wasn't so lucky. He stumbled his way down the street using buildings for leverage. As he closed the gap between himself and Jules Maes, Colby recognized the man: Dookie, the most famous of the Georgetown drunks. The tiny strip of Airport Way kept only six bars afloat with business and Dookie had been kicked out of every one, at least once. He rode around Georgetown as part of the Dead Babies Bike Club, a strange sort of entity that reconstructs bicycles into virtual kinetic art pieces. Some of the bikes got built up as high as three bikes, stacked and welded and somehow maneuverable. They race around Seattle sometimes impressing people with their drunken feats of balance. Grubby, dirty, and seedy might describe any one of the members of the club, but they were all interesting and fun nonetheless. Dookie displayed some of the less desirable traits on a regular basis.

"Oh shit man!" His voice bellowed in the doorway when he reached its precipice. He continued to laugh.

"You're more wasted than me, that's for sure." A puddle of spittle decorated the sides of Dookie's mouth. It was the sort of display that made you turn away and gag. Had Colby a napkin; she might have handed it to Dookie, that is if she weren't dead right then and being laughed at by a drunk. He continued his hysterical abuse for another moment or so until he took that final step forward and slid in the sticky pool of blood only recently abandoned by her dog friend.

"Hey!" He slowly began to ascertain the non-hilarity of the scene before him. Dookie crouched as close as he dared to Colby's body. "Are you alive?"

He covered his nose with his hands when he got a good whiff of her. That was rich; this guy with his dreaded hair and filthy clothing thought she smelled. Wonders continued to never cease despite death and its horrid lack of booze.

"Nope, definitely not. Fuck." He got up quickly and turned to run, but something stopped him. He scanned the scene for another moment in contemplation. Colby could almost see his mind working - little wisps of steam blew in streams out his ear. He wanted to take something too. It was as obvious as the lack of booze in her hand.

"Do it, you jerk." Colby dared him.

Nervous hands fluttered in deep contemplation. Eyeballs strained in the lamplight to find a label he wanted. Cigarettes, booze and beer beckoned him with the friendly salutation of free. But first, he needed to pass the threshold of the sticky puddle. Back and forth glances from body to booze set his mind in motion and he turned, reluctantly, and stumbled down the street to find help.

A surprised Colby hovered by her body and waited for the reinforcements to come. Jack, the dog, reappeared with friends. Apparently the little guy decided to throw a party in Colby's honor. She'd never been the guest of honor before. She thought she might have enjoyed it more if the guests weren't intent on devouring her.

Within a half hour and before the dogs could do too much damage, the streets filled with Georgetown folk. Dookie spread the news like wildfire. People didn't hesitate to show up to the scene with their cameras and sketchbooks in tow. Originally, Georgetown housed brewery workers. Cheap rent and dilapidated old buildings insured the arrival of artists and years later, they still occupied the town. The Yuppie infiltration still needed at least another decade to fully gestate before they could bend their minds around living so close to the noise and pollution of a train yard, an airport and a major highway. The artists barely clung to their community, but clung they did. Every incident provided aesthetic ideas and something as desperate as murderous death offered an inspirational fodder that one might not find again in a lifetime. Colby knew what it was to be a personality in Hollywood, then, with the Paparazzi hot for the picture of a lifetime.

The police finally arrived. Colby never felt such happiness over seeing a cop before. Her love affair with the law ended abruptly three years prior due to an unfortunate DUI incident. Oddly, that was also the same day her affair with Jameson took a turn for the worst. Now she just drank Jack Daniels, or did anyway. She frowned at the thought of her throat's current inability to swallow.

The cops shooed the artists away and Colby felt a wave of relief, in so much as a dead person could feel a wave, which, as it happened, wasn't much. But no one left the scene, they all hovered around the doorway, watching and waiting. The police line tape deterred the locals from tainting the scene any further. The Coroner busied himself with removing all the flowers one of the more colorful Georgetown hippies sprinkled over the body.

"I was there when that beautiful girl was murdered," Colby imagined her saying.

"How could anyone want to harm such a lovely girl?" She reminisced further.

"She was an angel and perfect in every way." She moved herself with the fake sentiment. If only people actually thought about her that way, the fantasy might be easier for her to swallow. As it was, the bile she created over the lie proved quite distasteful.

"That's it," she mused aloud, though no one heard her. "I'll never be able to change my image. I'm always just going to be that kind of annoying girl with a drinking problem murdered by the stinky guy." Would anyone even miss her? She had friends and family but she'd done a good job of alienating them over the years. Suddenly that "list of things to do and people to reacquaint with" became very important to her - so did the phrase "too little, too late."

"Feelin' better yet?" The old Cowboy's head floated up from the floorboard in front of her.

"Don't know." She looked down at the bottle of Jack that still hovered in her mid-section.

"Is that working?" He pointed to the booze.

"Not really."

"Well... yeah, I didn't think it would."

Red roses bleed,
Blue violets stink
man I could really use a damned drink.

She gave him a look of plain irritation. It quieted him. The bar buzzed with activity. Cop cars surrounded the place and the constant flicker of blue and red lights made the joint look like some kind of techno bar. Colby's body now laid on a gurney inside the building. After what seemed to be thousands of pictures and investigative probing, they loaded her inside the coroner's black body bag with the same grace a butcher might bag up a side of beef. The scene took on the look of a real crime scene; like *CSI* or something, but with less attractive cops. She saw the investigators dusting for prints and doing all the things they were supposed to, according to Hollywood, but she suspected it might all be a waste of time and her dirty assailant would never be brought to justice.

"Sorry sir, this is a crime scene, you can't come in here," Colby overheard one of the cops say in a most official manner.

"This is my bar," the voice replied. John, the Bossman, walked in like he owned the place, which he did. Another wave of relief washed over her - this one she almost felt. Finally someone came in to do something more than ogle her bloody body.

"What happened?" He asked.

"Well, it looks like someone came in and shot her." She watched him flush, a look of panic crossed his face.

"Can you ID the body?" The coroner asked.

"Sure." John said. She couldn't recall ever seeing her boss so serious. Usually he maintained a jovial attitude around all things. It occurred to Colby that she'd never really socialized with her favorite Bossman, least ways not enough to really understand his character and she regretted it.

Bossman and Cop walked over to the gurney. The coroner unzipped the bag, but before he could pull it away from Colby's face, John stopped him. A sudden compulsion brought Colby over to the spot with the three men. She needed to see herself.

"You could just show me her boobs if you want," John told the Coroner.

"Excuse me?" The Coroner looked appalled at the suggestion.

"Yeah, excuse me?" Colby responded as well, though no one heard her.

"You know, I mean, if her face is all gross and... um... dead, like. You don't have to show me that, just the boobs will do." John stammered out, his nerves caught up with him pretty quick, so he didn't realize the sleaziness of his request.

"WHAT A PIG." Annunciating each word, Colby got right in his face and said it. She didn't care if it took on a sickly green pallor.

"And you'll be able to identify her by her... breasts?" The Coroner, a ten year veteran to the job, immediately formed a memory of the interaction. In all his years, no one ever asked to ID a body by their breasts. He couldn't wait to share the story back at the morgue.

"Yeah." John lowered his gaze, suddenly embarrassed by his admonition.

"I had no idea that you were such a sleazy, disgusting, putrescent, despicable..." Colby wondered if the veins on her forehead still popped out when she screamed angrily in death. "Honestly," the rant continued, "one time you get wasted and show your boobs at a busy intersection and you're labeled for life!"

"You did what?" CJ asked.

"Slut! That's what they're thinking I am."

"I'm not one to judge." Matilda smiled.

"She has a tattoo on her left boob. I don't have to see the whole thing; it's just a chick riding a hotdog. I think you can see it without removing any clothing. People comment on it all the time," John explained further.

"Oh." The Coroner's expression flickered. The new Morgue story lost some of its luster.

"Oh." Colby gave a nervous laugh. She didn't mean those things she said.

"Well, you'll be pleased to know that she was shot in the stomach, so her face is intact. But if you prefer to ID her with the tattoo, I can certainly do that as well. She is much bloodier the further down you go, though."

John's queasy face returned. "Face is fine." A distinctive odor wafted up through the unzipped section of the bag. Quick and painless, like a band aid, John hoped.

The coroner moved the bag from Colby's face.

"I don't look so bad," she said.

"You look dead to me," Cowboy Jerry said.

"I don't know, I think that dead looks okay on me," she mused.

"Nobody looks good dead."

"What about those Goth kids?"

"What's a Goth kid?"

"Come on, you've seen them in here; the ones that keep themselves really pale."

"Well heck, that's everyone in Seattle. People out here are downright translucent at times." Cowboy Jerry laughed.

"They dress in black a lot."

"Oh, you mean them kids hanging out in the back music room? That is if you can call that racket they make music."

"No. Those are bands."

"Seems to me that's everyone else in Seattle," Matilda offered.

Colby took a moment to figure out her dilemma. How do you explain a Goth to a cowboy? She settled on: "Big shoes: giant colorful hair with lots of makeup."

Without missing a beat, Cowboy Jerry stared at Matilda and just sort of pointed. He opened his mouth to say something but Matilda hushed him up pretty quick.

"NO!" She shouted and disappeared.

"This is hard. Um, I don't know... they look like Vampires. Do you even know what a vampire is?" She cocked her head to the side like a dog might in a state of confusion.

"You mean them vampire worshipers?"

Colby laughed at the old guy.

"Yeah, them."

"Ain't nobody look good dead, even if it's on purpose?"

"How long have you been dead, Cowboy Jerry?" She took a good look at him then.

"I told you, since aught 8."

"Do you mean 1908?" The truth dawned on Colby just then; after taking a long survey at the style of Cowboy Jerry's clothing.

"Yep... what else would I mean?"

"Well you do know that it's now 2008, don't ya?" She didn't mean to sound insensitive. He looked dumbstruck.

"Naw, you're just joking with me." He laughed, then, an unbelievable chuckle.

"Look at that." Colby pointed to a poster on the wall, an advertisement for one of the bands that was coming to play the next evening in the music hall. The date said March 15, 2008.

"Sure is a pretty picture," he said, though he wasn't too sure what he was looking at. He pointed to another poster and said, "I like the one with the horse on it."

"Yeah, yeah, the pictures are nice but look at the date on it."

"What date? Where?" Confusion clouded his expression. The only time things came fast for the old guy was while he rode his horse.

"Right there." She pointed as sarcastically as her finger could muster, which wasn't very much as it turned out.

He shook his head and took off his hat so that he might run his fingers through his hair. If he were this confused over a date, she wondered what he might think of say a Rubic's Cube.

"I don't know what yer yappin' about." He looked away.

"It's right there," Colby insisted. "Read that, right there."

"Aw, hell." The old Cowboy disappeared.

"What's his problem?" Colby rolled her eyes toward the old guy's faded image. A few sparkles told her where he stood only moments before.

"He can't read," a deep male voice came from way atop the bar.

The actual bar, original to the first proprietor of the Jules Maes Saloon, came direct from France where it was hand-carved. Sturdy and beautiful, a customer couldn't help but recognize the craftsmanship. The only question Colby answered more often than, 'is this the original bar?' was: 'is this place haunted?' She decided not to dwell too heavily on that thought, since having bent almost in half to spy the face behind the voice; she now had something much more attractive to dwell on. The bar ran almost the full length of the restaurant with two intricately carved pillars to cap the ends. Mirrors filled in the middle helping the bar to appear almost twice as big, which really wasn't necessary since it did that on its own. The mirrors, pristine in their hay day, now displayed event posters and mandatory liquor licenses. The posters changed from week to week; however, one poster always remained up: Johnny Cash flipping off the world. It spoke of the general philosophy behind the bar.

A long shelf ran the length of the bar above. The new intensely attractive stranger lounged upon it like a Greek god, casually surveying the scene below. Colby found herself grinning like a child staring at a gigantic lollipop. She didn't think she'd ever seen anyone as attractive as that man. Shaved head, dark green eyes, an athletic body posed with heated sensuality in her general direction. Death suddenly gave itself a bit of a spit shine makeover and it didn't suck.

"I'm sorry, what did you say?" She sort of forgot the topic.

"Cowboy Jerry, he can't read."

"Well, that's dumb."

"That's one way to put it. Do you also like to refer to the Special Ed kids as retards?"

"I just mean, well, why didn't he learn? He's been hanging around this place for a hundred years, seems like you could learn a skill or something." Was she talking out loud? She hoped she wasn't.

"He's nothing but stubborn, as you may have guessed."

"I'm Colby." She gave the "few fingers" wave. Cowboy who?

"Bryce."

Silence stopped their conversation for a while. Colby wanted to hover up around him and talk some more. She felt silly shouting up flirtations, besides she knew how to play coy. Her current "single" status bespoke the truth on that count, but Colby showed great skills in completely disregarding the obvious, especially in her own life. Maybe she would have better luck in the spirit world.

"Geez," she whispered. The irony of the situation didn't escape her. She knew that in the 12 hours since her untimely death, she spent more time trying to live than she had during her 30 years of actual living time. Sadly, none of that understanding changed the fact that she felt quite desperate for some boink time with the hovering hotty above her.

"You know what's funny..." she gazed back up toward Bryce when she felt a little more under control of her voice. "Okay, never mind."

Bryce had disappeared, leaving her alone in a room full of people. A fleeting wonder survived momentarily in her thoughts: why did all the men in her death keep disappearing?

Colby turned her attention back to John. The subtle greenish hue had taken on a much more impressive color since last she noticed. His enormous deep breaths did little to help control his current skin pigmentation. Vomit seemed imminent as he couldn't quite purge the stench of bloody death from his nostrils. Every action of John, the Bossman, usually made her laugh, from the sway of his bushy beard and curly locks to his hilarious dance to his secret favorite music, the Indigo Girls. She always thought him to be a real-life Hagrid, from *Harry Potter*. She wanted to find him coaxing the spitfire out of a three headed dog, but had as yet to catch him performing any wizardry. Unless one counted his currently amazing ability to keep from hurling vomit all over the bar, despite the raunchy smell of dead flesh.

"It looks like she bled out pretty quick. I doubt there was a lot of pain," the coroner said. "She probably just kind of died."

"I guess that's comforting," John responded. His girlfriend, Vanessa, wanted to drive down with him to the scene after he got the call, but he'd convinced her not to. Now he wished she were there, being alone and identifying the dead body of your employee kind of sucked ass.

"So we guess that this was a robbery." One of the detective's came over to John with a small notepad and pen. "You're the owner right?"

"Yep." John said, happy to be concentrating on something else.

"Detective Oddball." The man presented a hand for the shake ritual. John, the Bossman, completely distracted by the detective's name, grasped the hand poorly like a 10 year old with leprosy.

"I'm sorry, Detective what?"

"Oddball, sir."

"Huh? Well, that's strange or rather - odd." John, the Bossman, actually cracked a smile. Finally, an ice breaker presented itself in the middle of all the chaos.

"Yes sir, it is. Now if you don't mind, I'd like to talk about the murder of your employee." Detective Oddball looked as though he wished to crack John the Bossman over the head with his billy club.

"Uh, yeah... right."

"What time does this place close?"

"2am."

Oddball perused the bar with sharp eyes. There wasn't a single thing about him that wasn't sharp from his high and tight hair down to his extraordinarily polished shoes. Everything was sharp like a tack, a pair of scissors, or an abrupt insult from a small Asian woman.

"Looks like a busy night." He directed his comment to the dirty glassware littering the bar.

"Colby wasn't exactly a clean bartender. It's possible it wasn't that busy." A sort of Bossman disappointment poured subtly from John's mouth.

"Hey," Colby muttered whilst hanging on every word. Now the truth came out.

"How do you mean sir?"

"Well, these glasses could just as easily been from the early rush as the late night crowd." An air of irritation rose in John's manner; an eye fluff that caused Oddball to narrow his own eyes to detective-like slits and ask that question that makes everyone act guilty.

"And where were you this evening sir?"

"Me?"

"Yes sir."

"Just a quiet night at home, Officer."

"Detective."

"Oddball."

"Right."

The two locked eyes for a minute, each attempting to understand the other's intent.

"Was anyone with you this evening?"

"Wait, you don't think that I...?"

"Is there someone who can verify your story, sir?"

"Ha ha ha ha..." Colby laughed.

"I...I... I didn't kill Whiskey."

"Whiskey? Who's Whiskey?" The detective perked up to the idea of a double homicide.

"Whiskey Tits - that's Colby. Her nickname - "

"Huh? Who the hell called me Whiskey Tits?" Her face screwed up into an inhuman expression.

"Your bartender's nickname was Whiskey Tits?"

A simple nod was John the Bossman's only response.

"How do you get a nickname like that and no one even tells you?" Colby took a quick look down her shirt, decided the nickname was great and promptly gave the boss a high five; though it really wound up being more of a middle five since Bossman had his hands more to the side.

"Sir, is there someone who can verify your whereabouts?" Detective Oddball didn't really believe this big hairy man to be the perpetrator, but he knew the man standing before him lied about something. He felt it in his demeanor.

"My girlfriend was with me the whole time." John silently thanked the great spirit of the eternal beyond for two things: his wonderful girlfriend for being by his side throughout the entire evening and technology for not quite creating the machine that turns thoughts into images for the cops to see and betray his real evening festivities. Far from legal, though not going as far as murder; John the Bossman immediately set his mind to remember the evening in a different manner as one that involved sewing and charity work... just in case. If anyone possessed the technology, it'd be this detective.

The answer satisfied the detective and he changed the subject.

"Judging from the empty till, we'd say she was probably counting money and the guy got into the bar somehow and robbed her. Can you tell us if anything else is missing? Maybe roughly how much money we might be looking for?"

"Sure." He looked around the bar and noticed a few empty spots where booze once occupied.

"There is a Jameson's bottle missing and a Captain Morgan... um... Bailey's and let's see... oh, yeah, a Maker's Mark." John looked through the cooler quickly and checked the stock below the bar.

"Anything else?" The detective asked.

"I can tell you that this guy is kind of stupid," John stated.

"Why would you say that?" The detective raised his eyebrow.

"Well, he didn't take any of the full bottles, just the ones on the rail - no caps to close them with."

"Interesting." The detective turned to the uniformed cop in the door way and motioned him over.

"I want you to take some men and look around the alley ways for some of those things." He pointed to the bottles.

"Bottles of booze?" he asked.

"No the things on top of the bottles, what are they called?" He turned to John with the question.

"Pour spouts... here..." John pulled open a drawer and handed them over to the officer.

"If you find any, don't touch them with bare hands - we'll need to print them. Grab some gloves and get to work." He dismissed the guy easily.

"What about the cash?" The detective turned back to John.

"Let's see." John took the long abandoned register tape and perused it briefly.

"Looks like she had a pretty good night... about five hundred in cash, six in credit cards receipts, hundred in credit card tips plus the four hundred we start our banks with... I'd say almost a thousand in cash." John shook his head at the loss of revenue, momentarily forgetting his dead employee. The expensive new kitchen gleamed a wink at John the Bossman in the soft light of the bar.

"Do all your bartenders work alone?"

"Yeah, but we've never really had any problems down here. It's a neighborhood where people all know each other."

"You've never had any problems with the transients from the train yards?"

"No."

"The crack heads from the alleys?"

"Crack heads? Are there crack heads in the alley?"

"Sir, there are always crack heads in the alley."

"Not that I'm aware of, I mean sometimes some creepy people make their way in but we shuffle them out pretty quick."

"What about the bikers from around the corner?"

"Magic Wheels?"

The detective nodded.

"No way, not to sound pathetic but they have a way of watching out for the white girl with the juicy ass in this neighborhood." John abandoned the tiny smile when he realized the cop didn't find his humor entertaining in anyway. *So much for trying to breathe a little levity into the situation.*

"You are aware that they had a shooting at their clubhouse last summer?" The officer stated.

"Yeah, I heard something about that."

"It's a pretty rough neighborhood to leave someone all alone to close a big bar like this, isn't it?"

"Yeah, it is. But to be honest, all of my bartenders are pretty capable of handling themselves down here."

"Not all of them."

Revising her earlier gratified response toward the police, Colby decided she didn't like this cop. In actuality, the whole situation might have been avoided if she had locked the damned door. She didn't want anyone to feel any guilt over her drunken behavior. One or two less shots during her shift may have altered her perspective on the importance of locking the door. But that message would never get relayed to the living; it would remain a secret between her and the stinky guy who killed her.

"Why don't you come away from all this?" Matilda sugested, but Colby didn't notice.

"Do your employees drink on the job?" The Detective hit upon the million dollar question. Colby cringed, ignoring Matilda for the moment, and awaited John the Bossman's response.

"They aren't supposed to." His gaze found the Jack Daniels bottle, knowing full well of Colby's affinity toward the spirit.

"Oops." Gratitude over abandoning her earlier post of Jack Daniels bottle shelf settled over her. The last thing she wanted was to feel the disappointed stare of her boss as he mused on her alcoholism.

"Colby had a drinking problem. I was planning on firing her," John revealed.

"Oh." Detective Oddball merely continued to write down everything John the Bossman said. He felt none of the devastation that Colby did. Being killed and fired on the same day had an unfair quality to it.

Matilda rustled in the background. "How long have you been standing, er…? I mean, hovering there?" Colby felt a sad defeat begin to settle upon her by then

"For a while."

"Did you watch yours - you know - when you died?"

"Yes. And I'll tell you it wasn't pretty. I didn't get what you might call a proper burial. They just kind of paraded my body through the streets and hung it out for a while to warn the good Christians against fornication and the devil and all that such nonsense."

"Whoa." Colby couldn't even fathom her words.

"Oh yeah. Things were mighty different in this part of town back in the day. It was that lousy Reverend Mark Matthews. He's the one that turned Seattle against us. He used to call Georgetown the cesspool of Seattle."

"Well it kind of is."

Matilda looked shocked with Colby's agreement. "Well, it might not be the cleanest or smartest or fanciest place in the Pacific Northwest, but at least it's got some charm to it."

"Charm?"

"Aw hell, yer right, but I sure did have a load of fun while I was here." Matilda whooped. "This place will suck you dry and spit you out, stamp on you and crush every moral you might have inside your tiny body, but you die without the heavy burden of having missed a thing in this world."

"Except booze," Colby pouted.

Cowboy Jerry Spins a Tall Tale

Adjustment came slow for Colby. She neither understood nor wished to fully comprehend the concept of death. She knew that she missed things and held on to strange compulsions and desires. Death proved to be absolutely nothing like she imagined it might. Though if the truth be told, she never really bothered to imagine what it might be like, except those few times she wished for it while puking in the toilet after a few particularly brutal binge drinking nights.

Her Golden Stiffy, as she came to regard Bryce, didn't come around as often as she wished he would. He seemed to enjoy his alone time, so she spent most of her beginning time with Matilda and Cowboy Jerry. Dozens of others surrounded her, but few came out to socialize, instead they hovered invisibly around wallowing in their deadness. Colby, having always been fairly social, decided to make the best of this death thing and stay close to the surface.

She couldn't understand why the dead were so depressing. When ghosts materialized they provided a colorful translucence to a room that felt sincerely tangible - like life really. Colby ascertained that a ghost's responsibility was to sort of fill the voids in the empty spaces of life, those parts of existence that just feel hollow. Since only a few weeks passed since Colby died, she had no way of knowing this ghostly beauty faded with time.

Jules Maes Saloon closed down for a couple days, a sort of "let's mourn Colby and clean up her blood" party. When the bar reopened, without pomp or circumstance, the neighborhood slinked in easily. Everyone wanted to talk about the murder. Colby became a celebrity.

"Enjoy it while it lasts," Cowboy Jerry said. "Soon enough they'll ferget all about ya."

He didn't say this meanly. His gruff exterior masked his sensitive side. Colby appreciated the guy for his cowboyness. Once he'd forgiven her for her cold taunts over his illiteracy, they became fast friends.

"I'm not really known for enjoying things without booze."

After her weeks of sobriety, she still thought of little else. She'd taken to hovering through people as they sat in inebriated states on their bar stools. The drunker they were the more she whooshed in and out of their bodies. Once she thought she felt something, but the other's just laughed at her when she voiced it with enthusiasm.

"I weren't never much of a drinker myself." The Cowboy ignored Colby's incessant whines about alcohol.

"Really? Why?"

"I didn't live round the big cities where they make the stuff."

"What about moonshine? Didn't you make booze in a bathtub in the middle of nowhere?"

"Oh sure, we had some of that out in the country. My brother tried to make a little distillery in the back yard, but the stuff tasted so awful he couldn't sell it."

"Did it get you drunk?"

"Well, if ya call running around the house in naught but yer drawers screaming that yer a chicken and need to be plucked - I'd say yeah."

"You thought you were a chicken?"

"Naw, not me - my brother," Cowboy Jerry insisted.

"Sure it was; it's always easy to blame the brother when he's not around to tell the truth."

"Truth telling weren't much of his specialty. He was a funny little guy."

"Was he like you?" She played along. The smallest discussion, no matter the weight of significance, always took precedence for Colby; anything to keep her mind off of booze.

"You could tell we was from the same Mama, but that's the only commonality we ever shared. We was as different as night is to the day."

"Let me guess, you were the work horse and he was the fuck up."

"In a sense, though I don't rightly know if I like yer term for it." He still disliked her foul mouth which is why she picked every opportunity available to her to use it.

"So? What was he like?"

"He was a real looker and good with the ladies. He used to cook up these get rich quick schemes so he'd have money to bring the ladies out on the town, which was much different in them days."

"I bet you were a real looker when you were young, eh Cowboy Jerry?"

"Well, I'll tell ya, a lot of ladies seemed to desire my company, if that's what ya mean. But I only had eyes for one lady, my Daisy." His eyes hollowed over, which is the Haunter's way of getting teary eyed. She'd seen it happen to some of the others and it always felt strange to see a ghost display an emotion.

"Back then, I took care of the farm," he continued. "It fell to me being the eldest when Daddy passed. That tore my mama apart and she joined him only a few years later. She sure did love him and never got over him leavin' her all alone."

"That's sweet." She pushed the image of Golden Stiffy from her mind. She'd not seen him since the first night but always spent a great deal of time fantasizing about his handsome face and other imaginary parts.

Concentrate, you're listening to a Disney story. She shook her head and tried to listen again.

"Well, my brother Jacob sure didn't want to help out on the farm. He'd spend hours out in his shed trying to come up with some crazy invention but most times just starting small fires and destroying copper pots and cast iron skillets. I couldn't tell ya what happened out there but it was always darn loud and darn smelly. One day he comes running out to the field with a piece of paper in his hands, yelling and screaming about how he'd done it. I didn't know what he was talking about, but he was excited as a coon in a hen house - less bloody though."

She didn't mean to stare at the bar longingly for a beer, but something about listening to a cowboy weave a tall tale made her damned thirsty.

"Anyways, he wanted to find his way to the city to patent some new invention with the intention of sellin' it to the Seattle Beer House. He claimed it would revolutionize something or other. Tell ya the truth, I couldn't follow a single word he said. I just smiled and nodded and wished him luck. The problem was he wanted to borrow the money from me to make his way there."

"Is this story about beer?" She got lost again.

"Pay attention Missy!"

She snapped to. "I am." Her defenses pricked up. "You lived on a farm, your brother's a genius and he wants to change the world with some great beer invention. I got it, jeez."

"The problem with my brother was he couldn't be trusted with money. That's why my mama and daddy put me in charge of the farm and finances. They both knew that Jacob would just run it into the ground, a' course, not on purpose but he don't follow the same kinda time line as the rest of us. He's like you - "

"A drunk?"

"Naw - well, maybe a little. But what I was gonna say is that he marches to the tune of his own cattle prod - if ya get my meaning. He's a bit different, is all."

"Cowboy Jerry, I believe you just paid me a compliment." Colby thought she saw the cowboy blush a little; but it turned out he just hovered through a red light.

"Don't worry, I won't let it happen again. So, he asks me fer the money to make his way to Seattle and I sez no. Fer weeks he works on me asking fer money. And then he turns to my sweet Daisy and works on her for a while. Finally we decided that it was worth the price of a train ticket jest to shut him up fer longer than 10 minutes about how we was ruining his dream and all that nonsense. Now the last time I loaned him money, he was meant to buy some supplies to make some invention or other but all he came back with after six days in town was a black eye, some busted ribs and a terrible case of the clap."

"They had the clap back then?"

"Shoot, they had them nasty diseases since Adam and Eve left the Garden of Eden - specially in a big city. It's easier to catch a dirty dinky than to catch a salmon, they say. 'Cept its worse fer pain - they ain't had no ointments or nothing to make it go away back then. You jest pee funny and deal with the pain, like a man."

"Oh to live in a time when your manhood was marked on how many eruptive boils you had on your ding dong. It kind of changes the concept of Penis Envy a little bit." Colby laughed.

"Well..., anyways..."

"Wait! I gotta know, did it clear up?"

"Did what clear up?"

"Your brother's balls? Did he ever pee right again?"

"I don't wanna talk about my brother's privates."

"Hey, you started this story."

"Yeah well, I didn't know you were gonna latch on to the only disgustin part of the story with so much enthusiasm."

"What are you kidding me? You've known me for weeks now, am I the kind of girl that doesn't enjoy a good conversation about one, genitalia, and two, the discomfort of others?"

"Aw hell!" Cowboy Jerry turned a lovely shade of translucent crimson.

"Holy shit! You cursed!" Colby pointed at him and laughed again.

"Dang woman, will ya jest listen? His pecker was fine!"

"Okay." She made the action of biting her lip to keep herself from laughing. She pretended that it tasted fleshy and whole, though it neither tasted nor fleshed.

"We all three, Jacob, Daisy and me, decided that we was gonna go with my brother into the city so's that everything would get handled right and the money wouldn't wind up lost forever. We were gonna be gone for no longer than a week and then with the massive fortune my brother thought he might make when the Beer Company bought his invention, he was gonna stay in the city and live large, and Daisy and me was gonna get on back to the farm."

"And your horse."

"Now don't go bringing up a sore subject."

"I find it incredible to think that you would refer to your wife with so much affection in the telling of this tale and yet, this is the first I knew that you were even married."

"Well, if ya just listen you might understand a bit more of my situation."

"Ugh, okay, okay..." Colby found herself staring outside into the dark recesses of the star filled sky, or at least as much as she could see out of the dirty windows, while Cowboy Jerry told of the train journey from Bumble Fuck to Co-Bumble Fuck. She thought it might be fun to try and count as many stars as she could, but lost count or interest after 10 or so. There sure were a lot though.

"...and that's when I seen em together and kissin."

Colby's head whipped around. "What? Who was kissing?"

"My brother was kissin' my wife. Should I say it again so the whole of this stinkin' town can hear?"

"Sorry. I didn't realize that your brother was such an asshole."

"I guess in this instance a cuss word is mighty appropriate." He took his hat off and rubbed at his temples to soothe away the nonexistent pain.

"So, what'd you do? Did you guys fight?"

"We yelled fer a long time. Daisy went away from both of us, she couldn't handle to watch us fightin' over her. Eventually we calmed down and started to talk it out. But Jacob kept calling me old, sayin' I was too old fer a bright young flower like Daisy and that he wanted to take her away from me fer that reason. They was in love and such."

"Were you?"

"Was I what?"

"Too old for her?"

"Since when is a man too old fer his wife?"

"Well, how old was she?"

"She was younger than you. Maybe in her mid-twenties."

The shock on Colby's face stopped Cowboy Jerry for a minute. He looked confused over her reaction. "Dude," Colby said.

"What?"

"You're like 70."

"I was 63 when I died, thank you very much."

"So you think that it's okay to marry a woman, hell, a girl who is thirty years younger than you?"

"I don't see nothing wrong with that."

"Did you, you know - stick it to her a lot?"

Cowboy Jerry definitely had Colby's full attention. She couldn't take her eyes off the man until he spilled some old cowboy sex scandals for her.

"I ain't gonna tell ya about my sex life. It's private."

"That's fine, I mean, it must not have been too good."

"Why would you say that? I mean we was jest fine."

"If you was 'jest fine', then why did she hump your little brother? And just how old was he?"

"He was 40. He came along quite a ways later than I did, my parents weren't expecting him and then there he was, like a surprise."

"He seems to make a habit of surprising people, eh?" Colby felt a real desire to see this brother of his, what was he really like? "So what'd you do?"

"Well it ain't that simple. I was married to the woman and had been for almost six months. We was making a life fer ourselves and getting along jest fine."

"Right, you said that."

"Jacob said she weren't happy. She wanted to live in the big city and be a real citified woman."

"So she came along for the ride to see what it was like."

"No, the whole thing was a sham. There weren't no great invention. There was jest the two of them runnin' away together and me being the sap with the money to get em there."

"So they wanted the money?"

"And my blessin' if you can believe that."

"That's ballsy."

"You can say that again."

"That's fucking ballsy."

Cowboy Jerry just rolled his eyes and let it go without comment.

"So, you're on this train headed to the city with a ton of cash and your brother and your wife tell you they want to run off together and they want your money to do it with?"

"Yep, that's about it."

"So, you gave them the money and let em go? You did, didn't you?"

"Well, they got the money alright, but it weren't me that gave it to em. You see after a time of yellin' and talkin' and yellin' again, my pride started swelling and I thought I might be able to prove to Daisy that I were a better, well you know stronger, man than my brother so the two of us started struggling around and throwin' punches. He was younger and faster but I was way more stubborn, so I took a hell of a beatin' before my side started twitchin' and I went down jest like that." He snapped his fingers but no noise sounded.

"He knocked you out?"

"No, my heart stopped beatin'."

"You died on the train?"

He nodded.

"Wait, if you died on the train, then what are you doing here?"

"Well, I only mostly died on the train. We pulled in to Georgetown right around that time and they had to put my body somewhere. They couldn't have a stinky corpse in one of the pricey compartments all the way back up toward Tacoma, so they carried me out into this building, which was just a storage building for the railroads in the beginning. It didn't become a saloon fer another decade or so. Anyways, I was still kinda alive but no one knew it 'cause I looked so dead. They never had a doctor come and check fer sure, so when I fully died, here I was in this dang building, left forever."

"Do you know what ever happened with your brother and Daisy?"

"Naw. I know he was pretty broken up about my dying. He cried over me fer a time, but I never felt a single salty tear from my wife. I also know they took all the money. Who knows what happened. I'm sure they sold the family farm and moved into the city to make their fortune."

"Does it bother you?"

"Which part?"

"Any of it? All of it?" Colby couldn't fathom the level of hurt he must feel every day.

"All of it most days and then others, I jest miss my horse."

Silence penetrated the room as it always does when the haunters tired of sharing their tales. The image of Cowboy Jerry began to fade.

"I'll tell ya," Colby heard his voice in whispers, "I'd say the reason we all is here now, together, is cause we all got something we jest can't stop harboring on. And if I been here sinkin' down with this feelin' of loss for over a hundred years now, I can't imagine I'm ever goin' anywheres."

"Cowboy Jerry?" Colby asked into the darkness before he completely disappeared for the night.

"Yeah?"

"I still think it was you who was the chicken."

The Short and Honorable Life of Tiny Tommy

A high pitched scream pierced the silence of the bar. Colby freaked: "What the fuck was that?"

A single florescent light illuminated the bar under the Plexiglas display case that held the liquor. That light coupled with the screeches sent little spasms of fear through Colby's psyche, an eerie feeling for a dead chick.

Alone in the bar, as she had been every night since her death, she felt exposed to the noises of the night. As a good Haunter, she failed. Fear continued to surround her even in death like that shroud of Jesus thing. Haunters did one amazing thing every night. They retired, which led to a kind of sleep mode where they completely disappeared from view. After weeks of diligent effort, Colby never got the hang of it, so she just hovered around restlessly all day and night. She liked to think of it as "guarding the hooch," like her favorite bouncer, Papa Lee. Being a hundred and thirty year old building, Jules Maes creaked with the best of them. Colby spent many an agonizing night listening in the dark. She disliked the honor of being the only Haunter in history to be afraid of the dark.

The scream sounded again.

"That was definitely a Haunter." Colby liked voicing her opinions aloud in uncomfortable situations. It made aloneness seem less vulnerable somehow. She tried to concentrate on her amazing new ability of telling the difference between Live Ones and Haunter noises.

A tiny form scuttled across the room in front of her. She took a good look around to figure out who it was, but the form flickered in and out of focus. Its movements became more erratic until finally it stopped and two eyes focused on her. Her heart stopped, or it might have if it were actually inside her hollow chest and still beating. The eyes glittered in the dusty air for some time before a face formed around them. Two hollow eyes floated in the middle of the room like some creature out of a comic book. The outline of tiny cherub cheeks and a pouty little mouth emerged. As it became more visible, the mouth opened wide and just as the rest of the small body reappeared in the dim light to reveal Tiny Tommy, another shrieking howl sent Colby flying across the room.

She ducked for cover. The wail manifested so much power Colby actually felt her own hollow form twitter in and out of focus.

"Fuck!! Kid, relax!!!"

He looked right through her. His bottom lip down to his chin quivered. He paced back and forth across the main floor of the restaurant. His body passed through tables and chairs, booths and poles. Though he stood barely as high as some of the tables, he didn't relent, just kept moving and mumbling to himself, a real ghostly freak out.

Colby watched for a while, waiting for someone else to come and take care of the situation, but no one showed up. It was just she and the boy on opposite sides of the bar. Thrust into unfamiliar territory, Colby laughed at the thought of her taking control of a precarious situation. Responsibility didn't suit her.

"Cowboy Jerry?" She whispered into the air. Maybe they just needed a little prodding to come out and help.

"Matilda?" She tried again.

"Golden Stiffy?" *Night in shining armor my ass*, she thought.

"Anyone?" No response, no reply, no help...

She turned her back on the suffering child and glided easily toward the back of Jules Maes to the Music Hall. Obviously, he needed help from someone and unfortunately for him, she was the only one around. Maybe if she took a quick peek around, she'd find someone with more experience to handle the situation. Children and she didn't quite mix, like the salad dressing that dead race car driver made after it sat in the fridge for too long. Her last experience with a kid horrified her. There was crying and pooping and an odd smell - wait, maybe that was just a diaper commercial she'd seen on TV.

"Do I have any experiences with children?" She questioned the darkness. "Maybe I'm thinking of dogs."

Kids were like pets to her, cute to look at and something that you always have to kind of clean up after. She had pets in the past. Maybe that information would be helpful. Of course she never owned a pet that she didn't give away after a few months to someone with a more responsible nature. None ever died on her, so that was a plus. Since no other solution, especially in the form of another Haunter, presented itself, Colby decided to push forward with her dog whisperer skills and see how they fared with the boy. Cautiously, she crept back into the main dining room in search of Tiny Tommy. He hovered in wait.

"Tommy?" She spoke softly, avoided eye contact and checked her pockets for a treat.

He sensed her presence - at least she thought he did since he stopped moving.

"Hey buddy." She moved closer and he turned to face her. Again, he seemed to look right through her. She had another bizarre thought. For a moment she felt like she was on the set of the movie *Damien*. She took a quick look around, and realizing there was neither a set of stairs nor a Big Wheel in the vicinity, felt safe enough to continue with the intervention.

"What's up, little dude? You're kind of freaking out a little bit."

His chin started quivering again. She saw it happening.

"No, no, no, no, no..." Colby put her hands up defensively as if she could somehow shove the upcoming scream back down his throat before it left. "Relax kid. Let's talk this out."

A more ridiculous notion couldn't have possibly crossed her mind. Talking out problems with a screaming five year old never worked for anyone. She remembered her own mother's solution to her prepubescent tantrums was to medicate her with peppermint schnapps in her hot cocoa.

She looked back at the bar with longing, but for the first time since her death, it wasn't for a selfish reason. At that point, drugging a small child took precedence over her own alcoholic desires. Death turned her into a maternal figure with priorities - what the?

She saw the scream rise in the boy's throat and braced herself for it, but she didn't give up entirely. "Wait, wait... sh, sh, sh..." Desperation filled her voice. "I know, let's sing a song! You like songs, don't you Tommy?"

He stopped; stifled back the sob. She was onto something.

"Yeah, a song. Sure, a song. Everyone likes songs... a song. A song? Wait, do I know a song?" Mayday, mayday!!!

The sob began anew.

"Okay, okay, okay - I've got one. I do - and it's a good one. Um, uh, oh yeah. Here we go." Colby put her arms up as if she were leading an orchestra and began.

99 bottles of beer on the wall
99 bottles of beer

Her voice quivered under the harsh strain of melody. Tommy halted his own vocal assault completely and really focused in on her. She continued:

You take one down, pass it around,
98 bottles of beer on the wall.
98 bottles of beer on the wall –

"Come on, you too – "

98 bottles of beer, you take one down -

He smiled that same shy smile that always graced his face and began to sing in so slight a whisper that she wasn't entirely sure he really made a noise. She trusted in herself and her "sing-a-long" skills and continued.

97 bottles of beer on the wall -

It took to about 95 bottles until she could hear him singing along, not just see his lips moving. By 90 he began to laugh and by 80 he stopped , looked her dead in the eye and said, "Your voice sucks."

He then ran toward her with his arms spread for a hug, passed right inside her and swirled round for a minute before bolting out of the room entirely.

"Well, I'll be." Cowboy Jerry crooned.

"Geez!" Colby jumped out of her spirit skin for a minute. "Don't you people knock before you come hovering into a room?"

"Sorry yer majesty. I'll be sure to send a message ahead when I'm about ta enter a room." He started to blur away.

"Hey! Wait a minute. Don't you dare disappear when I'm talking to you. Just where the hell have you been?"

"Since when is that yer business, Missy?"

"It's my business when you guys leave me with a screaming kid and no instructions. Do I look maternal to you?"

"It looks like you did jest fine." He shrugged his shoulders at her. "I wouldn't done no better. Do I look Daddy-ternal to you?"

"She did better than alright." An older conservative woman appeared. She wore an elegant black dress and her hair in an upsweep.

"Pearl Davenport?" Cowboy Jerry gushed like a schoolgirl. "I ain't seen you in a dog's age."

Colby's shock over Jerry's behavior toward the woman stayed her usual biting sarcasm, she watched as the Cowboy made a damned fool of himself.

"Good evening Jerry. It's wonderful to see you again."

"Where ya been keeping yerself?" His demeanor completely changed. He dropped his surliness and took on the drippings of a right and true gentleman. He might have been wearing a tuxedo and entertaining a party in a grand ballroom, except for his improper country twang. But suddenly it was more endearing than ever.

"Oh, I've been around." Duh.

"Well, yer still just as beautiful as I remember." Was he blushing?

"That's so lovely to hear. Lord knows that's something a woman misses hearing. People don't often describe the dead as beautiful."

"Well, that's 'cause they ain't seen you."

She smiled coyly at his compliments, thriving on it. Somewhere a gilded cage stood empty in wait for the return of this woman. A cage she no doubt spent her entire life in, surrounded by luxury and gentlemen callers, available to satisfy her every whim. Her entire spirit reeked of privilege.

"Miss Pearl, I could spend days telling you how beautiful you are." He moved closer to her and Colby felt vague recollections of the feeling of bile creeping up her throat.

"Okay, that's enough. I'm seriously gonna puke."

"Really?" Pearl looked alarmed and rather amazed.

"No, not really. But seriously, gross dude." She gave Cowboy Jerry the stink eye.

Watching a Grandpa figure try to mack on a teacher figure offered an uncomfortable feeling to Colby.

"You're quite crude, aren't you?" Pearl gave that haughty "down your nose" stare that the wealthy learn at an early age.

"You don't know the half of it." This broad did not affect Colby. Rich don't mean shit now. Dead was dead.

"No doubt you feel right at home in a place like this." She waved her hands as if to shoo the filth of the bar away from her.

"You could say I fit right in, mostly somewhere over there, under the taps." Colby smiled, years tending bar taught her how to deal with all types of people. The key to success was the old 'smile and nod' routine.

"Hm... well, despite all the slovenly common-ness about you, you do seem quite capable of handling difficult situations."

"Well gee whiz, that pretty lady just paid little old me a compliment." Colby batted her eye lashes at the woman, who continued to eye her coldly.

Pearl regretted her decision to make herself visible to the contemptuous bartender.

"Easy now, you speak nicely to this lovely woman." Cowboy Jerry came immediately to her defense.

"Lovely woman? Now I know you are crazy, old man." Matilda's laugh filled the room.

"Back She-Devil!" Cowboy Jerry yelled. "Don't bring your poisoned tongue here."

"Oh shush, you." Matilda eyed Pearl with a coldness that could only come from years of full on hatred. Colby saw the room chill to the point of frosty breath with the heated stares of the two women.

"Matilda." Pearl looked Matilda up and down, eyeing her with a hardened gaze. "You're looking well... satisfied."

"Why thank you kindly and might I say that you look as pretty and brittle as a glass figurine, yourself."

Fervent prayers to useless gods escaped Colby's lips in whispered tones as she begged in the darkness for these two women to regain their flesh. It promised to be the fight of the century; two women battle it out in true cat-like style, right there in Jules Maes. Colby laid down twenty bucks in her head that Matilda would kick some serious uptight bitch ass.

Though her mind filled with some of the best images she'd ever conjured, complete with American Gladiator outfits and bully sticks, Colby recognized a real intensity building. She, reluctantly, took it upon herself to lighten the mood.

"Man, things are getting a little tense in here," she stated while running over to her favorite spot on the bar. She let the Jack Daniels bottle settle into her chest.

"Drink anyone?"

Three sets of eyes rolled at the same time.

"What?" Genuine confusion clouded Colby's expression. She just didn't understand these people. Jack

Daniels always solved every problem she ever had; either that or a cup of mashed potatoes. Not a person on the planet, in whatever dimension they happen to be hovering in, had the capacity to stay mad when faced with a delicious cup of mashed potatoes. If those potatoes happened to be smothered in Jack Daniels gravy - well, you may as well buy a lottery ticket, sit back and wait to collect millions, because that was the golden ticket.

"You two behave." Cowboy Jerry scolded Matilda and Colby. "We don't never get to see Miss Pearl, so jest you mind your manners."

"Why are you out of your solitary confinement? Just felt like slumming it?" Matilda clearly refused to take Cowboy Jerry up on his suggested behavior.

"It just so happens that I was bothered by the screaming."

"Oh, I see so you came to prey on poor Tiny Tommy. He's just a boy. He can't help himself," Matilda shouted.

"I know that. I am not completely insensitive to the needs of others, especially a small child."

"Really? I think you are."

Once the shouting began there was nothing that anyone could do but wait until it ended. Colby was not alone in her joy of watching women fight, some of the other Haunters began filtering in, faintly. No one wanted to miss out. Colby scanned the hollowed images for Bryce but didn't perceive him. She noticed a few strange looking shapes in the dimmed light and motioned to Tiny Tommy. He glanced over and beamed at the sight.

"Ears!" He whispered excitedly; then returned his attention to the battle.

"Well, you don't know a thing about me," Pearl shrilled.

"You know what, you sure are right about that. But I do know that you are a woman who can never be trusted. I do know that you haven't got a clue about anything besides what you need and desire, and I know that you will never understand what true friendship is."

"Is there something I should know about these two?" Colby asked Cowboy Jerry.

"Best to leave that alone," Cowboy Jerry whispered.

"Why?" she whispered back.

"That there is a tale that'll rip yer insides out."

"I don't have any insides," Colby mused.

"Yes, and everything else has been so pleasant up until now," Pearl continued, unabated by Colby's general lack of silence.

"Why don't you just go back to your room and leave us all be?" An echoed resonance vibrated through every Haunter in the room as Matilda vocalized her feelings.

"Fine, I will. But I'm still gonna say what I set out to, whether you like it or not." Pearl lost her cool manner and just shouted in anger now.

"You!" She pointed at Colby.

"Me. I was just... I didn't hear anything. I just was standing here." Crap, she wished she knew how to disappear.

"I came here to say that in the 50 years that I've been hovering around this old dilapidated bar, listening to that poor child scream time and again with his nightmares, not one of us has been able to ease his suffering until you. I don't know how you did it but you brought that boy around and I am ever so thankful for it."

The words that came out were lovely but the way she screamed it in Colby's direction left her wondering how to take the praise. "You're welcome." She sort of shouted back.

"Fine. That's all. Now goodnight." She disappeared.

"And good riddance," Matilda shouted into the air.

"Honestly woman, yer a plum mystery to me. She come down here with the best intentions and ya hang her out to dry."

"This is none of your business and you know it."

"Can't ya never forgive her?"

"Forgiveness? I know what forgiveness is, Cowboy Jerry, but does she?" Matilda disappeared.

"Dang fools." Cowboy Jerry disappeared as well.

Colby found herself alone. All the screamers, cowboys and ears vacated the scarlet clad room with the end of the skirmish. An overwhelming sense of discontent plagued the newest Haunter. With only a pea-sized amount of brain matter left undestroyed by malted hops and spirits, Colby simply couldn't understand anything that just happened.

"Okay then, good night," Colby said to the emptied room. She looked down at trusty old Jack Daniels. He would never leave her so abruptly.

"It's been a while since we've seen that." Tiny Tommy's head popped up in front of her feet. Colby yelped, startled for the 10th time that hour.

"What's that?"

"The way that Mattie and Miss Pearl yell at each other. It used to happen a lot more often."

"Oh really? Do tell, my young friend." Finally - some dirt.

"They had some big blow out a long time ago."

"A blow out, you say? About what? Money? Friendship? Men?"

Tiny Tommy shrugged his tiny shoulders in response. Either he didn't know or he wasn't telling. "I kind of missed all that."

"How do you miss two banshees like that howling at each other?" Colby refused to believe him and intended to spend the rest of eternity winkling it out of him, if necessary. Secretly she hoped it wasn't necessary, she had such a short attention span.

"I spent a lot of time disappeared in the beginning."

"Did you miss your Mom?"

"In as much as I could miss a woman who murdered me, I suppose."

"Oh yeah, right. Why did she do that again?"

"Because I was a very bad little boy." He laughed.

"Can I ask you something serious?" Colby had an itch that needed scratching.

Tiny Tommy eyed her with the most curious, juvenile expression; it softened her intent. Though she still had a stinking suspicion that her best friend might be the devil, incarnate, but dead.

"Is your middle name, Damien?"

"I don't have a middle name."

"Do you like to ride Big Wheels?"

"What's a Big Wheel?"

"Do you have a tattoo of 666 on your head somewhere?"

"Wait a minute. I know where you're going with this crazy talk. Just cut it out! I'm not the stupid devil," Tiny Tommy stated in no uncertain terms.

"Because if you are," Colby continued,"I just want you to teach me a couple things."

"Like what?"

"Possession - I think that's a good one to start with."

"This is about getting a drink again, isn't it?"

"Sort of - not that I don't think it's totally wicked that you're like Satan and everything."

"Well, if I actually was the devil," Tiny Tommy played along, "I'd probably try to help you with your other problem first."

"How do you know about my problem?" Paranoia reared its ugly head.

"Everyone knows about your problem."

"Sweet." What could be worse, Colby wondered. Being made fun of by a bunch of neurotic dead people or being alive? It was a toss-up. But with life there was booze and with death, just a permanent AA meeting.

"You're making it into too big a deal. If you relax, you'll be able to do it."

"Oh sure, it's just that easy. Wait, what are we talking about?"

"You know, your problem..." Tiny Tommy nodded knowingly.

Absolutely no understanding crossed Colby's mind at that moment. She stood staring in blankness down at her little friend, awaiting an explanation.

"The problem you have with vanishing."

"Oh! That problem... I hate that problem."

"It's really easy to fix. I bet that song you sing will work for you, too."

"Speaking of which, why were you screaming?" Quick Change Magee; at your service.

"I don't know. I don't ever really know that I'm doing it. It's like I'm sleep walking or something."

"Are you telling me that you sleep walk?"

Tiny Tommy squinted at her as if the answer pained him. "Yes?"

"Who ever heard of a Haunter who sleepwalks? You're dead."

"A what?"

"A Haunter."

"Clever." It took a lot to impress Tiny Tommy. Colby puffed up at the compliment. She knew she liked him for a reason.

"I know, but seriously you are dead."

"Really? I thought I was just slow to develop."

"How old did you say you were?" Every time she spoke with this kid it felt way too adult. She certainly never thought a kid this small could formulate such complicated thoughts.

"I died when I was five."

"You're like a genius. How'd you get so smart?"

"I've been dead for 65 years, you tend to learn a thing or two, and you know... boredom."

"That's what I said." Colby now knew the boy was a genius because he agreed with one of her own thoughts before she ever voiced it aloud to him.

"Well, I guess you might be a little smart too." He winked. "So how come you always got whiskey in your chest?"

Madame Ms. Matilda Pinnell

Weeks or months or years passed without incident. Colby tried to keep up with the passage of time but found it almost impossible. The longer she endured her haunted half-life, the easier it became to understand why none of the others had a clue as to the year or day either. It took a great deal of effort to figure out such things.

The whispers and tales of her death long subsided and the bar meandered back into a lazy haze of drunken debauchery. Each night stretched into the next as the same repetitive conversations, behavior, music, and lives played out their tired games over and over. And the longer Colby sat at the bar to listen, the less interesting her death seemed. She longed for something new and exciting to happen.

"I want something new and exciting to happen," she said to Cowboy Jerry one day.

"Yeah, me too." Tiny Tommy never left her side now. The two got along easily enough but they sometimes drove the others a little crazy with their constant crooning. Once they tired of the beer song, they moved onto such great hits as: "Margaritaville" and "Hotel California" and any other song featuring booze.

"Maybe we should sing another song." Tiny Tommy brightened at his own thought.

"NO!" Cowboy Jerry raised his hands in protest. "Fer the love of all that is pure in this world, I beg you to keep quiet."

"That's not very nice." Colby felt the insult.

"You know what's not very nice?"

"Yeah, I know, I know... my voice." She stuck out her tongue to the old man. "But that shouldn't stop me from doing something I enjoy."

"Actually, that's exactly what should stop ya."

"Well, you wouldn't know good singing if it came up and handed you a twenty."

"I know bad singin' fer free." Cowboy Jerry pointed with both index fingers directly at Colby.

"Well you're just a... a... jerk!"

"That might be the nicest insult I's heard from ya yet. I don't know whether to thank ya or say the same on back to ya."

Colby sensed a change in her relations with the ghostly group quite some time ago. She couldn't understand how it happened but somewhere along the way, these strangers took on the role that her family fell short of. She never imagined that death might be the one thing to take the loneliness away. Now companionship filled the bar and her half-life like a never ending Long Island Iced Tea. The loss of any semblance of privacy, though bothersome in the beginning, no longer struck her as odd. The need for privacy disappeared the moment she stopped breathing. Haunters never require the use of a bathroom for butt zit popping or going number two. Embarrassment lay in speech and deed for the Haunter, no boogers, strange growing hairs, green food bits caught in teeth, or stinky body odor affected their unchanging appearance.

She enjoyed Tiny Tommy's company the most. The two could just hover together without saying a word for days, then look at each other and burst into laughter over nothing. She felt protective over him, like a little brother and best friend all rolled into one.

"Hide and Seek!" Tiny Tommy shrieked.

"Again? Don't you get tired of that game?" Colby asked.

"Hide and Seek, Hide and Seek!" He jumped up and down like any normal five year old.

"Alright, alright. Do you want to hide or - " Tiny Tommy disappeared so fast he didn't hear the rest of her question.

"Guess he wants to hide first." Cowboy Jerry laughed.

"Wanna play?" Colby asked.

"Naw, ain't my style. I think I'll jest set here for a while."

"You can't fool me; I know you're just checking out boobies."

"Well, that's jest jest jest insultin'," Cowboy Jerry stuttered.

Colby nodded. Though Cowboy Jerry appeared a harmless old man, she knew what lay inside the heart of every man - a blatant desire to stare at some bodacious ta-tas. Even Colby couldn't help but stare when a particularly perky pair bounced by. Boobs held power and it's a rare man or woman who can turn in the face of such awesomeness without a tiny peek and a hint of desire.

Colby relaxed for a while, checked some of the posters on the wall and looked at her nails wishing for the hundredth time since she died that she'd bothered to repaint her nails that day.

"Shouldn't you be countin' er something?"

"It doesn't really matter. Tommy always hides in the same place anyway."

"Takes some of the fun outta the hidin' don't it?"

"He doesn't seem to think so. He laughs just as hard every time I catch him."

"He's a squirrelly one."

"Yeah, isn't it great?" Colby smiled and zoomed off through the building to find her little friend.

She took her time in pursuit of her miniature man-child. She floated here and there before she headed toward Tiny Tommy's favorite room.

Though Colby knew Jules Maes Saloon to be the oldest bar in Georgetown, it wasn't until she possessed the ability to visit the many decaying layers of the building that she fully appreciated what that meant. Corpses lined the nooks and crannies of the building like raisins in a Kellogg's product, rivaling the body count at the local graveyard. Rats, birds, cats and what appeared to be a rather large snake greeted Colby whenever she passed through the floorboards and walls. In the beginning, Colby's misgivings gave pause to her passages. Eventually she stopped stressing over the other bodies and began to wonder why she never saw any

Haunter animals in the building. Brittle bones and feathers provided the only historical documentation that these creatures ever existed.

"Hey Maurice. Hey Kitty, kitty. Want some milk or something?" Colby teased the skeleton of what must have been a cat at one time. He sported a jingle bell around his neck with a nametag that labeled him: *Maurice.*

"Not hungry, huh? Catch you next time." She floated away without a second glance.

She floated up into the apartments above the bar and whooshed through as quickly as she could. The new found ability to fly offered no joy; it didn't matter how fast she moved within her hollow form, it always felt the same. No adrenaline rush; no nervous stomach and no dizzy feelings betrayed her body. These should be the times she loved most as a Haunter - she could fly! But feeling nothing in return for the gift ruined the glory.

She did find the upstairs tenants, a sculptor and a painter, vastly interesting. Doing a simple fly-through seemed near impossible; she always found herself slowing down to peruse the general splendor of the apartment. Artists offered hours of entertainment to the every day Haunter without much of a social agenda. Their manners and projects, often hilarious, gratuitous and vulgar always diverted.

"Artists," She muttered under her breath.

Colby didn't think she'd ever seen a space more jammed with stuff than up in their apartment. Trinkets lined countless shelves; newspapers and books cluttered the stairwell leading the live people up into the overly full living area. Toys, paintings, sculptures, engines, candles and drawings flowed like the waters of Niagara throughout the entire apartment. Smoke soaked fabrics, including curtains and drapes, betrayed a few vices, nicotine, marijuana and patchouli. The stinking scent of habitation wasn't something Colby could enjoy anymore, though she doubted she ever did. The poor life of the modern day bohemian usually stank to high heaven and no amount of Patchouli ever masked the stench of body odor and turpentine. A lack of tang kept her interested in the couple.

Since Tiny Tommy awaited her arrival elsewhere, she delayed her desire to linger in the apartment and continued on. Despite her new ability to keep awful quiet when wandering into a room, at least to the living ears, Tiny Tommy always knew when she was there. She heard a noise in the corner and recognized the sound of stifled giggling. As if on cue, she hurdled around the corner to scare him in his usual spot but found nothing there instead. He always hid right there, behind the big ugly yellow vase.

"Tommy." She began looking around the room with determination. His child-like laughter silenced; something that rarely happened.

"Yoo whoo.... Tommy... where are you?"

She twirled around when she heard another noise at the other end of the room, but saw that one of the windows in the room was open. The wind blew lightly into the room ruffling some papers on the desk.

"You better not be invisible right now. You know that's not fair." He loved to gloat with his "disappearing" skills, something that irritated Colby to no end.

"Tommy. Olly, olly Tiny Tommy free." Her voice cracked in a dreadful reminder of her intense lack of soulful melody. She ignored the fact completely, a habit the other Haunter's did not appreciate.

"Rooaaarrrrr!" Tiny Tommy reappeared and rushed at Colby.

She turned around and bent down like a football player, ready to block the little body from passing through. It never worked. He tumbled right through. She closed her eyes as he passed, wishing she might feel something and wondering why she never did.

"Did you feel that?" Tiny Tommy asked.

"No, not that time either."

"But I bet I scared you that time." His giggle filled the room. It sounded like one of those wind chimes that used to piss her off, except now she didn't mind it so much.

"That was a good one. Pretty tricky changing your hiding spot on me." She felt an overwhelming urge to tickle the boy, maybe a hair tussle?

"I bet you can't catch me," he said and took off through the wall.

"Damn."

Tiny Tommy sped away like a crafty well-designed bullet, a Sniper bullet, deliberate in both target and speed. Colby needed extreme speed if she wanted to keep up with him. Catching a glimpse of his form, she picked up the pace. In the Haunter's world, bigger didn't make anyone faster than another. The longer a Haunter stuck around, the better their abilities became. She never saw anything in the world move as fast as old Cowboy Jerry. It made sense since he resided at Jules Maes for 100 years, so Colby convinced herself that it must be the truth.

She kept pace with Tiny Tommy longer than usual. To his delight, every time he thought he lost her, she appeared behind him with a determined look in her eye. She almost caught him. His form raced ahead of her but only inches away.

"Gotcha." She reached for him and her fingers came dangerously close to his form, but just as she might have won the game, he took a nose dive down to the first floor.

"Come on." Colby whirled around before she passed through to the next room. She dove down after the boy and caught him directly below her. She over shot her mark and landed in the basement. Her head popped up between his feet. She laughed uproariously. The last time she remembered laughing so hard, it ended with gooey milk ungraciously squirting out her nose.

"Shhh." Tiny Tommy put his finger to his mouth to stop her from making noise.

"What is it?" She whispered back looking around.

"Matilda." He pointed toward the far corner of the restaurant; a room they'd magically retuned too. Matilda's form paced back and forth in the corner of the restaurant.

She muttered almost incoherently to her self. The only word Colby could make out was, "Pearl."

"We should go." Tiny Tommy began to sink through the floorboard.

Colby's curiosity got the better of her. Without a second thought, she approached Matilda.

"Hey Matilda."

"What do you want?"

"I don't know. I guess I just came to see if you wanted to talk about anything."

"You mean you came to see why I was talking to myself?"

"Well, that too. I've noticed you've been doing that quite a bit lately."

There wasn't a day that'd gone by that didn't see Matilda off in a corner working something out all by herself. No one spoke about it but everyone noticed. She'd hovered holes in the atmosphere and by rights should have had a face full of worry lines with all her fretting. Her beautiful pale face glistened in the red light like a ruby; a very angry ruby.

"I guess I've had some things on my mind."

"What have you got to worry about? You're dead." Matilda's cutting gaze stopped Colby for a moment. "Sorry. Was that inappropriate?"

Tiny Tommy's eyes peeked out of the floor where moments before he'd disappeared.

"Why don't you just go away?" Matilda asked.

"I'm really sorry. I didn't mean to hurt your feelings or anything. I just wanted to, you know..."

"Nose into my business?"

"Yeah, I guess so."

"Well, what is it you want to know?" Even her bustle looked deflated.

"Whatever you want to tell me, and if that happens to be everything, I have a mind to listen." Colby smiled big, hoping a smile might prove trust. Oddly, it worked. Not because Colby had any real ability to persuade with charm, but because after sixty years, Matilda simply needed to spill her guts.

"Everything, huh? You want to know about the time I stubbed my toe on that old trunk and my toe nail nearly fell off when it turned all black and full of puss?"

"Okay, maybe not everything. Why don't you tell me about Pearl?" Colby held her breath as she said the name, unsure of how Matilda would react. Anger flashed over her face at the mention of her nemesis.

"That damned woman!" Matilda began. "If ever I had a mind to beat the hell out of someone, it'd be her. I'll tell you that much."

"So you knew each other then?"

"We were married to the same man, Mr. John Pinnell."

"Isn't that illegal?" Laws changed all the time, so she asked this delicately. If she had a dollar for every time she misquoted a historical fact, she might be able to buy herself a real education.

"Sure it is, but you gotta understand the time we lived in. Things sure were different, especially in this little town. I guess it was the coming of the railway that really saw the change. It turned Georgetown into a railway town and what with the brewery here and so many people depending on a job at the place, it was only fitting that the town had to annex itself from Seattle when the law passed prohibiting the sale and manufacturing of intoxicating liquors within a mile of the city."

"Is that the Olympia brewing company?"

"No. Back then it was called the Seattle Beer Company, unless I miss my mark Olympia brewing company was probably in Olympia." That *you're an idiot* look crossed Matilda's face.

"Oh yeah, right, duh... But which one are you talking about?"

"It's a ways down on this same patch of road." Matilda pointed out the window to Airport Way.

"Oh, right. That was the old Rainier building."

"Whatever."

"That's a giant coffee warehouse now. You know how Seattle folks love their coffee."

Matilda merely nodded. Coffee in her time was about as tasty as a steaming hot cup of dirt.

"They painted it all these retro pastel colors. Every time I drove past it I used to be reminded of *Willie Wonka and the Chocolate Factory*, but if Willy had a lobotomy and wasn't really that creative anymore."

"Who's Willy Wonka?"

"He's this chocolate maker, inventor of the everlasting gobstopper, and caretaker of Uumpa Loompas."

"Uumpa whoompas?"

"You never read *Charlie and the Chocolate Factory*?"

"I thought you said his name was Willy?"

"Anyway, it's a really cool story about this poor kid who wins a golden ticket to visit a reclusive chocolate factory."

"I was telling a cool story," Matilda mused.

Colby lowered her head in shame.

"Where was I?"

"We were talking about coffee." Eager to forget her lack of story propriety, Colby offered what she could to belay her idiocy.

"No we weren't. Coffee is not a part of my story." Matilda's eyes searched the room for a memory of what the hell she'd been talking about.

"Beer!" Triumph laced Colby's response.

"Yes, beer; well, around the time that Georgetown annexed itself from Seattle, things started getting pretty hairy around here. Georgetown became the place where people came to cut loose, unwind if you will from the strict rules of the city. Just as there were dozens of societal rules in Seattle, there were no rules at all in Georgetown. It became a virtual orgy of the senses in any way you might think right here on this tiny stretch of road. In its hay day over twenty five saloons operated 24 hours a day. Reverend Mark

Matthews, famous in his day as an advocate of temperance, called Georgetown, the cesspool of Seattle."

"Oh yeah, you said that before."

"Well it's true, isn't it?"

Tiny Tommy nodded in agreement.

"Okay," Colby agreed. Far be it for her to disagree with the general consensus. "Georgetown is a cesspool."

"I said... was," Matilda corrected.

"No, it still kind of is."

Matilda imparted a queer look to her fellow Haunter.

"And you were here for all of that?" Colby changed the subject.

"Well, not really. I was still a young girl living in Seattle with my family."

"Were you rich?"

"We did alright. Daddy was in the publishing business and things were just starting to get going for him."

"What about your mother? What was she like?"

"She was just like every other mother in the day, pretty and organized. She kept a clean house and did what she was told."

"That sounds boring."

"You can say that again." Matilda shook her head with a sad smile. "I would have gone plum crazy if it weren't for my brother William. He was the only light in that constrictive town. We used to go out on adventures, which basically meant get into a lot of trouble, all the time."

"Was he a boozer?"

"He liked to take a few down, but that wasn't his downfall. William liked the horse races. He used to take me there, though very few women ever went. But I became known there as William's sister and the men took good care of me, mostly because I wasn't one of those stuffy women that thumbs her nose at a good time. I could hoot and holler with the boys and they respected me for that. And that's where I met John Pinnell."

Colby perked up, ready for the sleazy interesting part of the story to begin.

"He's the one that brought real prosperity to Georgetown. You see he was one of the first Saloon and Brothel owners in the town and when he started to see a real profit from it, he invested in the Seattle Race Course. John was smart as a whip and could turn a dime into a dollar with the flip of a wrist."

"Was he cute?"

"Handsomest man I ever saw. If I were to ever use the word *dashing,* it might be in reference to him." Matilda's smile lit up her entire face, evidence to the enormous love she felt for her long-dead husband.

"How did you two hook up?"

Colby glanced at the bar. A Jack and coke went along with the telling of a story like potatoes went along with eggs and bacon.

"He always had a kind word for me. He'd bring me gifts when he knew I'd be around the track, but the truth was, my father did not approve of such a notorious man giving me attention. So we had to keep things quiet. We'd meet secretly when we could and he was in love with me, but there was nothing I could do without leaving my family entirely to requite it. William was all for me abandoning the family but I just couldn't. I loved my Father dearly."

"That's a pickle." Colby smiled with satisfaction after 30 years attempt to use that phrase. She'd done it, yeah for her!

"John was a bit older than I. He was a man full grown with a successful enterprise, and he started to think those thoughts about how he needed an heir to leave it all too. Since I was so reluctant to wed the man, his attentions started to turn toward others."

"Pearl?"

"Well, no, definitely not at first. As proper as my family was, and they were more progressive than proper, her family was twice as bad."

"Did you two socialize?"

"Sometimes we'd find occasion to be at the same party and we'd have to say a kind word, but never because we cared the least bit for each other. But she was a looker back then."

"I bet you were too."

"What do you mean were?" Matilda's hands smoothed back her hair and she shook her bustled fanny at Colby, making her laugh.

Colby didn't think she'd ever seen a woman in her time nearly as beautiful as Matilda. It wasn't just about her perfect features; straight Roman nose, cherub cheeks, heart shaped mouth or blue within blue eyes. Everything about her reeked sensuality. Matilda was a proud woman and as sure of herself as any man. In Colby's society, people gravitated toward such confidence; however, the same could not be said for the society of Matilda's time. If Colby had to estimate an age for the prostitute, she'd say 38 or so.

"Do you want some fries with that shake?" Colby tried to keep the jovial moment alive but she could tell that Matilda didn't understand her inference.

"Go on." Colby urged instead of trying to explain.

"John went in search of a nice proper family to become a part of, but none of them would have him. Sure the men would spend hours in his company when the horses and whores were around, but when it came to polite society, he may as well have had a face full of boils. But then something happened that changed everything - the Great Depression."

"Oh shit! I forgot about that."

"I imagine a lot of folks would like to forget that ever happened, but as it turns out, Mr. John Pinnell was one of the few Seattle citizens that didn't lose his shirt over the whole affair. I wasn't so lucky. I lost everything and everyone."

"What happened?"

"Well, first the Depression happened and it seemed like a dream. It took almost a full year for it to affect us here on the west coast. But when it did, it was like gangbusters. My father managed to stay ahead of it for a while. People needed their news and he'd made the transition to newspapers just in time. The bottom fell out maybe a year and a half later. By that time William had been sent to war. He didn't make it and Mama died of heartache a short time later. Then my Daddy was trampled to death trying to get pictures of a Communist rally on the Capitol steps when the riot broke out. That left just me, penniless and alone. That might have been the most scared and heartbroken I'd ever been."

"That sucks."

"You're right, it did. And I didn't have many people I could turn to. Most everyone I knew had fallen to the streets during the Depression, and I was pretty reluctant to ask if I could share a box with anyone along the river. I went to the only man I knew whose luck hadn't exactly run out."

"John."

"Yep. I figured if he'd have me, I would marry him right then and there. It turned out I was a bit too late. When all levels of society disappeared and dozens of *Proper Families* were just desperate to hang onto what wealth they still had, a man like John Pinnell became well liked. He'd had his pick of any woman now and he'd done his best to find a good and proper one: Pearl. I think it was his pride that made him choose her. She came from a family known throughout the whole state as the most strict and moral. It tickled him to know his seed would be a permanent part of that family's history. The family didn't like him, but he kept them in the money and they never had to beg, borrow or steal for a thing. When I came to John, he took me in. Pearl and the family found out about it pretty quick and came down pretty hard on him. They wanted him to abandon me, but he refused. For everything that had happened between us, since we'd met so many years prior, he still loved me. I think if I had gotten to him before Pearl's family did, he might never have married her. I would have been the one and only Mrs. John Pinnell. But I was caught up in the same misguided society as Pearl, so we were both to blame in the end."

"So when did you marry him and why did you become a prostitute?"

"I was never a prostitute. That was a lie concocted by Pearl's family."

"But you told Cowboy Jerry..."

"I say those things because I know it irks him." She winked at Colby.

"Weird."

"They tried to save face by turning me into a painted whore. John put me up here in the brothel so I wouldn't have to sleep on the streets. The brothel wasn't running at the time, no one had money for such things. Besides the depression hit so hard, that sometimes the only release you had from your own suicidal thoughts was to fuck like a dog on the street. There were a lot of freebies happening out there."

"Sounds fun."

"I suppose it does, if dirty sex is your thing."

"Isn't that everyone's thing?"

"By the time the War ended, and therefore, the Depression, John had two sons with Pearl, a place in society, two thriving saloons, and a live-in mistress. I hadn't meant to become that, but it just sort of happened that way. He had a family with Pearl, but his life and love was with me, he used to tell me that all the time. When the boys come back from war, they had a thirst that couldn't be quenched no matter the amount of booze or broads. Once again, Georgetown became that place. I'd already taken on quite a bit of responsibility with the saloons and the brothels as well. It seemed the girls always came to me with their problems and I was always there to sort them out. Then John's health failed. It was during this time that John started to regret some of his decisions in life. He wanted to marry me; he said it one day and I, of course, just laughed at him, as I had for the past 20 years of him asking."

"You laughed at him?"

Tiny Tommy listened intently. He always wondered about Matilda's life but never found a cause to ask her. He curled up comfortably underneath Colby's legs and sucked on his thumb, ineffectually.

"Hell yes, I laughed. Talk about too little too late."

"But you said that you denied him first."

"That was different. Times were different then."

"Did you have any children?" Colby changed the subject.

Matilda turned away at the question. A genuine pain lit her face for the briefest of moments, but she pushed it away. Though she anticipated the question, she still wasn't prepared for it.

"You don't have to answer."

"It's alright." She sighed as if her lungs were full of the biggest breath she'd ever taken, but there was no air and thus no breath to let out really. "I did have a little girl but she died before she was born."

"Sorry." Awkward; nice job Colby.

"You'd think after 70 years, it wouldn't hurt so much to remember."

"I had a hangnail once, I totally understand."

Tiny Tommy crawled over to Matilda and curled himself underneath her. She smiled down at the boy, pushing her grief aside. Dwelling on old pains, though a favorite pass-time of most Haunters, only made things worse.

"Anyway, he wanted to marry me and I laughed because he was already married with two children. Plus he was responsible for an entire household of high society folks. Marrying me seemed like a bad idea since he didn't want to go through a divorce."

"No divorce?"

"He said he just wanted to make things right between us and marry me."

"That's like illegal, right?"

"You're right, polygamy was not legal, but for some reason, I just didn't care and I said yes. We got married and never told a soul."

"Very romantic."

"When he died, he left me the last saloon still running and this brothel."

"So you owned Jules Maes?"

"No. I owned the saloon at the end of the block, but the brothel was upstairs. John owned the whole town by the time he passed on."

"That's pretty impressive."

"Well, not really. Shoot, I could have bought the whole town for a song. It wasn't worth much by that time. Now women didn't own much back then, and women with my reputation didn't own anything at all, but John saw fit to hand the business over to me. Pearl found out about everything and she hit the roof. She was humiliated in the eyes of high society and did everything she could to take everything that John had left me. She hired lawyers and did wind up getting the saloon, which was no big loss for me, since the 24 hour status of things had gone tits-up many years past. It was mostly a restaurant and that seemed like too much work for me to keep up the supply of beef and eggs. I let that one go."

"I can't see Pearl running a restaurant."

"She never wanted to run it. She wanted to burn it to the ground; along with anything I ever shared with John."

"She's pretty vindictive."

"And how! Pearl tried to get the brothel next. We fought fiercely, she with lawyers and me with my big mouth, and just when it looked like I might up and lose the fight, she pulled away. She gave me full ownership of the brothel and sent papers over to the fact. I didn't understand it. But my Daddy always mentioned something about a gift horse and not looking them in the mouth, so I took it and never looked back. About three months later I learned why Pearl had done it when I started getting visits from the local zealots."

"She sent the religious folk after you?"

"Oh you bet she did."

"I once got stuck talking to a Mormon all afternoon."

"What's that?"

"People that believe that Jesus was a Native American and all their holy documents were read out of a hat."

"Sounds about right." Tiny Tommy, though just a child when his life ended, had very pointed opinions about various religions and their necessity.

"They started campaigning in front of the place, scaring all the girls. They canvassed the town with posters of me and called my girls *whores* to their faces. We had a couple riots and beatings, but the cops were on our side for a time. But when they also turned on us, things got ugly, real ugly."

"I thought you said it wasn't a whore house."

"It wasn't." Matilda's expression betrayed some hidden secret.

"You're lying, aren't you?"

"Do I look like the sort of woman who would lie?"

"Uh... yeah."

Matilda pondered a moment or two before she made her final decision on how to end the story. As it turned out, she decided to be completely truthful.

"Alright... it was a whore house, in the end. The men started coming back with money in their pockets and the girls in the house wanted some of it. I just managed the girls to make sure nothing bad happened."

Colby's complete attention was on the woman before her; she chose not to comment on the obvious poorness of her management style.

"One night, I wake up to windows shattering, so I come high tailing it down the stairs to figure out what's going on. There's a whole string of people with gasoline cans and fire torches just standing and staring. I get real nervous. The girls are crying and screaming behind me. Pearl is out front telling us to send me out and no one will get hurt. What the hell can you do in a situation like that? I calm the girls down, tell the bitch I'll be out in a minute, and try to figure out what to do. I tell the girls to get dressed and go out the back. Leave as quickly and quietly as they can. I just want them to be safe. I can tell by the look in the eyes of the people out front that that is the last thing I'm gonna be."

"I never intended for them to hurt you." Pearl appeared out of no where.

"I don't want to see you now. This is my story, not yours."

"It's our story! Why is it always just about you? I lost someone I loved too."

"Well, you may have lost someone, but you have a funny way of grieving for him - by killing me."

"I was angry. I didn't mean for things to go so far." Pearl's usual composure disappeared at the angry accusations.

"What happened?" Colby preferred to judge for herself.

"I came out of the building and people started throwing things at me. First it was rotten lettuce heads and vegetables, but when they ran out of that, they started throwing rocks and dirt."

"You came out all venom, spitting like a wild animal," Pearl defended.

"I did not. I came out civil, trying to buy time for the girls to escape through the back door."

"You busted through that door like you were on fire, with a shot gun in your hand as I recall."

"It wasn't loaded."

"I beg to differ. You almost fell over when you shot it up in the air."

"That gun did have quite a bit of kick to it."

"There see! Tell the story like it was; not like you wanted it to be."

"Well, I only had a couple shells, then..."

"See!" Pearl pointed at Matilda with an accusatory finger. "A wild animal!"

"I was defending myself; any normal human being might have done the same thing."

"Are you accusing me of being abnormal?"

"Well, look at you standing there. Even in death you're all nervous and uptight - too afraid to relax and have a good time."

"Oh, I'm sorry; I didn't realize death was supposed to be a big old party."

Tiny Tommy eased away from the two quarreling women. He didn't fear any harm, but too, he didn't wish to interrupt the flow of hostility. This interlude offered a nice break from the norm; free entertainment. Colby and he exchanged knowing looks.

"The way you treat everyone around here, it's like we all have to die over and over, every damned day."

"I'd prefer it if you did die every day!" Pearl's voice took on the shriek of a Banshee.

"Killing me one time just wasn't enough?"

"That was all your own fault. You were the one with the shotgun and sour attitude."

"You brought a crowd of people with pitchforks and torches like I was the Witch Bride of Frankenstein."

"If the corset fits..."

Matilda disappeared and reappeared instantaneously nose to nose with Pearl. Every ounce of her spirit longed to hit, spit and commit serious injury or anything else that ended in it.

"I am not a whore." The words erupted like a growl from a trapped wolverine, not desperate, but as if understanding soon it would lose a foot to escape.

"That's fine. I can think of a few other words for it, if that one doesn't suit you." Pearl didn't back down.

Tiny Tommy and Colby hovered ever closer to the two feuding women, not wanting to miss a single word. Ears appeared all over the room, like floating fleshy butterflies soaking in the argument like nectar.

"Lady if I could, I'd rip the heart right outta you; but I don't rightly know if you ever had one to begin with."

"You ripped it out years ago when you took my man!"

"He was my man first!"

"NO! Mine!" The two women began circling each other, pushing translucent fists into each other's bodies with complete dissatisfaction. Punching the abyss with vain attempts to quash the argument of the century; neither felt uplifted for their efforts.

"You left him!"

"I never left him."

"He never would have found me if you hadn't!" Pearl stopped when she heard her own words, understanding the truth of it. Real torturous pain registered on her face. If she could weep, she would have flooded the world with her tears. "You were all he ever talked about. All he ever thought about. I could see it in his eyes whenever he'd come home from you. I just knew that if you'd ask him to, he might have left me and gone to you."

"Don't you think I knew that too?"

"Well, why didn't you then?" Curiosity stayed Pearl's anguish momentarily.

"You had children together. You were married in the society and your family made certain that I was just another floozy living in Georgetown. What was I suppose to do? Convince the whole town that my reputation was a fake; kill off your children and family and then you so I could have him? That's utter nonsense. I had a small part of his life and that was enough. It was his idea to marry, not mine. I think the only reason he did it was because he hoped it might help to secure my rights to some of his property when he passed away."

"Go back to the part about the yelling and throwing of rotten things..." Colby was all for the two ladies settling their differences, but first she wanted the juicy gossip. Two harsh looks pierced Colby. Tiny Tommy giggled beside her. Matilda turned away from Pearl and for no apparent reason, continued her story.

"Before I knew it, the girls who were trying to get out of town were caught escaping and brought round to where I was. By that time, I'd been tied to a pole and subjected to some vicious words, along with a fair amount of saliva. The Zealots tied the girls up right alongside me."

"It was no more than they deserved."

"We all get by, the best we can. I can't begrudge a woman a choice she makes, especially if it puts food on the table."

Pearl tried not to think too long on this philosophy. Being a woman of good breeding, the sort of behavior Matilda condoned horrified her. If the tables were turned and it were she who wound up on the streets, she couldn't say what her own decision might be. She was ever so thankful for never needing to make painful choices.

"I couldn't stand to watch the other girls suffer, so I made a deal with them. I said that I would take on the punishment for them all. They found their scapegoat and let the others go with the understanding they could never come back. They left me there; every single one of those girls whom I kept from starving on the streets, left me behind with an angry mob."

Matilda's laugh, pregnant with bitterness, sounded hollow in the caverns of Jules Maes. She gazed out the window as if the whole scene happened before her eyes just then. Reliving the moment in all its painful glory.

"Not one stayed to help?"

"Not a one. But I don't blame them, not really. They were children. They couldn't crawl their way out of a paper bag if I didn't show them."

Matilda's gaze found a new target: Pearl. The more she thought on the events of that fateful day, the more she knew where the real blame lie.

"We didn't kill you. You were alive when we left." Pearl defended her actions from that day, still so sharp in her mind despite the many years passing.

"You're right. I was alive when you left. I was a bloody, swollen mess of a woman with barely enough life left in my bones to pull myself back into the building. I might have lived. I might have survived and found a life outside of

Georgetown if that man hadn't come up after me when everyone else went away."

"What man are you talking about?"

"The old preacher." A serene smile crept across Matilda's face, as if in retelling the tale she needed to accept her fate all over again.

"Reverend Jeffries?"

"That's the one."

"Why would he stay behind?"

"Why does a man do anything?"

"No. He was a reverend, a holy man."

"Maybe by your standards, but certainly not by mine."

A twinkle of understanding passed between the rivals. Tiny Tommy groaned in response to the tragic end of the tale, but Colby, poor Colby; so intensely unintelligent when it came to the art of subtlety, missed the point entirely. "I don't get it. What did he do?"

"Colby." Tiny Tommy planned on explaining the whole thing to his rather dense friend later, but she just couldn't keep her mouth shut.

It pleased Matilda to explain further. She didn't want Pearl to misunderstand in the same manner, though the likelihood of such a thing occurring seemed rather improbable. She did continue the last tidbit of story, her eyes fixed on Pearl's all the while.

"He had another goal in mind, quite a selfish one that he probably did not share with anyone else in the parish. He finished the job for everyone with me, but not before he took me like the whore you said I was."

Pearl couldn't take it; too many years of unpleasantries had already passed between the two women. Stifling a sob and thus betraying a real human side to her gruff exterior, she disappeared.

"Fucking hell!" Colby said.

"You got that right." Matilda gave a hearty laugh. For some reason it was genuine, though Colby was hard-pressed to find humor in the story.

Tiny Tommy didn't know what to consider. Every Haunter had a tale to tell and knowing that each ended in murder, it's a fair assumption that those tales aren't happy. He loved and admired his Matilda, more than he did his own mother. But the story she told curled up his ghostly insides, and he felt a strange sadness creep inside him and burrow a little hole.

"Anything else I can tell you?" Matilda asked. Her voice waivered, both tired from the long account and restless from decades of resentment.

"I guess that about covers it."

Matilda started to vanish but Colby called her back.

"Wait a second."

"Yes?"

"Why is Pearl here? I thought she lived in a mansion somewhere in Seattle? Why did she die here?"

"Lord knows why but about fifteen years or so after my own death, she came to stay here. She died here, in her sleep, nice and peaceful. If she'd known she was going to have to spend all eternity with me when she woke up dead, she might have picked a better place to die."

"I bet that was some fucking scene to watch."

"Let me put it to you this way: whenever I feel down about the bad things that happened in my life, I like to remember the expression on old Pearl's face when she floated out of her old dead body and ran face-to-face into me. It was the most joyous day of my death. She about died all over again."

Colby didn't know whether to laugh or cry.

The Day the Haunters Came Out to Play

"Happy Halloween!" Colby shouted loudly through the household, attempting to wake the living and the dead.

All of Jules Maes bustled with activity. Every year the bar hosted a special celebration called "Cabaret Macabre" to entertain the Freaks and Geeks of Seattle. Generally speaking, Halloween tends to turn everyone into a Freak and Geek as women dress like sluts and men act like devils. During the fiendish holiday, booze ran a little too free, sometimes inciting vomit to pour from mouths like water from a spigot; babies to be conceived, though almost never intentionally, and a lot of people suffered the same fate as Colby except the murder weapon usually was a bit more "car-shaped" and its driver often clung dependently upon a beer bottle whilst driving. Halloween is the Live Ones excess and the Haunter's favorite holiday.

She circled around the Live Ones loading in gear and decorating the bar with hay bales and skulls. Already in the early afternoon, the bands arrived for sound check and pre-show whiskey shots. Some came dressed in costume, while others looked as though they'd only just woken up, dressed in bedraggled clothing with sleep marks still indenting their cheeks. Drum kits followed upright bass, followed accordions, the bevy of instruments did not adhere to the usual "Emo" band structure. Cabaret Macabre never hosted the usual suspects of musical genre; instead it championed the underground punk gypsy sound with a touch of folk and a smidge of sexy, dirty, death waltzes. Not for the faint hearted, its fans ran the gambit of crusty gutter punks to Aristocratic Goths.

Tiny Tommy rolled his eyes at the growing crowd. He never enjoyed Halloween.

"What's your problem?" Colby asked.

"Nothing." His disinterest was obvious by the listless sound in his voice.

"Come on! It's Halloween. You should be excited."

"And why is that exactly?"

"Because you're a kid! All kids like Halloween."

Tiny Tommy stared at his friend with a great amount of irritation.

"Well, you look like a kid," she mused.

"You look like a drunk."

"Point taken."

For the first time in a long time, she wandered away from Tiny Tommy. She couldn't explain it but she felt genuine excitement when it came to Halloween. Now that she was dead, celebrating it seemed even more important. The other Haunters seemed to agree. Many of them began appearing early in the day and sort of flew around the room in sweeping motions. Colby didn't recognize most of them. Even after all that time elapsed, Colby still hadn't met half the Haunters that called Jules Maes home. The comparison to family couldn't be more realistic. These new found Haunters could be her East Coast family that she only saw every six years or so. Obviously not enough to keep the ties strong to her discredit, and they looked like such fun people.

Colby lost herself in the Haunters dance as she watched the lucid flow of spirits above her head. A tuba passed through her body as a hulking beast of a man clammered through the music hall with purpose, but Colby still managed to keep her attentions upward. She wanted to join in the fun but suddenly felt shy as she didn't recognize a single individual. Waiting with watchful repose, Colby drank in the scene. Since this type of drinking was the only possibility for Colby, she attacked it like an alcoholic pirate might a bottle of rum. Each of the Haunters looked as if they dressed for the event with their various time-period garb, not a one matched the other above. The group got along easily. Smiles adorned their faces and indeed their very lightness of spirit. It appeared as though they could float right out of the building and straight up to heaven, if in fact, that was the way. Colby had her doubts and far too ready a belief in irony to not think that maybe the direction was the other way.

A familiar face sailed by her. Though she had no heart to skip a beat or stick in her throat at the sight of him, the muscle memory felt the same despite her lack of flesh. Bryce! She watched him for a minute, building up courage and a game plan. Tiny Tommy hovered in the same corner that Colby abandoned him to only minutes earlier and watched also. Whatever happened, he knew it'd be awkward and hilarious. Bryce, unaware of any stalking, watched the bands setting their gear on stage with an unhappy look in his eye. A deep sense of longing plagued the man, and Halloween only made things worse with all the decadent happiness surrounding him. One of the band members, a swarthy dark-haired rogue with a gold tooth, set his guitar into its holder on stage and Bryce gravitated toward it, without thinking. He stroked the air where his hand should have felt wood and thought if he could cry, now might be a good time.

"Hi Bryce!" Colby decided the exuberant approach to be best. She couldn't have been more wrong. His sour expression gave voice to a much nicer response than his mouth might have. Colby simply wouldn't be deterred. "Guitar, huh?"

His eyes narrowed, her smile widened, and Tiny Tommy's giggle sounded like a hyena through the room.

"So what have you been up to?" Colby's smile didn't wane.

The golden-toothed rogue appeared, filling in Bryce's hollow form with his own. He removed his guitar from the holder and the Golden Stiffy reluctantly hovered away from the stage. Colby followed him, not willing to let him go without at least a few words.

"Do you mind?" Bryce inquired when he noticed he couldn't lose his little shadow.

"Nope."

More snickers sounded from Tiny Tommy's area. Bryce stopped, turned abruptly on Colby and stared at her with a bit more venom than he felt. "What!"

Caught off-guard, she blurted out the first thing that came to mind: "Happy Halloween!"

Tiny Tommy couldn't hold in his laughter any longer. He burst, erupted if you will; like Mount St. Helen's but with less smoky residue. "Do you mind?" Colby shouted across the room to her young genius friend.

"Nope!" He shouted back.

"Wait!" Colby rushed over to Bryce who'd attempted an escape when her attentions turned.

"What is it Colby?" This time he feigned interest. Hey, it was a start.

"Um..." At a loss, she looked around for a solution to the question. What was it? This guy was good. To his credit, he did give her a few seconds of thoughtful consideration before he lost interest again. "Dance," she said, when he tried to turn again.

"Dance? Dance, what?"

"Would you like to dance?" Her voice was dainty and pure, somehow. It didn't hurt as much as a girl such as herself might think. She pointed up, toward the other Haunters, who still swirled above their heads. An occasional "whoop" sounded betraying their merriment.

Bryce craned his neck to watch for a moment. More than anything he wanted to forget his anguish, but dancing seemed a trivial thing to relieve such intense pain.

"Looks fun... doesn't it?"

He didn't reply. His fate couldn't be reversed, shouldn't be reversed by any small amount of pleasure he might derive from his haunted half-life. Painful remorse saturated his existence and he could ask for nothing better. But right then, he really wanted to. A yearning for joy, real-honest-to-God joy overcame his faculties. Colby sensed it, like a lioness recognizes the weakest member of a pack, and attacked.

"Come on, what have you got to lose - just that sour expression?" She smiled and he didn't cringe or look away. He smiled back and put his hand out toward her.

"Holy crap!" Tiny Tommy continued to moderate the events as they happened.

Colby ignored her teeny friend, clasped the air around Bryce's extended hand with certainty and the two floated toward the dancing wraiths above.

"I think I just pooped my pants - spiritually."

To Bryce's credit he managed to keep the disgusted look off his face when he turned to Colby with a tidbit of advice. "Maybe don't say anything else," he offered.

"I can do that."

The bartenders cranked the tunes loud for the pre-celebration while a few afternoon patrons trickled in and out to both warm themselves on the chilly Seattle afternoon and fill their bellies with fried goodness. John the Bossman piddled around carrying enormous trays of food in various stages of prep. Since Colby's time, there remained two constants: someone always felt deserving of a free drink and the kitchen always maintained an "understaffed" status. Georgetown didn't breed workers with real stick-to-it attitudes; most all of the cooks worked (and often were fired) at every restaurant in town. John the Bossman didn't mind. The tiny Buddha belly he'd acquired over the years pronounced clearly his proclivity toward food and its many uses. He never shunned a prep shift and often excelled at it.

Colby wished the Live Ones could see into her dimension. Disney-like magic happened around them every day and they simply couldn't see it. She trained an observant eye upon the other Haunters around her and found them almost impossible to focus in on; happiness shimmied their bodies in and out of perception. One young, gangly lad dressed as a short order cook waned away moment to moment but his smile; a bright toothy grin, remained behind no matter how far away he seemed. Happy Haunters; Colby didn't realize such a thing was possible, yet as she too indulged in playful camaraderie, she surely couldn't deny it.

From out the corner of her eye, Colby noticed a fairly solid Haunter approach her and Bryce. A sick sense of jealousy arose when she noticed the woman, a rather wild looking blonde, staring intently at Bryce. She looked hungry, like Bryce were a steak and she, an anemic badly in need of some iron. Colby tried to dance Bryce around so that both their backs faced the woman, as if to say: *go away, scary blonde ghosty*. Bryce didn't move - the blonde kept coming and Colby waited for the inevitable.

"Hello," A breathy voice whispered. Luckily the music drowned her voice out; though Colby heard it plain as a scream, she chose to ignore it. "Hello!" The voice persisted.

Bryce stopped, turned and, without meaning to, rolled his eyes when he recognized the Haunter before him.

"Hi, Chelsea," a rather irritated Bryce responded. Colby wanted to kiss him then. She just knew he was falling for her and his reaction to this woman, despite her rather ragged appearance, proved it.

"Bryce, dance with me!" The blond sounded so pathetic that Colby actually felt a little sorry for her.

"Oh, sorry Chelsea. I promised Colby this dance." He turned away from her and Colby was all smiles. That moment turned into the best moment of her death. She had a boyfriend!

Her happiness lasted only moments before Chelsea's high squeal of misery pierced through the otherwise jovial scene. Every one stopped, including the Live Ones below. At the exact same moment that Chelsea let her squeal loose, the house speakers sounded an equally piercing squelch of their own. All of Jules Maes felt Chelsea's misery for exactly 1 second, then promptly forgot and carried on with the good times. Though Colby wanted to know who Chelsea was, she didn't want to know bad enough to interrupt her date, so she threw the thought of the strange woman to the back of her mind and pretended not to hear the insistent sobbing that seemed to linger in her head.

The music switched - a slow mournful tune crested the Haunters for a moment. They stared at each other as if to figure out how to feel about the sadness that suddenly overcame the dynamic of the party. The bartender below ran over to the stereo and quickly changed the music to something livelier. A universal sigh and delighted uproar sounded, reinvigorating the room, and the Haunters continued hovering above, now with more buoyancy.

Another woman approached Colby and Bryce; this one a bit more familiar. Matilda rushed up, full of spunk and whooped like the others around the couple.

"Oh my! We haven't seen a party like this in a dog's age, have we Bryce?" Matilda winked and Colby thought she saw Bryce melt a little. She tried to dance between the two of them, using her strategic skills from the previous encounter to no avail. Bryce just moved out of the way and smiled at Matilda. Colby wondered how Matilda managed to make her breasts appear even fuller; suddenly hating herself for being so plain.

"It has been a while, Mattie." Bryce winked back a bit too flirtatiously for Colby to handle.

"Colby, you don't mind if I steal this little charmer away from you?" Matilda asked out of politeness, never really anticipating a negative response.

"Well... I..." Colby started, with one hand on her hip and the other snapping in the air like she'd seen on *Jerry Springer* when the girls want to fight.

"No, she doesn't." Bryce and Matilda just spun away from her without really taking her thoughts or feelings into consideration. Deflated, she fell toward the ground where Tiny Tommy waited.

"Sorry," he offered.

She gave him the hard, inconclusive stare that generally encompasses the question: *why?*

"I thought we had something special."

"I guess now you know how Pearl feels."

Right about the time Colby might have nodded her head as if to concur with her small friend's sympathies, she noticed that Pearl danced primly nearby with none other than Cowboy Jerry. Despite the charming nature of the interaction, with CJ taking on the role of Romeo and barely able to lift his eyes to meet his Juliet's, Colby felt irritated over the whole thing. As if the ground dropped away from her again, Colby found herself hovering halfway between floor and basement. Her head suddenly the same level as Tiny Tommy's.

"Cheer up! It's Halloween." Tiny Tommy sounded as excited about it as he had before.

"Don't mock me." She now shared his misery.

Colby spent the next hour or two wallowing and watching. Matilda didn't leave Bryce's side. The two laughed together easily, like some annoying Hallmark card. She watched the Haunter's appear and disappear on their dance floor or plateau as the case were. All shapes and sizes presented themselves. Colby should have been up there introducing herself and getting to know all these new people. Instead she stared and wallowed.

"A gambler, a maid, a short-order cook and a prostitute walk into a bar - " Her voice cut through the silence she and Tiny Tommy shared.

"Mattie's not a prostitute, remember?"

"I'm not talking about her." Colby pointed up where the newest Haunter appeared, a girl clad in sleazy lingerie. Her perfect body annunciated the form of her outfit as it should, with all the ruffles and peep holes aptly displayed. Her face might have been pretty but from Colby's view, it looked almost clownish painted with too many bright colors. A creepy smile settled upon Tiny Tommy's face as he gazed up to the pro's goods.

"Clementine." He breathed her name heavily onto the air, like a zephyr might say the name: *Titanic.*

"See! She's tainting children." Now Colby's pointed finger became accusatory.

"Whore!" Colby continued.

"Yes, please." Tiny Tommy sighed again.

"Honestly, all men are alike."

Tiny Tommy's head swirled around unnaturally as the flawless behind of the sexy Haunter did the same boogie. He neither heard, nor remembered his friend.

"This is uncomfortable... pretty graphic too."

"Isn't it great?"

"I'm talking about you." Once again, Colby's voice lost its resonance in Tiny Tommy's head.

"Ugh," she replied to her own irritation, in her best Charlie Brown voice. She began noticing the other male Haunters losing sight of their partners. All eyes turned to the scantily clad vixen. Even Bryce seemed less spellbound by Matilda's attention and turned his attentions elsewhere. She took it in stride.

"Hey there, Clementine."

"Matilda." She purred like a perfect pussycat.

Bryce coughed lightly to remind Matilda he remained by her side, but wouldn't be opposed to meeting this rather enticing young girl. She laughed at him, but made the introduction just the same. Colby didn't like the way he acted around her, so nervous and sincere. She turned to Tiny Tommy to voice her opinion only to realize he'd finally decided to engage the party above and spend time with the delightful, wanton charmer.

Left alone to continue her tortured wallowing; Colby contemplated the liquor shelf again. Even her pal Jack Daniels chuckled in her general direction.

"Boy, that girl always could command the attention of a room." Matilda's voice stayed Colby's sudden desire to abuse alcohol.

"What's her story?" Frustration tailored her question with enough venom that Matilda raised a curious eyebrow.

"Is that a hint of jealousy I detect?"

"Maybe."

"Don't let her worry you none."

"That's easy for you to say; it's not your boyfriend up there flirting like an idiot."

"Who's that now? Tiny Tommy?"

Colby laughed so hard she snorted.

"No," she sputtered. "Bryce."

Now it was Matilda's turn to laugh out loud.

"What's so funny?" Colby asked.

"What's so funny? Well, I mean - you and Bryce?" Judgmental disbelief laced her response.

"It just so happens that we have a very strong, committed relationship," Colby countered.

"Yeah, I can see that."

Colby refused to hear the sarcasm involved in that particular statement.

"How long have you two been together now?" Matilda gave Colby the benefit of the doubt.

"About an hour or so."

"If it makes you feel any better, she died from a rather painful case of the Clap." Matilda fibbed a little. What harm could it do?

The most genuine smile Colby ever experienced, let alone shared, addressed the sheer glee that overcame her. Matilda gave her a famous wink along with the characteristic sly smile.

"How do you know that?"

"I was there when she went."

"Was it painful?" Please, please, please.

"Torturous."

"Good." Colby decided to stop feeling sorry for herself and get back to having fun. She refused to harbor on the couple for another minute, even when they spent the bulk of the evening together.

Tiny Tommy rejoined her eventually, mumbling under his breath, "That boy is a menace."

"Which one?"

"The one you keep throwing yourself at."

"Oh, Bryce, huh?"

"Yep, that's the one." He shook his little head in the most exasperated fashion.

"What did he do?"

"Cock block."

"Excuse me?"

"I was having a perfectly lovely conversation with Clementine, and he just came along and took her away. Cock block."

"Oh, I get it." Ever slow, it took Colby even longer to realize that she'd suffered the same fate at the hands of Matilda earlier - but without the boy parts. It pleased her to know that Tiny Tommy suffered too. He seemed to lead such a sheltered half-life that sometimes it became almost insufferable to her. Rather than rub in his pain, she turned her attention to the bar where two men wearing a fake boat on their shoulders meandered across it. They sang a song in harmony, played instruments and fake rowed. Colby had never seen anything like it and couldn't tell if she were impressed or just confused.

"That's odd," Tiny Tommy observed. For fun he joined the minstrels in the boat and for no apparent reason started to laugh really hard at the ridiculousness of the scene. It never took much to pull Tiny Tommy out of his funks. He stayed with the bar top nautical engineers until the song ended, then flew around the room fast to clear his head.

"Better?" Colby queried when he returned.

"Much."

The night carried on as any other blissful affair might. By the time the Haunters stopped their mystical eddy, the party below obtained the full swing status of. Costumes pranced in and out of doorway after doorway. Goblins, vampires and whores caroused through the building in harmony. Colby had trouble distinguishing Haunter from Live One, since they all seemed to be both jovial and dressed alike. The music began, not in the music hall but on the tiny stage at the front of the restaurant. A tiny band called the Peculiar Pretzel Men bellowed entertainment to the colorfully clad masses. Located so close to the bar assured them a crowd and the lead singer roared coarse melodies while the drummer coaxed dulcet rhythms and the horn player humped the ground, quite literally making love to some iron. Cheers rose high for the trio as clapping proved impossible with so many hands laden with beverages. First rule of the night: drink; second rule of the night: listen.

Colby watched the band from above. A strange desire to hover inside the singer's body while he crooned over took, but his abundance of sweat relieved her of that thought. The horn player stopped attempting to pulverize his instrument, so he held no fascination for Colby either. In the end, she settled upon the drummer whose simple movements heightened her mood to one of specific pleasantry. About half way through their set, Colby jumped out of the drummer and swirled around with pointed glee. Not one frown occupied a single person's face, regardless of their live or dead status.

Spying Cowboy Jerry smiling in a corner, Colby confronted him over his obvious good time.

"CJ, are you actually having a good time?"

"Course I am."

Though the prudish Pearl's presence eluded the old boy, he maintained his jollity just the same. He hovered dangerously close to a few other cowboy costumes.

"Are you sticking with the boys tonight?" She asked, motioning toward his cohorts.

"I didn't know I was so darn popular."

"Don't worry, you're the best cowboy - these guys are just posers."

Cowboy Jerry looked right through her as he tried to sort out why she thought those boys looked like a pretty flower. Knowing that any explanation might involve more confusion from his liquor-deprived afterlife mate and some sort of laughter at his expense, he chose to ignore the observation completely. Cheers sounded around him as the band finished their last song and the sweaty singer shouted for the patrons to continue on to the music hall for more bands. Except for the never ending line at the bar, the patrons complied. The Haunters followed, eager to continue with the festivities as much as any Live One.

The band in the back started up immediately, not wanting to waste a second of the crowd's attention. A blaring accordion announced the onslaught and another sweaty singer crooned melodious agonies toward the gaudy fans. An upright bass beset with the lumbering clod from earlier steered the dancers in the right direction, while guitar and drums helped govern the path. A real slut of a female slammed on her tits with fervor while the words 'kill yourself' rang over the speakers. An aptly titled song for just such a morose holiday, this band knew how to cater to its followers. Something wasn't right about the scene. A vacant spot on the stage signaled the absence of someone - a lone banjo sagged woefully against the wall.

Unbeknownst to everyone except the missing banjo player and his angry girlfriend, a great disaster took place right outside the front doors of Jules Maes. It wasn't until the police arrived and shut everything down within minutes of entering the building that his absence meant anything at all. He and his girlfriend shared a rather dramatic relationship. In a characteristic struggle, the two managed to plow down the main gas line in Georgetown. In reality, she plowed it down when she attempted to run her banjo boyfriend over with her rather pathetic VW bus.

The police and rescue teams arrived in record time and managed to evacuate all of Georgetown. So Jules Maes went from one amazing party scene to completely abandoned in no time flat.

The band remained behind for as long as they could, feigning a desire to pack up their gear, but when the police spied the members in the Green Room attempting to spark up a Doobie, they threatened to arrest them on the spot.

"There is a gas leak. One spark and this whole town is going to blow up. Do you get that?" The cop looked a little annoyed.

"Why don't you just back off with that attitude man?" The drummer had a particular distrust for any police type figure. The cop pulled out his gun; thought better of it and pulled out his bully club instead. The entire band, including the unharmed yet terribly responsible banjo player, grabbed the drummer apologetically and made a hasty retreat through the back door. Without a second thought to their gear, they high tailed it out of there. The cop took a deep breath to steady himself and exited the back door also. It took twenty minutes to evacuate.

"It's a good thing they got everyone out," Tiny Tommy surmised.

"Why's that?" Colby pouted. The party was just getting good. She'd seen three pairs of naked breasts and two guys with their pants around their ankles.

"I don't think we'd have enough room for all those people if they died."

The Haunters Next Door

Cowboy Jerry sat in the front window and stared forlornly across the street. All morning long, a deep crease in his forehead betrayed an equally deep sense of pondering.

"What' up CJ?" It was Colby's fifth attempt to get his attention. She'd left and come back so often that she grew dizzy from the constant rotation. This time he turned away from his gaze and looked right at her.

"Did ya ever wonder what happens after this?"

"After? Is there an after? I thought this was the after."

"I used to think so too, but lately I've had cause to reconsider."

"Does it have something to do with that building you keep staring at?"

She used the term 'building' loosely. All that remained of the old Ice House was a little pile of rubble, a tiny edifice and lots of dirt. Colby turned her attention to it, but focusing on the thing felt like the most difficult challenge of her death. Another unfortunate side effect of being totally dead was the inability to truly focus on something outside your own entombment. In the beginning it was easy. She remembered trying to count the stars through the window, but the longer she remained a Haunter, the fuzzier things became. She thought looking outside must be what it felt like to have your eyes covered in cellophane.

"Can you see that over there?" He pointed to the north end where a half of one wall still stood.

"Not really, what am I looking for?"

"A Haunter."

Colby smiled at CJ's use of the term *Haunter*, pleased with herself. Coining the phrase brought to light her apparent avant-garde side and she found it pleasant.

"We can see Haunters in other places?" She found the fact fascinating; one, because she'd never thought to look for others elsewhere, and two, because she actually could. When she focused hard, she made out the form of a woman across the way. Long blonde hair framed her face as genially as terror hardened her eyes. Colby wondered at the cause of such blatant fear.

"Holy Shit! I see one," Colby shouted with delight.

"There used to be a whole lot more over there," Cowboy Jerry responded with much less glee.

"What do you mean used to be?"

"The building's almost gone now, ain't it?"

A wealthy benefactor bought the building a year or so prior and began the demolition just before Colby's untimely death. She remembered the day the giant cranes came in to get started, the swell of dust took days to settle. She couldn't remember a more catastrophic loss to the neighborhood, or at least that's what the locals called it. Personally, she could care less. But the neighbors were all upset about losing the historical landmark, a building that had been condemned for fifty years and served no real purpose. Colby always considered it an eyesore. She believed the neighborhood to be more upset over the impending condos that would take over. Everyone bitched about the loss, but did what they could to bypass security and steal some of the priceless bricks and old sturdy lumber that held up the decayed building, just the same.

The artists of the community didn't want to see their precious slum redesigned into a pricey Yuppie commune, which condominiums would undoubtedly herald. Colby thought that bringing more business, reputable business, into the neighborhood might not be a bad thing in the end, but always kept that opinion to herself lest she warrant a lengthy lecture on the sanctity of historical remembrance. She preferred to not care.

"Yeah, so?" She recalled hours of useless conversation over the building. Thousands of people flocked to old Georgetown to take hundreds of pictures of a building that nobody even noticed until its removal.

"So it used to be like here - a home to Haunters like us. And that one there is the only one left."

"Where did they all go?"

"I can't say for sure. But I've been watching them disappear one by one."

"Maybe they just disappear like we do when we don't want to be around anyone."

He raised his eyebrow. "What do you mean *we*?"

"I'm learning alright. Give me some time and I'll get it." Why wasn't death the end of all humiliation?

"Anyways, they don't disappear like that. It's not pretty what I seen. It looks to be a sight more painful than death. If I could hear them, I'd think they was screamin' in pain. Keep yer eyes out fer that one. She'll be the last to go."

Colby looked out the window again. This time she really focused on the lady and she didn't look happy. Even a thousand snakes crawling up her arms and a million ants in her underpants wouldn't necessarily warrant such a pained expression. "Shit!"

Colby spent the rest of the day watching and waiting. Assuming it might happen while she watched gave her cause to really stare long and hard. In the back of her mind, she understood the reality of the situation; even a single remaining brick from the decimated building gave the woman something to cling to. Simple theories didn't elude Colby, especially with her new ability to reason without the unfortunate side effects of alcohol swaying her intelligence.

"I guess if the building were to be demolished, the souls inside it would do the same. We're all tied here for a reason." Matilda materialized and empathized with the ghostly figure across the street.

"Do you think we could get her to come over here?" Colby pondered.

"And jest how the heck do ya propose we do that? Send her an invitation fer some tea and crumpets?" Cowboy Jerry laughed out loud.

"More like Whiskey and chicken fried steak."

"Mmm. I love's me a good chicken friend steak." Cowboy Jerry licked his lips like they were smothered in the bacon lard gravy.

"Did they even have that back then?"

"Naw, but I can imagine what it tastes like."

"I assure you it's impossible to imagine how intensely delicious a fried piece of steak is. Not in your wildest dreams could you begin to understand the feel of grease leaking down your face after your first succulent bite." Colby's ghostly body shimmered at the thought of it.

The wall clock said 6:15, happy hour at Jules Maes. The restaurant bustled around them with booze and food flowing freely. She rushed over to a table that'd just gotten their food order.

"Come here, CJ." She motioned for him to follow. He did reluctantly. The crowd whooshed through and around them, spilling beer through them.

"There! See that? That is a chicken fried steak, slathered in gravy with mashed potatoes. Looks good, doesn't it?"

"Aside from it looking like a shriveled up piece of squirrel meat, minus the fur o'course, it do look mighty tasty."

"Now, watch this guy eat it. Look at his face."

The man at the table, obviously a laborer of some kind, scored off a huge piece of the steak and shoved it into his mouth. Colby wasn't entirely sure how he fit it in there but she was impressed that he didn't choke on it. A genuine smile lit up his face at the flavor. She imagined the laborer used the same face for all types of reasons: buying his first power tool, getting his first blowjob, and killing his first fuzzy thing. This guy reeked of masculinity, from his dirty wife beater down to his paint stained cover bibs. Simple and pure, he enjoyed cheap beer, sleazy women and good fried meat.

"He does look happy." Cowboy Jerry looked on with something akin to jealous admiration.

"That's fucking good." The guy nodded his head to his buddies. His voice sounded far away and hollow. It took effort to bring the Live Ones close to your perception in the Haunters' world. Colby gave up that thought so long ago that she'd almost forgotten she existed in the same building with them. There might be hundreds of people walking through her and she barely noticed them on any usual day.

"What's that?" Cowboy Jerry's eyes took on the gaze of a lunatic. He'd forgotten about food and how satisfying it could be.

"Meatloaf."

"And that?"

"Lamb burger with gorgonzola cheese and fried onions."

"I'll take two of those."

"I'd like a salad." Matilda played along. They hadn't played the *I'm still alive and damned hungry game* in a long time.

"Salad? What are ya crazy? Who ever heard of a dead person who's watchin' their weight?" Cowboy Jerry rolled his eyes.

"I happen to like a salad." Matilda wouldn't be upset by his indignant remarks.

"I want some salmon," Tiny Tommy piped in. "That was my favorite when I was a boy."

"When you were a boy?" Colby snickered.

"Shut up and respect your elders young lady."

Both Colby and Tommy burst into a fit of laughter.

"What do you want to eat, Colby?" Tiny Tommy asked when he had his laughter under control.

"Pork Chops with a Jack Daniels cream sauce - no wait, just the sauce."

"They got a name fer you."

"A beautiful flower?" she smiled.

"An alcoholic."

"Aw hell, I thought we were having fun here. Lighten up CJ."

"I guess I could use a toot on an old pipe, myself." He didn't mean to let go of the fight but sometimes it took too much effort to keep up his crotchety old façade.

"That's the spirit."

"We used to have the best barbeque parties in the summertime, during my time here," Matilda mused. "Most times the whole town would follow their noses to old Jules Maes. We'd roast a whole pig on a spit out back. We'd have some fellas playing their instruments, and we'd dance and drink for what felt like a whole week. Those were good times."

"Nothing brings a town together like a good barbeque," Colby agreed, but she was really just pretending to know what she was talking about. She'd never experienced any sort of real town pride before. She didn't even live in Georgetown during her life - she commuted from Ballard. She didn't even like Georgetown, which made her eternal damnation in the bar she least enjoyed working at while alive so painfully ironic.

The noise of happy hour faded into the background again. Countless people passed by and through the group, but they enjoyed the quiet solitude that always surrounded them.

"Did you really like it here?" Colby needed to know.

"I loved it when John was alive, but it lost its luster pretty quick when the townspeople murdered me."

"I hate it." Cowboy Jerry spoke forcefully.

"I never really thought about it," Tiny Tommy said.

"That sucks, little dude. Did you ever go anywhere outside of Georgetown?"

"Nope."

"And you're stuck here forever."

"So are you, idiot!"

"Oh yeah." Colby dropped the insensitive bitch act when she realized she suffered too.

"Maybe not." Cowboy Jerry gazed through the front window again.

"I don't see why we can't get that lady over here. You know that Vampires can only come in to your home if their invited in by the head of the household."

"Why do you always bring up vampires?"

"They're very popular. You're the oldest, Cowboy Jerry, why don't you just invite her over?"

"What should I do? Jest shout on over to her and see if she ain't got other plans er nothing?"

"We've got to do something, she looks so scared." Matilda floated in the big bay window and watched the woman across the way. Matilda's form looked funny as her body hovered over a thin, raspy woman drinking a bud light. Her bustle and the woman's head merged into one creepy elephant man shape.

The woman across the street locked eyes with them just then. She waved frantically. Colby waved back but the others were too stunned to react. Colby raced out the door but only got as far as the front walk before blindness hit her. The atmosphere became like a tunnel of light that bounced her backward. She couldn't penetrate it. An intense pressure pulled and pulled her hollow form each time she tried to touch the tunnel. She only lasted a few tries before she backed up and fell through the doorway back into the restaurant.

"That was fucking crazy!"

The Haunter across the street became forgotten for the second time.

"Colby!" Tiny Tommy shouted at her. "Where did you go? How did you leave the building like that?"

"What do you mean? That was easy. Like this." She wandered through the door again and came right back in.

Cowboy Jerry, Matilda and Tiny Tommy all stared wide-eyed at her. For a moment, Colby wondered if she'd grown another head. She stifled the impulse to check her shoulders.

"Can't you guys do that?"

"Uh uh."

"What happens when you do it?"

"It's like this tunnel of light comes along and slams into you, it kind of knocks the wind out of you." Tiny Tommy looked frightened at the thought.

"That happened to me too, but out there, not at the door."

"Oh, I git it." A light of understanding brightened Cowboy Jerry's face. "It's a cause ya died half in and half out the door. So you can kinda go outside."

"Am I the only one?"

"Far as I know, ya is."

"Cool. I'm finally unique."

"I guess that means that you have to be the one to invite the Vampire over to play." Tiny Tommy giggled.

"Fine. I was gonna anyway."

Colby exited the door again and felt alone for the first time since her death. She found a place that no one else could go, a secret place all her own. She took a good look around. Cigarette butts littered the ground, some actually making their way into the old coffee can pseudo-ashtray. A couple stood nearby smoking and talking, their conversation fleeting in and out of Colby's ears. She thought it might be time to watch the sunset, and in fact, she could have if it weren't pissing down rain in the grand and glorious Seattle tradition. She longed to feel the rain on her face. She held her hands out and saw the rain pass through her. It didn't seem so long ago that she'd wished for just such a super power. Never Get Wet Girl, a super-heroine with the power to stay dry in any deluge.

She looked down on the sidewalk she stood upon, searching for any remnants of blood, or maybe a dead body line. She'd been dead too long now for such things to remain, but still she searched. The glint of brass caught her attention and she looked down on the side of the building to see a tiny plaque. *In Memory of Colby 2008.*

"Oh, that's so nice."

"Hey!" A shout brought her attention back to the business at hand.

She looked up, fully expecting it to be one of the smokers on the sidewalk shouting about some bullshit, but it wasn't. The woman across the street jumped up and down, waving as if Colby were a helicopter and she was in Vietnam hiding from Charlie.

"Oh yeah," Colby whispered, then shouted, "Hey!"

"Jesus Christ. What the fuck are you doing over there? I've been yelling for ten minutes." Was this bitch really going to start out like that?

"Sorry. I got sidetracked by something shiny." It felt like a very good reason, so she voiced it.

"What!?"

"Nothing, it wasn't about you. I mean, um.. Uh.. What's your name?" Time to change the subject.

"Jackie."

"Hey! I'm Colby."

"What?"

"Colby. I'm Colby." Why was Colby so hard to annunciate? If she had a dollar for every time someone asked her what her name was and then had to repeat it a hundred times, she'd have a couple bucks.

"Okay, great. Are you gonna help me or what?"

"Sure... how?"

"How the hell should I know?"

"Well, what's the situation over there?"

"The building's almost gone and I'm the last one left."

"Where did everyone else go?"

"Disneyland? How the fuck should I know? I'm still here, aren't I?" Jackie, the angry ghost, left Colby feeling less than charitable with her help.

"You're kind of hostile over there!"

"What the fuck does that mean? I'm over here hanging on by a couple of bricks that I had to beat some other ghosts off for - "

"Haunters!" Colby wanted to wow her new friend with the new preferred nomenclature.

"What?"

"We're called Haunters."

"What the fuck ever you call yourselves. Why don't you haunt your way across this fucking street and help me!!"

"I can't cross the street!"

"How'd you get outside then?"

"It's kind of an interesting story actually..."

"You know what. No! I don't want to fucking hear it. Why don't you get your pansy ass back inside your little warm happy building and get together your little Haunting friends to figure out a way to get me the fuck out of here. I see them watching me right now! Go! Go!"

Colby peeked her head back in through the doorway where her three companions waited to hear the neighbor's status.

"She's not very nice," Colby said.

All three chirped at the same time, wanting to know what was happening.

"Hang on." Colby went back outside to her new friend.

"Well?" The blonde devil spoke with all the venom of hell in even her easiest of questions.

"We're gonna need some time to figure this out."

"Perfect. Hey guess what, idiot!? That's one thing I don't have a lot of. So, hurry the fuck up!!!"

Colby reentered Jules Maes. "Man, what a bitch!"

"I bet she's real nice and you're just saying that." Cowboy Jerry never believed anything Colby had to say about another person.

"Trust me dude, even you would have a serious problem with this particular cunt."

The swoosh of a hard slapping hand passed through her face from two directions, one was Cowboy Jerry and the other Matilda.

"We do not use words of that nature in this place." Matilda rarely angered over anything that didn't have to do with Pearl, so this stopped Colby in her tracks.

"Sorry." Even though she wasn't in the slightest bit sorry, an apology felt warranted because she did respect and love Matilda. Words of vulgarity had no real value to Colby, so she never understood when people found them offensive. In her mind calling a woman a hag and a cunt were one in the same.

And thanks to Colby, Cowboy Jerry and Matilda now shared a common thing, after all those years. They both disliked the word cunt. Colby opened her mouth to point out the fact, but thought better of it. She didn't wish to be air-slapped again and be further demoralized.

"What happened?" Tiny Tommy pulled the subject back around.

"Her name is Jackie and she's holding on to the last few bricks to try and save her own skin. She wants me to go over and get her and bring her here."

"Well, yes, we have to try and get her over here somehow."

The two adults committed themselves to the task of saving the blonde bimbo across the way, but Tommy sided with Colby.

"I don't know. She's a real spitfire."

"It'd be good to have a spirited woman around."

"If you think I have a potty mouth, you should hear the profanities that came from her."

"No one can hold a candle to you." Once again, Cowboy Jerry zinged a hidden meaning compliment her way.

"Fine, we can bring her over here and you guys can deal with her, but I just don't have a clue how to do it."

"How far do you think she can get?" Matilda asked.

"I think she's stuck where she is. She doesn't strike me as the kind of woman that would put herself into an uncomfortable position for too long unless it served her purposes."

"Let's try and be a bit more constructive here."

"Fine." Colby crossed her arms and leaned back to listen, but that was all the effort she was willing to put in.

"It's a shame we don't have any rope er nothing."

"Ghost rope? What are you gonna do Cowboy Jerry? Lasso the little Philly?"

"I could if we had some rope." Never tell a cowboy he can't lasso something, they take that stuff real personal.

"I'd prefer to poke her with a really long stick." Two sour looks and one giggle were pretty much the reactions she expected.

"There's gotta be a way."

The pacing began. Both CJ and Matilda crossed each other time and again, thinking. Occasionally they would look outside while muttering to themselves, then shake their heads and continue to think on the problem.

"I know, she can throw us her long golden hair and I can pull her over just like Rapunzel," Colby spoke to Tiny Tommy.

"That's a good one. Or maybe she can just jump over and you can catch her." Tiny Tommy laughed so hard he snorted.

"That's it!" Matilda stopped her pacing.

"What?" All eyes turned to her.

"She can jump over."

"I was joking," Tiny Tommy explained.

"I know, but I bet it would work."

"I don't see how." Realism clouded Colby's sentiment.

"What if she thought really hard about wanting to be over here, obsessed over it like we all seem to do, and then just jumped? We could catch her. If we all think about her coming over, it could work."

It sounded reasonable enough. They didn't have access to a soul-extracting crane. Blind faith and the hope their abusive neighbor spent time practicing her long jump skills provided the only final options.

"What the hell? Sounds good."

Everyone agreed. Colby remained so certain as to the failure of the plan that she agreed to it immediately. Still she wished she could save face and prove how terrible this woman was to everyone else. They spent some time hammering out the details of the rescue. The time came for Colby to return to her isolation chamber and talk to the banshee.

"This plan is complicated. I wish I had someone to help me explain it to Jackie." The intricacy of the plan muddled inside Colby's not so expansive frontal lobe.

Then by some miracle the front door of Jules Maes opened and stayed open. A late delivery guy with a huge order passed through them, all smiles and apologies. Papa Lee, the ever chatty security guru held the door open for the man with a friendly smile.

"Quick!" Colby hustled everyone over to the door. "We can all see and hear her while the door's open."

Colby stepped onto the threshold and waved at Jackie while the others crowded as close as they could to listen and shout back some advice over the transfer.

"Where in the fuck have you been!?"

"Sorry," Colby half-heartedly shouted.

"I've been sitting here and waiting for fucking ever. Do you think this is fun for me? Do you think I enjoy sitting here in this wretched hovel of a building waiting for you? Is this some kind of fucking game for you? Jesus Christ. Did the mutants over there come up with anything or are you all just a bunch of fuck ups?"

"Colby?" Cowboy Jerry whispered in barely audible tones.

"Yeah?" She turned around to face her friends inside the building, each with a more horrified look than the other.

"Hey! Are you listening to me? I'm fucking talking to you, you little bitch! Don't you turn your fucking back on me! Hey! Hey!"

With the banshee levels Jackie achieved, Colby knew if she had any blood left in her spirit it might begin to spew out of her ears.

"Why don't you just come back inside?" Matilda extended her hand toward Colby.

The delivery driver finished bringing in the boxes and shut the door, drowning out the vulgar onslaught from Jackie.

"Sorry," Cowboy Jerry said, simply. He took off his hat and scratched at his receding hairline.

"I'm sorry too." Matilda shook her head. "You were right, she is a real cunt." Matilda laughed and disappeared. Cowboy Jerry left next. Colby and Tiny Tommy hovered alone in the restaurant.

"I think there's a band tonight. Do you wanna go sit in the Jack Daniels for a while?" Tiny Tommy always knew how to make her feel better.

"Does the Pope wear a funny hat?"

"What's a Pope again? I never get that joke."

"Honestly, kid, will you grow up." They laughed together.

"Oh excuse me." A girl with a tray of drinks moved out of Colby's way.

Both Colby and Tiny Tommy stopped in their tracks. They stared at each other with shock. "A Live One just spoke to us!"

New Blood

"Thanks Ruth." Walt gave the waitress a dollar from the pile on the table.

"Sure thing, Walt."

The lure of an easy buck brought many an attractive female to the bar business. It took patience and balls to make it though. People waved, whistled and shouted at you nonstop. The bar regular typified the phrase: *a blessing and a curse.* They knew Ruth and Ruth knew what they drank, so words were meaningless most of the time, especially during a busy night. The level of expectancy on both parts made things difficult at times. The monotony of it never seemed to bother the regulars nearly as much as the staff.

Colby disliked all the regulars, as she remembered it. In Georgetown the regulars ran the gambit. They ranged from wealthy builders, to engineers from Boeing, to poor skate punks with shitty art degrees. To her credit, Colby had completely forgotten about the job, but it didn't take much to remind her of those painful bar years. She'd done it for years, but never well. In the beginning she wanted to do well so she worked hard and expected tips to reflect that work. They never did. She did less and made the same. Then she started drinking and forgot to care. She still made the money, so she lowered her standards and became a lousy bartender. Lazy, lousy and lemony fresh might have described her. She used to freshen up during a sweaty night with lemons on her temples and neck. For the first time, she found something to be thankful for in death. She never, ever, ever needed to wait on another person ever again. That revelation caused a massive smile to erupt on her face.

Tiny Tommy pulled her from her revelry; otherwise she'd spend the entire afternoon reflecting on how amazing death and unemployment really was.

Ruth scurried around the restaurant, grabbing empties and plates along the way. She took a few orders and smiled at a few people who waved at her impatiently. She took the busy nights in stride, did what she could, and tried not to piss off too many people.

"Hey Ruth, are you still dating that guy?" One of the crusties shouted over in a manly way. Colby thought she saw a club under the table, the Neanderthal man's Spanish Fly.

"Of course." She rolled her eyes in a charming manner at the man.

She'd only been working for the company for a short time. She barely learned the computer system and already she'd been asked out by about 5 or 6 different regulars. Ruth never worked in a bar before, so she didn't understand the way things worked. Her sweet demeanor caught the clientele by surprise, and her stunning good looks prompted many a man and woman to turn a grateful eye. Hazel eyes mixed with flaxen hair intensified a perfect oval face. Her body was lean where it should be and fluffy in those other places that mattered. The regulars rewarded her good looks with crooked, toothy smiles and an extra coat of Old Spice.

"Well, when you're ready for a real man - " he smiled and pointed to himself.

"She'll be sure to look anywhere but here!" Colby shouted.

Ruth laughed.

"See that?" Colby poked her elbow through Tiny Tommy. "She heard me. I just know it. She saw us and just heard me."

They rushed over to the server station. It'd been build beneath a stairwell and provided a bit of privacy for the server to collect her thoughts. Working a shift at Jules Maes meant enduring a great deal of useless banter, sometimes you needed a break. When they came up behind her, they heard her humming to herself.

"Oh hey." She blushed slightly at being caught off-key humming, just like Colby used to do. She looked down at Tiny Tommy and frowned. "I'm sorry, but you know you can't be here."

“Can you see me?” Tiny Tommy whispered.

“Of course I can see you, but the real problem is if my boss sees you. You have to be twenty-one to be in here. Sorry.” She turned to Colby. “You’re going to have to take your son out of here.”

Colby and Tommy snickered at each other. “She thinks we’re mother and son.” Colby laughed.

“Well, whatever you are. You have to go.” Colby marveled at her sweet voice.

“Miss! We’re ready to order.” An entirely sour voice interrupted their conversation.

“Hey Lady, where’s my beer?” That one sounded like a frog eating a goat.

“Ruth, you gonna deliver these drinks or what?” Hot Ass, the bartender shouted over to her.

“You better leave before you get in trouble.” She ran past them to pick up her drinks at the bar.

“What the fuck are you doing?” Hot Ass asked.

“I was just talking to that lady.”

“Well it looked like you were just picking your ass.” Hot Ass thrived at being a hot, smart ass.

Colby and Tiny Tommy hovered away into the music hall. They wanted to keep their eyes out for Ruth, but they didn’t wish to get her in trouble either. So they waited until the end of the night so they could talk with her.

Around 1:30 the place cleared out, leaving Ruth and Hot Ass to finish up the night. They locked the door, which ruffled Colby’s feathers for a minute. She hated watching other people do that one thing she should have done. It made her feel all stupid again. Hot Ass drank down a beer while Ruth worked on some paperwork. She excused herself to go to the ladies room and was gone for only a minute or so when she sounded a blood-curdling scream. Hot Ass dropped his beer and it shattered. He bound to the ladies room to see what happened and found Ruth shaking and pointing at nothing.

“What? What is it?”

“There was a man!”

"Where?"

"In the ladies room. I just saw him. He was right there." Her face paled to a ghostly white.

"Which way did he go?" Hot Ass's male savior gene kicked into high gear. He looked ready to kick some ass in his fist forward, leg wide stance.

"That way." She pointed to the wall.

"He went through the wall?"

"I know it sounds crazy, but that's what I saw."

"Okay. Well, I'll look around."

"I'm coming with you."

The two started plodding through the restaurant. Hot Ass carried the baseball bat from behind the bar. In case any trouble arose, he'd be ready for it. That was, if a baseball bat might counteract any trouble a man who could walk through walls might offer.

"Who was it?" Colby asked.

Colby and Tiny Tommy came flying when they heard the scream. They stayed in the bathroom while the Live Ones explored the restaurant for the culprit. Laughter sounded from the wall.

"That's old Milton." The expression on Tommy's face showed his distaste for the Haunter.

"I've never met him."

"Naw, probably not. He mostly stays in here."

"The Ladies Room?"

"Yeah, he likes to watch the ladies take their panties down."

"Yer damn right I do!" A creepy old guy's face poked out of the wall. He had a mouth full of teeth none of which were straight and his hair matched his eyes: feral.

"What do you do that for?" Colby asked. Tiny Tommy shook his head feverishly but it was too late. Milton pulled his whole body out of the wall and revealed himself. The only thing he wore was a pair of penny loafers.

"So's I can do this!" He jiggled his junk in a most upsetting way.

Colby covered her eyes. "Gross!"

She dove out of the bathroom with Tiny Tommy in hot pursuit. Milton's laughter followed them all the way out to the bar.

"You could have warned me. Fuck!"

"Yeah, fuck is right."

"Well, I don't see anyone." A Hot Ass voice sounded from the game room. Colby and Tiny Tommy jetted out of view.

"I'm telling you I saw someone."

"Well, what was he doing in the bathroom?"

"Something disgusting." Ruth shuttered to remember the satisfied expression on the man's face.

"Oh that? That's just old Jake."

"Name's Milton!" The Haunter screamed from behind three brick walls at a man who couldn't hear him. But Ruth heard him.

"You don't know about old Jake?" Hot Ass's mannerism took on a tall-tale-telling stance. Hot Ass had a lot of stances.

"Milton!" Screamed the voice again.

"Well, rumor has it there was a guy who used to come in here to look at the pretty call girls that used to work upstairs, but he never had a dime to spend on it. So, he'd come into the bathrooms and listen for the moans upstairs so he could – um - well, you know. That's old Jake."

"It's fucking Milton!"

"I think his name is Milton." She pointed to the sound of the voice.

"Milton? That's a dumb name. It's definitely Jake."

"AHH!" Milton refused to be ignored.

Ruth cringed to the sound of the screams. For the life of her she couldn't understand why Hot Ass didn't respond to Jake's shouts. Maybe, she thought, Hot Ass merely looked to lure the man out with this fantastic story. Suddenly she looked on him as a savior.

"So, when was the last time anyone saw him?"

"Oh there's usually a sighting of him once every couple of years."

"Should we call the cops now?" Ruth whispered. "I'm pretty sure he's listening to us right now."

"Cops?"

"Do you want to nab him first and then call the cops?"

"Cops don't respond to ghost stories." Hot Ass laughed at her. Ruth was confused, so he elaborated. "Jake's not alive."

"MILTON!!" Milton came diving out in all his naked glory. Ruth's scream caught in her throat. Fear paralyzed her completely. He headed straight for Hot Ass and flew right through him, then he did the same to Ruth. As he passed through her a little sparkle fluctuated through him, and he paused for a moment afterward and smiled at her. He came right up to her and whispered something to her that made her fear disappear. He shot off like a bolt of lightning. That's when Ruth realized her companion had been talking the whole time, completely unaware that anything out of the ordinary occurred. "...and that's how they found him, naked in the bathroom with his dick in his hands."

"He wasn't naked. He was wearing Penny Loafers, maroon ones," Ruth corrected him.

"So you have heard this story."

"I guess so." Ruth couldn't understand the emotions she felt right then.

"Yeah, well, anyways - there are lots of ghosts that live here in Jules Maes. Or at least that's what the regulars will tell you. Of course, I don't put much stock in a bunch of drunks." His reasoning was sound.

"I hope I get to meet them all." Ruth looked into the room expectantly.

"I'm sure you will. Come on, let's get out of here. We still got time to make to last call at the 9lb Hammer. You up for it?"

"Okay." She followed without much thought.

They turned out the lights and walked out the front door.

"Good night." Ruth whispered in to the darkened restaurant before she shut the door completely and locked it.

"Holy Shit!" Colby exclaimed the minute she felt comfortable to do so.

"What just happened?" Tiny Tommy felt the same overwhelming joy that Colby experienced.

"We just had an encounter - that was awesome. We have to tell the others. Cowboy Jerry! Matilda! Pearl! Bryce! Milton! Anyone that can hear me? Come quick!"

Colby needed a cowbell or triangle to round up the troops. Yelling was so primitive. She didn't even know who else to call. She'd just found out about the house pervert. Why didn't she ever know about him?

The Haunters rounded quickly. Cowboy Jerry came first, then Pearl, then Matilda.

"What's all the yelling about?" Pearl asked.

"I'll tell you but we have to get everyone here first," Colby said.

"Who's everyone?" Cowboy Jerry asked.

"I don't know. Cowboy Jerry, you're the one most likely to know everyone. I only just met the guy in the bathroom."

"Milton?" Matilda shook her head at the thought of him.

"Yes?" He appeared at the sound of his name, smiling with all his teeth.

"Ugh, can you at least cover yourself up?" Pearl asked.

He looked around with uncertainty then just covered his genitalia with his hands. "Better?"

"Fine, fine." Pearl turned her back to him in dismissal.

"Cowboy Jerry, can you help us round up the others?"

"Well let's see now - there's Dolores, the old house maid, she died of a heart attack jest like me."

"Oh Dolores. I haven't seen her in ages." Matilda smiled.

"Dolores?" Colby shouted. A translucent figure emerged into the room.

"I'm here." She smiled kindly. She wore a maid's uniform, in white and blue. She adorned her head with a bright kerchief, which made her chubby cheeks seem fuller. She looked like a stereotypical black maid. Her image didn't materialize like the others; instead her form glistened with a faint hollowness.

"Don't forget about Stewart. He is quite the gentleman. He was stabbed during a card game when he called out a cheater." Pearl stood primly by waiting for things to get started.

"Stewart?" Colby yelled again.

"Ma'am." A well dressed man appeared next to her. He dipped his hat toward her and took his place between Cowboy Jerry and Pearl. When Pearl's hands fluttered toward her face in a typical female flirt; Cowboy Jerry didn't look pleased.

"Who else guys?"

"What about Chelsea?" Tiny Tommy piped in.

A universal groan resounded through the room.

"What's wrong with her?" Colby perked to the name; a vague memory loosened in her mind, but she couldn't pull it forward.

"Well, we kinda asked her to leave," Cowboy Jerry explained. "She was a bit hard to deal with."

"Is she mental or something?"

"You could say that," Stewart replied. "It's not Christian to speak of people when they aren't here to defend themselves, but she had a bit of the crazy about her."

"She cried all the time. We couldn't get her to stop." Matilda remembered being elected the one to try and talk her down from her stupor. She failed miserably.

"How did she die?" Colby wondered.

"Electrocuted. Her radio fell into the bathtub. It was a bit of bad luck and she didn't let any of us forget it."

"Hm... well, I'm sorry but this does pertain to all of us. We really need to call her." She paused to be sure they all agreed, and then sent out the bellow for the crazy woman to hear. Ears appeared instantly.

"What's with the ears again? Chelsea," Matilda offered in soothing tones, "we want the whole you."

"I didn't think you'd call me too, but here you all are, just waiting for me. It's so lovely to see you *all* - ," she started crying; sobbing so hard that she developed the hiccups.

Colby recognized her immediately.

"Chelsea! You need to stay calm or else we'll kick your sweet little petooty right back where we called you from," Matilda warned.

"Alright, I'll be fine." She covered her mouth with her hands and tried to relax.

Colby looked up expectantly toward Cowboy Jerry for the next name. He delivered. "Bobby!" He shouted.

A strapping lad appeared wearing a cook's white apron and his token gigantic smile. He waved to everyone.

"How do?" He asked Colby.

"I do okay." Colby stared at Bobby with expectation.

"What?" He looked around in discomfort.

"Well, how'd you go?"

"Oh right - struck dead by a 50 pound bag of sugar." He moved into the group of Haunters waiting for the meeting to begin.

"Gerald!" Cowboy Jerry shouted again.

A man in a cheap suit and tie appeared. He was bald and fat. There were grease stains on his tie and Colby thought she saw the sparkle of a silver tooth.

"Choked on a bone at my table," he said, by way of salutation.

A few other hollow forms appeared with no shouting or invitations and shuffled into their spots to listen to what the new girl had to say. Colby looked around the mini crowd and noticed someone missing, Bryce, her Golden Stiffy, Suspiciously, Clementine, the shameful minx also did not appear.

"Bryce!" she shouted.

"Oh, yeah, where is Bryce?" Tiny Tommy reiterated her thought aloud.

"Bryce!" He didn't answer or appear.

"Is anyone else missing?" She asked the others; taunting them to say the name of the harlot. Every man in the room recognized her lack of attendance, yet for some reason, none mentioned it. Heads shook back and forth. "Alright, let's get started. Tiny Tommy and I have something amazing to tell you. We've had a real encounter with a Live One."

"Aw hell, I'm leaving," Gerald looked annoyed.

"Wait!" Tiny Tommy put his hands up in protest. "At least hear us out before you disappear."

"Fine, but this better be good." If Gerald still had that bone he'd choked on, he might have shoved it down Colby's throat just then.

"I don't respond well to pressure," Colby whispered to Tiny Tommy.

"You'll be fine." He nodded.

"Um... yeah, we had a real interface with the living." She hoped to keep the Haunters rapt with excellent use of vocabulary words.

"What exactly are you saying?" Bobby asked. "We've all been around the living for our whole death, so we have all encountered them."

"But she encountered us right back. She spoke to us and actually saw us."

"Oh, you mean like a psychic? Cowboy Jerry, you remember that psychic that came in here? Must have been about twenty years back. Oh he was a funny one. He had on the cape and everything - called himself Nostradamus or some such nonsense." Dolores had the kind of laugh that was contagious, but Colby stayed focused on the discussion.

"No! Listen. She's not a psychic. Her name is Ruth and it's like she's one of us or something."

"But she ain't?" Cowboy Jerry was confused.

"She's a Live One." Tiny Tommy's patience wore a little thin.

"That is simply not possible," Pearl chimed in.

"We know, but it happened. She nearly scared me to life."

"That's dumb." Tiny Tommy's disappointment at her analogy injured her further.

"Well, it was scary."

"I know I was right there when it happened."

"Fine."

"If you two are done," once again Matilda wished she might be able to slap the shit out of Colby, "can you tell us exactly what happened?"

Colby gave Tiny Tommy a look of annoyance. She never enjoyed corrections in life, why would she suddenly find it affable in death? "It happened right after we let the lady across the street go."

"What lady?" Milton asked. "Is she pretty?"

"No Milton, she was a fucking lunatic, okay?"

"That's my kinda girl."

"What?" Chelsea listened in for the first time, obviously thinking they were talking about her.

"Focus buddy! You're part of this too." Colby couldn't help but notice that Milton started to play with himself.

"Anyway," Tiny Tommy continued, "as soon as y'all retired away, Colby and I were just minding our own business by the door and a woman with a tray moves to avoid us and says 'excuse me' just like that - like she saw us standing right there."

"That's impossible," Pearl said.

"That's what we thought too, so we waited around until everyone was gone and came back out to try and talk to her, only, Milton got to her first."

Every eye turned toward the naked Haunter. Confusion clouded his vision as he couldn't decide the general emotion being poured toward him. Some faces looked angry, some sad, some confused and old Dolores looked disappointed. He kept quiet and blurred his body into a semi-state of invisible.

"Milton! Don't you dare disappear. You tell us what you did." Matilda sounded too stern. Colby envisioned the woman as his mother, taking the young Milton by the ear and scolding him.

"I just did what I always do."

Chelsea let out a girlish giggle. She'd never admit to anyone that she sometimes liked to watch Milton watch the girls. She developed a crush on the pervert some time ago, mostly because she thought she might have a chance with him. They had matching lunacies.

"That behavior is disgusting, young man," Stewart stated. His shoulders puffed up like a bull.

"What would you have me do? I'm a naked man in penny loafers doomed to wander this building forever like this!" He raised his hands in anger and though everyone tried to look away, they were all confronted by his comical nakedness. Most of the expressions in the room remained motionless, but Colby broke. She laughed so hard she might have popped an eye blood vessel if she had any full of blood.

"Stop laughing. It ain't funny!"

"I'm sorry." Colby tried to gain control of her laughing fit but found it rather difficult. "You're right."

An unintentional snicker escaped Cowboy Jerry's lips which caused Colby to lose control again and before they knew it almost everyone in the room laughed. This angered Milton. He jumped up and down with irritation but it didn't help his cause. The only thing funnier than seeing a naked man in Penny Loafers was seeing the same one jumping up and down like an angry schoolboy. He disappeared completely.

"Milton! Come on. We're sorry."

"No you ain't." The air around them spoke without his naked body to accompany it.

"Well, anyway," Colby finally demanded control from herself, "Ruth saw Milton in the bathroom and she screamed, so Hot Ass came on in and tried to help her, but he didn't see Milton at all."

"Don't you mean Jake?" Milton pouted, invisibly.

"Oh yeah, they thought that Milton's name was Jake for some reason."

"It was that last psychic. He said there was a ghost in the bathroom and his name was Jake." Dolores maintained a crisp memory of the old psychic.

"But Ruth heard him talking because every time Hot Ass said the name Jake, Milton screamed out a correction until finally Ruth said, 'I think his name is Milton.'"

"Well, but... that's probably just a coincidence," Stewart said.

"Coincidence? How can that be a coincidence?"

"And who's Hot Ass?" Chelsea inquired.

"The bartender," Colby answered.

"But why do they call him Hot Ass? That's not his Christian name."

"No, probably not." Colby rolled her eyes at the annoying woman. "It's called a nick name - like when we call you crazy cry-baby loony lady."

"No one calls me that." Chelsea's bottom lip quivered.

"For Pete's sake, maybe it's because he has such a hot ass! Or maybe because his girlfriend calls him that. What does it matter?"

"It's just odd, that's all." Chelsea shrouded herself in indignation.

"Listen here. We've all been tricked by the living before, every single one of us came to think that someone saw us or heard us and we get ourselves all worked up over nothing. It's just not possible." Stewart continued with his argument undeterred.

"We can prove it," Tiny Tommy said.

"And how are you gonna do that?"

"We'll just go talk to Ruth."

Colby looked on with growing admiration to her young prodigy. Genius didn't quite describe the amazing cognitive ability of the boy. He qualified as an uber-genius.

"Brilliant!"

"Fine. Let's get this over and done with. I'm awful tired of being so damned illuminated." Gerald waved his hands impatiently to Colby and Tiny Tommy.

The entire group materialized into the restaurant, except Colby who had to float through each level of the house in order to reach her destination. She'd hoped she might be able to disappear with everyone else by just being near a group of Haunters all doing it. But that did not cure her inadequacies. She felt the stares of the entire group when she rushed through the far wall to join them. A few raised eyebrows told her of their disapproval. Luckily more important matters pressed them, and her inadequacies remained on the back burner. The Haunters materialized into a darkened restaurant.

"Shit. I think we missed her," Colby said into the darkness.

"Hello?" A voice sounded from the game room. The Haunters waited as they heard the tepid footsteps of a Live One come closer. Ruth's face emerged in the vague night light. She held the old worn baseball bat in her hands.

"Ruth?" Colby tried not to scare the girl.

"Hey, where did you guys go?" Ruth wore her irritation like a button on her sleeve.

"It's funny you should ask that, 'cause we can't go any where'," Cowboy Jerry explained.

Ruth felt silly holding the baseball bat. She swerved through the crowd of Haunters to reach the bar and return the bat to its rightful home. This action put the Haunters in a confused state of awe.

"There's so many of you." Shock engaged her face like the emergency brake in a Buick.

"Crazy right?" Colby felt the same, since she'd only just met many of them that night.

"I don't understand. I mean, you weren't here, clearly or else I might have seen you, so where do you go?"

"We're always here somewhere. Sometimes we can just disappear from view but we're always around," Colby explained as if she were an expert.

"Some of us can." Pearl wasn't going to let Colby claim any sort of authority on the subject.

"I've almost got it, you know," Colby defended.

"Sure you do."

"Anyway, I was trying to convince some of these non-believers that Tiny Tommy and I had a real encounter with you. But no one believed us."

"I know what that's like."

"We've been discussing our options."

"Discussion is always a good idea. I've been having my share of discussions on the subject as well, with the regulars... my therapist." Ruth looked around for Milton's stringy nakedness, but he'd abandoned the Haunters party and retired to his place in the toilet.

"You see a shrink? I always wanted to." Colby often thought her problems might be solved with the help of a professional and more to the point, his drugs.

"Colby!" CJ chastised.

"Sorry." She shut her rambling mouth, for the moment.

"So," Ruth tried to sort her thoughts aloud, "you're all dead and I'm not crazy."

"That pretty much sums it up," Colby agreed.

"At least the dead part, you might still be crazy," Chelsea snorted.

Ruth didn't look too thrilled with the answer.

"Don't listen to her, she's fucking nuts," Colby whispered to Ruth.

"Call it what you will, but I think we must all be a little on the side of nuts if we're still hanging out in this hell hole."

"Manners," Pearl chimed in with her sweet as pie voice. "This is our first Live One; perhaps we might try to be a bit more hospitable. My name is Pearl, Pearl Davenport Pinnell."

She curtsied delicately with all the reserve of her station.

"And I'm Matilda Pinnell." If she could have given Ruth a hearty handshake, she might have, but only if she could have elbowed Pearl in the ribs while doing it.

"Oh! Are you sisters?" The injured looks of the two women answered the question for Ruth and the question she'd asked shut them both up.

"I'm Cowboy Jerry." CJ turned the subject quick as he didn't wish to insult their new host with any sort of cat fight yelling match which had a tendency to happen when the two women stayed together for longer than a few minutes.

"He's the oldest Haunter here and I'm Colby, the youngest." Colby followed Ruth's gaze down to Tiny Tommy. "I mean I'm the most recently dead. I guess Tiny Tommy is the youngest, though he's been wandering this building longer than you or I have been alive."

"I'm 65." He used his fingers to show his age like a 5 year old might do.

"Nice to meet you." They all looked expectantly at her. "Ruth." She pointed to herself with embarrassment. "I'm Ruth."

The rest came forward to offer their salutations and get a chance for one-on-one interface with their first Live One. A million questions crossed the minds of everyone, both alive and dead, but the situation was too strange to offer much clarity.

"It's great to put names to some of your stories. Now when people ask, I won't have to lie anymore." Lies never came easy to Ruth.

"People are askin' about us?" Cowboy Jerry felt like Ruth had just dangled some reins in front of him. He lit up like a boy riding his first bull.

"You'd be hard pressed to find a single person in this town that doesn't think there's a ghost spooking around somewhere in here."

"Haunters," Colby corrected as she always did. She knew she needed to be pretty militant with her corrections if she expected the name to stick.

"Haunters? I like that."

"It's a good one," Colby boasted.

"I think people are more willing to believe in the Haunters now because so many witnessed the last death."

"Murder," Colby corrected again.

"Right."

"Did they ever catch the guy?" Colby stopped caring about real life so long ago she probably missed the guy being brought to justice.

"I don't think so."

"That sucks. What am I just another fucking statistic? Another unsolved death in a string of the same at this stupid restaurant?"

"Join the club," Matilda said.

"We're talking about me right now, okay?" Emotions flooded back when Colby remembered her intense anger over her untimely death. She glowed brighter for a moment in the dark bar and took on a harsh flesh tone.

"If it makes you feel any better, you're not exactly forgotten."

"What do you mean?"

"There's a whole wall dedicated to you at the Kristof Gallery around the corner, pictures and everything."

"Pictures? What fucking pictures? What did my Mom send baby pictures of me or something? Oh god, there's not a naked one is there?"

"No, nothing like that. It's pictures of, you know, that night." Ruth regretted this conversation almost immediately.

"Dead pictures?"

"Yeah." Oops.

"There are dead pictures of Colby adorning an art gallery wall? Just anyone can stop by and look?" Pearl's obvious disgust at the thought carried through the sarcasm in her voice.

"Not just anyone, but everyone! There are lots and lots of people that come by to look. It got voted 'coolest gore displayed by a gallery' in *The Stranger* this year."

"I've never heard of such an offensive thing."

"Things have changed quite a bit since your time Pearl. We don't hang prostitutes in the street anymore either. Now we celebrate them by putting them on TV and

Magazine covers." Colby didn't want to be the only one in pain, so she lashed out.

"Sounds like I was alive during the wrong time." Matilda winked a thank you to Colby. She always appreciated someone else zinging meanness to her husband-sharing murderer.

"Did I miss something?" Ruth queried.

"It'll take months to get up to date on all the drama of the dead." A faint beep sounded throughout the building.

"Oh shit!" Ruth said. "I have to go. That's the alarm. I only have about a minute to get out before it turns itself on."

Ruth rushed forward and grabbed her stuff off the bar. She'd been on her way out when the Haunters stopped her. She ran out the front door trying not to drop anything along the way and waved goodbye.

"See you all tomorrow," She shouted and pulled the door shut behind her.

Colby followed her and poked her head out the door before she'd locked it completely. It startled her.

"Hey Ruth, how is that you can see us and no one else can?" Colby asked.

"I don't exactly know." She clicked the lock in place and pulled her key out.

"You seem to be taking it pretty well. If I had seen a Haunter when I was alive, I'd be drinking the visions away."

"Not to belittle your 'deadness', but you're not the first Haunters I've ever met."

"There have been others? Cool."

"Once I got used to it, yes. But the beginning was pretty scary."

"I bet things might have turned out differently for you if Milton had been your first, huh?" Colby laughed a little.

"You're right about that. I don't even think my brother could have persuaded me to pursue these 'friendships'. And he's pretty damned persuasive." Her eyes glazed over for a second but before Colby could ask about it, she turned and walked past Colby's limitation mark.

“Bye.” Ruth waved without turning around but Colby saw her dab at her eyes before she turned the corner.

Golden Stiffy's Secret

Things took on a different sort of excitement for the Haunters as they all came to know Ruth. Since their introduction, she brought back a spark to the dead folks, one they hadn't felt in quite some time. Engaging the living in such a personal way made them all feel slightly free, as if their half-life finally had some purpose. Almost everyone caught on to the zeal of the time, but Colby's concern over Bryce began to occupy her thoughts. His absence dragged on for far too long. Clementine remained profoundly absent as well which caused more consternation than Colby readily admitted.

"Do you have a boyfriend?" Colby asked Ruth one day.

It was Thanksgiving and Jules Maes closed down for the entire day. Thanksgiving didn't deter Ruth from visiting her friends and enjoying an entire day of relaxed conversation with them. Her usual day became much more difficult when faced with the horrendous task of carrying on the semblance of normalcy. The Haunters didn't realize how odd she appeared to Jules Maes customers when she seemed to have in depth conversations with herself. Ruth's satisfaction over her new other worldly friendships blinded her to her own actions. It wasn't until Colby overheard some regulars talking about how odd they thought Ruth was; that the Haunters even thought about the difficulty. The Haunters decided to remain clear of Ruth during business hours.

"No, not really. I guess I have some contenders but it seems like I'm always too busy to care about that really."

"That's my one regret in life. I never loved anyone."

"Never?" Amazement filled Ruth's voice. "But you're so old."

"I'm not that old."

"What are you late 30's?"

"Early, thank you very much."

"So you made it to your *early 30's* and you've never loved anyone?"

"Well, I guess I probably loved people but they didn't really love me back."

"Did they just fake it or something?"

"No, but I was so wasted all the time that I never really noticed if I was missing out on anything."

"Ah, yes, the eternal drunk."

"That reminds me, when are you gonna let me take a shot with you?" Colby looked eagerly to her benefactor. She knew that Ruth drank some, not nearly as much as Colby did while she worked; but still, she'd seen the woman throw back a shot or two since they met. She just wanted to be there when she did it next time, but her request seemed very off putting to Ruth. "It just weirds me out."

"Come on, it'll only take a second."

"Will it shut you up?" Ruth was tired of this non-stop request.

"Totally."

"And you won't ask me to do it again?" Ruth prodded further.

"I can't guarantee that."

"NO! You get this one time and one time only."

"Well that's not fair." Colby turned away in despair, though she still hadn't even gotten one shot and already thirsted for more.

"Hey! You're lucky I'm even considering it. Milton wants to be there when I bone someone. Not just bone, but you know, when I suck him off."

"Yer damned right!!!" Milton popped his head out of the nearest wall. He always listened in.

"Go away." Ruth said easily. Her fear of him dissipated many months prior.

"One shot," Colby continued, undeterred.

"Fine. Consider this an early Christmas present."

Ruth wandered over to the bar and looked over the bottles. She grabbed the bottle of Crater Lake.

"Vodka? Gross!" Colby protested.

"What's wrong with vodka?"

"It's too easy, I'm not gonna feel a thing."

"Well what do you want?"

"Jack Daniels." Colby hummed the name as if it were the name of a lover.

"Absolutely not. I can't stomach the after taste; it's like eating potato salad at a white trash picnic."

"Turkey? For Thanksgiving? Come on, that's appropriate."

"Oh good, pick something worse than Jack. How about rum?"

"A shot of rum? What are you a fucking pirate?"

"I am a little Spanish."

"No." Colby put her foot down. "Tequila?"

"I said Spanish! Not Mexican! Besides that will make me puke."

"Galliano?"

"Very funny, you know that bottle has been there since the bar opened in 1930. No thanks."

"Pick something!"

"How about Jameson's?"

"Oooh, yes!! Please!" Colby thought she must be frothing at the mouth like a rabid dog. She hadn't felt anticipation or excitement in forever.

Ruth poured the shot into the glass and looked at Colby, waiting. They both just stared at each other for a minute.

"Are you coming or not?" Ruth asked.

Colby dove into her body and felt that strange tingle that she always felt when she was near Ruth. Ruth took the shot down and Colby felt the liquid rush through her like water through a drain.

"Yuck!" Ruth grimaced at the flavor of the harsh spirit.

"Spirits for the spirits!" Colby cried with pleasure.

"Oh no, you didn't." Tiny Tommy materialized just in time to see Ruth put down the shot glass and Colby come tumbling out of her body.

"Yes!" Colby shouted.

"There'll be no living with her now."

"But she's so happy," Ruth protested, immediately feeling the hazy effects of the booze.

Colby whirled around the bar and gleefully singing "99 bottles of beer on the wall". Her smile took over her entire face. Tiny Tommy and Ruth just watched, shaking their heads. Ruth finally disengaged her gaze when her neck began to ache from the strain of staring upwards.

"Yes, she's the happiest drunk in all of Deadville."

"What about you? What makes you happy?" Ruth asked Tiny Tommy.

"I don't really think about it. I know what makes me laugh and what makes me feel sad. But happy? I don't know if I've ever known what that word really feels like, so I can't simulate it in death."

"I know what you mean. I haven't felt happy in so long that I wonder if I could recall the feeling myself."

"Why are you unhappy?"

"Because of my brother."

"Is he a jerk?" Colby had stopped her rejoicing to join the conversation.

"No, he's quite the opposite."

"What's the problem then?"

"He went missing some time ago and no one's heard from him since. It's all very suspect."

"Were you close?" Colby recalled Ruth's misty eyes the last time she spoke of her brother. It all made sense.

"We were as close as two siblings could be. We talked all the time. And then one day he vanished and I got the worst feeling of my life."

"How long ago was that?"

"Almost eight years now."

"So he's probably dead?" Colby stated the obvious. Tiny Tommy tried to kick.

"What?" Colby saw him do it and for the life of her couldn't understand his rationale.

"That's okay," Ruth said to Tommy. "It doesn't really bother me that much. I mean, it would be really great if he were still alive, but let's be honest, I can see him and talk to him either way."

"True." Hey, a positive side to the death of a sibling.

"How are you gonna find out for sure?"

"Well, that's part of the reason that I'm in Seattle, looking for my bro."

"You're not from here?" Colby wasn't a native either, she grew up in Montana.

"Nope, we're from Chicago."

"Ah, the old windy city, I know it well." Colby pretended to know more than she did. She pretended a lot, it seemed.

"Anyway, Bry moved here from Illinois to pursue his music career," Ruth said.

"Didn't you just say you were from Chicago?" Colby scoffed.

"Idiot! Chicago is in Illinois," Tiny Tommy corrected.

"Right, sorry. That shot went right to my head." Colby's embarrassment showed but she continued talking as if she weren't the dumbest person in the room.

"A lot of people move here for just that purpose. Everyone in Seattle is in a band, most of them suck."

"There are some good ones."

"Sure there are." Colby scoffed. She'd heard some of the worst music ever made in the backroom at Jules Maes and no one in Seattle could deny it.

"There are. Bry was in one of the good ones. He sent me a couple CD's and they sounded really good. I bet they would have made it."

"Maybe they did make it and he got hooked on drugs and forgot everything, including family."

"I don't think so. That's not his style."

"Drugs destroy lives, lady, believe it." Colby knew first hand the torture of drugs, she tripped on acid once.

"Anyway, I've been trying to find clues as to his whereabouts since I arrived a year ago, but I keep coming up dry."

"We'd help, but ya know, we're dead."

"Hey thanks." Ruth rolled her eyes and wished she hadn't given in to Colby's shot request.

"Where is everyone else?" Ruth wanted to talk about something else. Every time she started thinking about her brother she always got upset. She didn't want to cry, it was sad enough that the only friends she had to spend the holiday with were dead. She looked at the turkey TV dinner she left to thaw on the bar with disdain. She missed the smells of the holiday.

"They said they'd be down by noon. It's almost time for everyone to wake up."

"Noon?"

"Yeah, about noon," Colby repeated.

"Do you even know what time noon is anymore?"

"Yeah. Noon is when the sun is out."

"Okay."

"She's just mad because she can't disappear," Tiny Tommy remarked.

"Still haven't figured it out, huh?" Ruth asked.

"I just don't care anymore. I wasn't very good at math either and it never held me back. This is just another thing that I will never master, why should death be any different than my life?"

"If you would just concentrate, you could do it," Tiny Tommy argued.

"Tommy, I will not have this discussion." She shushed him with a rigid finger in the face. "This is a holiday and we will only have happy talk."

"Sorry Mom," He joked.

"Too late, you're grounded - no TV for a week."

"What's so great about TV again?"

"*South Park... Top Chef... Project Runway*?" Colby couldn't believe she had to tell the ghost of a five year old about the wonders of television. "You're hopeless."

The others arrived after a time and the group spent the afternoon talking about holiday memories. It pleased most of them to reminisce. Every single one of them found it easy to recall at least one happy holiday. Pearl spoke of her lavish childhood Christmas' before the big crash.

Dolores told opposite stories of growing up poor and happy. She spent her life surrounded by family and friends who loved her.

Cowboy Jerry had a funny story about his horse.

The mood remained jovial throughout the day but something weighed heavily on Colby's mind. She worried about Bryce. She didn't want to alarm the others and she didn't know if he'd just disappeared himself away. She excused herself after a while and went in search of him. His privacy be damned, this was a holiday and they should all be together. He hadn't even met Ruth yet.

Tiny Tommy came along, since she didn't have the slightest clue as to where to begin. Tiny Tommy took her right to him. He sat, perfectly visible in a dusty old chair, in the furthest upstairs space. At one time the space encompassed the whole of a larger room, but it appeared someone erected a wall to conceal a miniscule part of it. The three Haunters barely fit into the spot, but that didn't deter any of them from meeting.

"You knew where he was the whole time?" Colby whispered.

"Yeah, of course." He shrugged his shoulders at the ridiculous question.

"Jerk."

"What did I do?" He grumbled to himself.

They poked their heads into the tiny space. Bryce looked up but didn't acknowledge them.

"Bryce, what are you doing up here?"

"Guarding."

"Guarding what?"

"Just guarding."

"Okay that's fine, but you know what today is, right?" Colby tried to keep the mood light and fun. His vacant eyes glazed over her as if she weren't there. "It's Thanksgiving. Everyone's downstairs in the restaurant hanging out and having a good time."

"What's so fun about a food holiday when you're dead?"

"Lighten up, dude."

"Did you just tell me to lighten up? You telling me to lighten up? That's a laugh."

"At least you're laughing."

"Just go away. If I wanted to talk to anyone, I'd be down there in the social room. But I'm not, am I? I'm here, alone in a quiet dark room." He folded his arms together as if it would bar the two Haunters from him.

"All alone?" Colby couldn't resist the question. She looked around with intent nonchalance, but hadn't spied the little hussy anywhere around.

"Do you see anyone else?"

"Haunter's can be pretty tricky, what with the disappearing thing and all."

Tiny Tommy cleared his throat, preparing his voice for an insult. When he saw the pathetic love-like expression on his friend's face, he held back. He wasn't a complete monster, after all.

"Who else would be here?" Bryce had no idea of the insane and obsessive story Colby concocted in his absence. It was probably better that way.

Colby sighed. "If I had a dollar for every time one of my relationships started like this, I might have been able to buy another life for myself."

A slightly fearful look took over Bryce's face. Tiny Tommy backed his face out of the space and disappeared. He had a funny feeling about where their conversation might lead and he respected Colby too much to watch her make a move on a dead guy.

"Jesus Colby." Bryce wasn't in much a mood to deal with her, but for once she didn't care.

"What? I'm a woman, you're a man. We're stuck in this hell hole together. Can't a girl ask for some companionship from time to time?"

"I thought that was what Jack was for?"

"Jack? Who the fuck is Jack?"

"Jack Daniels."

"Oh him, he and I broke up a couple of years ago. Maybe you heard about it."

His face didn't crack. No smile, no humor, just sorrowful death lined the creases of his pale face. "Colby, why can't you just leave me alone?"

"Because I want a boyfriend."

"And I'm the lucky guy?"

"Well, it was a tough race between you and Milton. I gotta say Milton was pulling ahead. Get it? *Pulling ahead?* Heh? Heh?"

"Yeah, I get it, it's a dick joke."

"Tough crowd," she said to her imaginary friend.

Silence threatened to consume them but Colby wouldn't allow it. She kept right on talking.

"You need a break from all this melancholy. Just come downstairs and hang out for a little while."

"I don't want to."

"Ten minutes and then you can come right back here and sit in the dark for all eternity if you want."

"NO."

"You don't have to be my boyfriend, just come out of this closet!" She shouted. She looked at him with intensity then, as if a light bulb turned on. Understanding flooded her puny little brain.

"I'm not gay," he said.

"You sure? You're awfully sensitive."

"Fuck! Leave me alone!" He stood and yelled directly in her face. Without the danger of bad breath or spitting, Colby felt nothing less than the thrill of close proximity. He did care after all. Past experiences dictated that only those who truly cared screamed obscenities in her face.

"But you haven't met Ruth yet," Colby grasped at the last straw she had to bring him out.

"Ruth?"

"Yeah, you've been up here so long, you missed all the excitement."

"What? Another dead broad?"

"No, a Live One. She can see and hear us!" Colby clapped her hands together. The gesture was, of course, completely ineffectual.

"What?" Shock registered on his face.

Colby remembered seeing shock like that on another's face once, the guy she smashed in the face with a 2x4, quite by accident. She rejoiced in the knowledge that Bryce would never suffer such injury by her hand. "Yeah, it's a crazy story really, but Tiny Tommy and I met her. She works here." Finally, she commanded Bryce's full attention. Impulsively, Colby's hands went to the buttons on her shirt and she spread her lapels open revealing her boobs.

"Why didn't you say so?" Happiness tore across his face, and he sped off so fast that he dove right through her and down to the main restaurant before Colby could react.

"I knew he cared." Colby didn't realize that Bryce left the space so fast he never saw her boob flash.

Downstairs the party raged, like a Dead Guy Mixer. All the Haunters interacted together nicely and even Pearl and Matilda seemed to be getting along. Bryce gazed around in amazement. For some reason, all the Haunters bubbled over with smiles, and lively chatter filled the room. He'd missed a lot during his self-confinement. He didn't see any new faces, though he searched pointedly. Colby caught up to him quick, she liked to play Chase the Golden Stiffy.

"Where is she?" He asked.

"I don't know. She was here when I left."

The party-goers noticed Bryce's entrance and let out a cheer.

"Bryce!" Matilda smiled at him. "Well, we haven't seen you in so long; we all started to worry for you."

"Hi, Matilda." He smiled shyly. Colby kept her eyes on the flirtation. She wouldn't have Miss Big Overflowing Boobies eye balling her man, especially after they shared such an intimate moment.

"What's all the shouting about?" Ruth came back into the room carrying her microwave dinner. She stopped mid-step when she saw Bryce and dropped the dinner on the floor where it exploded across the concrete.

"Oh damn! I was gonna eat that with her." The brevity of the situation was completely lost on old Cowboy Jerry.

"Bry?" Ruth whispered.

"Ruthie?" He whispered back.

"Bry!!! Oh god, is it really you?" She ran to him and tried desperately to touch him but her fingers slipped right through his translucent body.

"Ruthie, I knew you'd come. I just knew you'd find me." Bryce's eyes hollowed with emotion. The only thing he wanted right then was to hug his little sister.

"So wait, Bry is Bryce?" Colby asked.

"Keep up moron." Tiny Tommy shook his head at her for the second time that day.

"Wow, what are the odds?" Bobby said, though he had absolutely no idea what was happening. It bothered him that he and Colby had so much in common just then.

"This place is like a soap opera. I am thoroughly confused." Colby pulled at her hair but the act alone didn't solve her frustration, since she felt nothing.

"What's there to understand? Ruth's brother disappeared somewhere in Seattle, so she came to find him and she did. *Voila.*" Tiny Tommy recalled more than a hundred scenarios he needed to explain to his dense little friend.

"This would be easier to understand if I had a shot in me. Ruth?"

"What?" She hadn't heard a thing Colby said. She just kept touching the air around Bryce's face and laughing, the two caught in a magical sibling moment.

"Shots?"

"Colby!" Everyone shouted in unison.

"Jeez," Colby responded.

"I told you it was a bad idea," Tiny Tommy said to Ruth.

"Spill it." Ruth successfully ignored everyone in the room for the first time since she'd started working at Jules Maes.

"What do you want to know?" Bryce didn't have a clue as to where to begin.

"Why here?"

"My body's stuffed upstairs."

All the little voices and cackles in the background quieted. Even the mouse, recently apprehended in the trap, stopped squeaking. In his defense, he wasn't really interested in the story, he actually died.

"Your body's still here?" Ruth's face displayed sheer horror. Eight years of searching and she never would have found him if it hadn't been for these Haunters.

"Nobody noticed a corpse in this place? Hello! I thought we were supposed to be all in tune with our environment and stuff." Colby chastised everyone.

"It's stuffed inside a fake wall, which is not exactly in plain view of the public."

"Yeah but the smell of a rotting dead corpse, I mean, my God, it must have been absolutely horrible."

"Colby!" Tiny Tommy gave her that look again.

"It's not like we could smell it." Bobby said.

"Yeah, but man if we could, it'd be like a hundred times more powerful than rotting meat mixed with rotting vegetables. Plus are there like maggots and stuff? Holy shit, it must be so gross!"

"Colby!"

"Sorry. What about the Live Ones upstairs? Do you think they can smell it?"

"Maybe that's why they burn so much patch-oly incense," CJ reasoned.

"Of course, they probably don't know the difference between the smell of a dead guy and their own dirty bodies." Stewart wrinkled his nose, though he'd never smelled a hippie before, by all accounts he held rather low expectations.

"Hey, I have an idea. Let's stop talking about how smelly my brother's remains are."

"Good idea." Bryce agreed. He remembered why he never socialized with these people. Their lack of social graces mirrored that of a retarded ten year old, especially his new fake girlfriend. He wondered at the odds of her forgetting about their relationship.

"How did you wind up dead?" Ruth asked. She'd lied when she said she didn't care if he was dead or not. She really cared a lot just then because she wanted to hug him more than anything.

"It's so stupid."

"Good," Colby blurted out. Once again all eyes turned to her. "I just mean, I don't want to be the only one that's stupid. I mean, whose death was stupid."

"We know what you meant." Tiny Tommy felt it was his responsibility to keep Colby quiet, but he definitely believed the first part of her statement way more than the second.

Bryce decided to simply ignore Colby. It worked just fine. "The band was doing really well. After self-funding the first three albums, we finally got signed to a major label. We planned a tour for the summer and everything began to look good for us. Unfortunately our guitarist, Danny, got into a bit of trouble with drugs. Money became an issue for him, as well as his affair with his drug dealer's girlfriend. From there things just escalated like any damn drug movie you've ever seen. I was the one that wound up dead."

"Sex, drugs and rock and roll, baby. Living the dream." Colby nodded in understanding.

"It was more like a nightmare."

"You say tomato..." Colby refused to believe that any life involving alcohol and drugs could be all bad.

"Mom and Dad are gonna freak out." Ruth envisioned the conversation she'd have ahead of her. They'd have to come out and claim the body for a proper burial, after all this time. What a shitty ending for such a great guy.

"Oh God, Mom and Dad? How are they?" Bryce marveled at his own forgetfulness.

"Just the same, I guess. They're getting older. Dad retired a couple years ago and they were planning a trip to the old country next year."

"The trip they've been talking about since we were kids?"

"Yeah, if you can believe it, they are finally going." The siblings rolled their eyes to each other. In their minds, a trip to Ireland equated to *Imagination Land* for their parents; the trip always planned but never taken.

The Haunters stood around for a while, watching Ruth and Bryce as they caught up on their news. After a while it became boring for them, so they began to fade away, one by one. Only Colby remained behind. Even if she could disappear, she wouldn't have, since she too wanted to spend every second with her new boyfriend. Eventually Ruth became tired and though she protested over Bryce's insistence that she leave and get some sleep, eventually she did and that left Colby and Bryce alone together, at last.

"Well, what should we do?" Colby's attempts at sultry sexpot were paltry at best.

"I think it's time to say good night." Bryce didn't want to be completely rude and just disappear. After all, Colby did get him to come downstairs.

"But it's so early. It's not like you have anywhere to go."

"Yes, but I need some time to think."

"You can think with me around."

"Goodnight Colby." Bryce insisted.

"I could show you my boobs again."

"What? NO!" Though he was hard pressed to remember her doing that before, he didn't want to dwell on the thought for too long. The very nature of it seemed perverse.

"Well, fine, I can take off my pants if you prefer." She started unbuckling her belt.

"I'm really tired. I gotta go. Bye!!" He dissolved instantly.

"Oh, wait! Okay, bye." She frowned into the empty room. "Men are so fickle."

She looked around wishing for party remnants to clear away. Mindless cleaning soothed the soul sometimes. But, a gathering of Haunters left no mark. One empty pint glass sat upon the dishwasher, Ruth's. Other than that, not a single clue remained to tell the patrons of Jules Maes that 15 people socialized for many hours on that very spot.

Colby felt lonely. She paced up and down on top of the bar for a while and then her eyes caught the glimmer of old Jack and she gave in. Months passed since last she nestled her ghostly form along the liquor shelf but tonight she returned to her old ways.

"Hello Jack. I missed you."

The Return of Stinky Bum

"Holy Shit!" Colby screamed so loud she thought sure the Live Ones might have heard her if it hadn't been Honk Fest. The better part of nine marching bands blared all manner of instruments through the entire downstairs of the restaurant.

Colby didn't notice the High School Marching Band uniforms, or dorky guys trying to pick up on slutty girls with tambourines, or even the fifth rendition of "When the Saints Go Marching In". Today she only had eyes for the slovenly man seated quite brazenly on the last bar stool.

The man looked awful, as though he hadn't showered in some time, perhaps since the last time he'd visited the bar. With the Burning Man crowd that that evening, he fit right in. A sort of dusty grim settled onto his exterior making everything dirty about him, especially his eyes. He sat at the bar, scanned the crowd, looked up ladies' skirts and generally oozed all over the psyche of all those who surrounded him. He'd already lifted two wallets from within the crowd. Jackets and bags left haphazardly behind while the members of the Marching Bands trolled along Airport Way begged to be rifled through. This event read as pure gold for old Stinky Pants.

"Ruth!" Colby came right up beside her while she stood behind the bar, pouring drinks.

"That'll be 8 bucks," Ruth said to the man dressed like a hambone. Ruth glanced down his costume and wondered where the guy planned to drink his eight dollar drink from. No holes made themselves evident. As much as she wanted to know the answer, she knew the dangers of actually asking the question; it always led to an answer and sometimes those answers scared the crap out of Ruth. A man dressed like a hambone probably retained a vast reservoir of scary answers. Ruth had enough problems forgetting some of the grosser sights of Jules Maes; the Live Ones defied the fright level of the Haunters hands down.

"Ruth! Ruth! Ruth!" Colby chanted.

The pork product handed her a twenty and she turned to the register to make change. "Not now," she whispered to Colby. "I'm busy."

The line to the bar wrapped around into the other room; it was the most colorful and ridiculously dressed line that Colby had ever seen at Jules Maes before. It looked like Clown School collided with Marching Band and the result, a grotesque intermingling of mismatched color swatches that pained the eyes. They thought themselves rock stars, you could tell by their demeanor. "I'm with the band" was written all over their geeky little faces. No doubt they all had at least one bottle of Proactive safely tucked away in their instrument cases in case of a sudden zit outburst. Judging people like this was too easy. So Colby did the only thing she could - she turned back to Ruth and tried to get her attention again.

She'd gone on to the next customer, another in a long line of *I don't know what I want and when I figure it out I still won't have my money ready and when I do have my money read I'm gonna hold it in my hands and carry on my conversation with my friend before I hand it to the bartender* people. Man, they sucked.

The music stopped for a moment, so Colby took the opportunity: "Ruth!"

"Stop it!" Ruth turned and looked right at her. The anger in her voice bubbled over.

"What?" The girl at the front of the line looked offended. Ruth took a second to observed her outfit, which literally reached across and slapped her with its hideousness, before she made the decision to keep her apology to herself. The Honk Fest participant's outfit proved entirely more offensive than anything Ruth could ever say aloud - ever. Screaming lilac wig, star glasses, boa and some silver crinkle shirt thing thrown in the mix. Colby wanted to slap her right back.

"Nothing. What can I get ya?" Ruth tried to smile through her irritation, but feeling it pointless, moved on and just worked instead.

"Um...." The girl looked lost, abandoned and completely incapable of making a decision or counting money. Ruth moved onto the next person.

Colby wouldn't be ignored. She started diving through Ruth, over and over, screaming her name.

"Fuck!" Ruth said all the sudden. Everyone at the bar just stopped and stared at her for. They didn't know what to do. Even the Stinky bum looked a little on the frightened side. But he quickly hid his face in his beer to assuage his fear.

"Hot Ass, I gotta pee," Ruth said and left the bar. Colby followed Ruth into the bathroom. "What? What is so damned important that you couldn't let me do my job for five seconds?"

"He's here." Colby's eyes widened in fear, maybe anger. She hadn't given herself any time to assess her feelings on the subject. She functioned on adrenaline alone. Everything about the scene touched a nerve. His callous attitude, filthy clothing and general position in the restaurant mirrored a scene from a not so distant past.

"Who's here?" Ruth dropped her pants. She really did have to pee. A snicker sounded through the wall. "Go away Milton!" Ruth shouted at the wall with anger. "I'm in no mood."

"Sorry," he hollowed back.

Ruth turned her attention back to Colby expectantly.

"It's the Stinky Bum. He's sitting at the bar right now."

"Which Stinky Bum? I lost track of who's who two hours ago."

"The one who killed me. He's here and he's sitting at the fucking bar right now." A shocked look crossed Ruth's face. The look appeared while Ruth wiped herself, so Colby felt compelled to tell her again, in case her shock drew from another, more private, source. "My murderer," Colby said, with feeling.

"I heard you." She stood up and pulled her pants up along with her.

"Call the cops. Have him arrested."

"It's not that easy. I mean, how can we prove that he's the one who killed you? And are you absolutely sure that it's him?"

Colby's look of certainty showed a loathing for Ruth's doubt. For once, Colby didn't feel like the dumbest person in the room.

"Okay, sorry. But I can't go out there and say that the reason I think this guy murdered you is because you told me so. People are really not going to believe that."

"Well, he's been lifting wallets all night. I bet he has about four of them by now. You can call the cops on him for that and then just casually mention the whole murder thing."

"Ah! Theft! Now we're talking." Ruth exited the bathroom and went straight to the phone. She pointed the guy out to the bouncers, Papa Lee and Country Mike. She mostly wanted to keep the guy in the building, but she feared the two bouncers might befriend him and let him go. She tried to relay the stern message that the cops were indeed on the way and the gentleman of stench would be going with them. Her bouncers, big gushy teddy bears, always gave people the benefit of the doubt, which often necessitated Ruth's mean side to surface.

It took a long time for the cops to get there which led Ruth to wonder if they even knew where Georgetown was. They seldom made appearances down there, except during times of gunshots. The Honkers kept Ruth busy. Colby stood watch, literally standing on the guy's head while wishing she could pee on him, or do something else really nasty. She didn't want to disturb Ruth further, but she started growing restless as the minutes tricked by without the appearance of the Fuzz.

By the time the cops arrived in Georgetown, things bubbled over into a mild state of chaos. The Marching Bands had taken the party to the streets and displayed a rather blatant disregard for the police and their desires to enter Jules Maes. They practically barred the door with their bodies, so sweaty and colorful. Over-privileged white folks danced their monkey dances using hoola-hoops and their inability to copy anything resembling rhythm. The Stinky Bum tried a few times to leave, but Ruth kept him inside by giving away a couple drinks. This made Colby sick to her stomach.

"What are you doing?" Colby yelled at Ruth.

"Do you want him to leave?" She whispered. There were only about 20 people left in the bar, so her conversation might be overheard.

"No, but he doesn't deserve fucking free stuff!"

Cowboy Jerry, Matilda, Bryce (who rarely left Ruth's side these days) and Tiny Tommy all floated around the man, watching him like a hawk. They couldn't have done anything even if they wanted to, but it made everyone feel better just by keeping an eye on him. He got up and started moving around the bar again.

"He just got another one. This one looks fat. Gawl, these kids need to take better care of their stuff." CJ watched Stinky Bum take a wallet right out from under a table.

"Hey! What are you doing?" Jerry Garcia asked. At least it looked an awful lot like Jerry Garcia. Dressed like a band leader, in sort of muted black with rather dramatic satin threaded shoulder pads, the man revealed his life long dedication to the craft of Marching Band. He claimed responsibility for the ruin of many a youth to the rhythmic dorkiness. Events such as Honk Fest helped everyone involved feel like rock stars, though that couldn't be further from the truth.

"What? Hmmph - " Stinky Bum wandered away without really saying anything. Ruth saw Jerry Garcia walk up to the bar and knew it was all going to come to a head right then.

"You gotta get that guy outta here. He's being really disruptive to the flow of tonight. We have a really great vibe going on and he's kind of shitting all over it."

"Yeah, I see what you mean." She had her eyes on the guy. He'd sat back down at the same seat he'd been in all night and just looked at her with a crooked smile.

Jerry got disrupted by loud noises when a few stray horns came barreling by. He frolicked off to relive the glory days of queer frenzy and forgot all about his problem with the Stink. Obviously the man's mushroom trip kicked in just then. If Ruth weren't constricted to keeping Stinky Bum in the building and having the bands perform until their set time ended, she would have kicked every last one of her illustrious patrons out on their collective bottoms.

"Hey Barkeep!" Stinky shouted. "How about another?"

"Sure." She poured him a whiskey shot, Jack Daniels.

"Come on! Don't you dare give my Jack Daniels to that slimy piece of Stink." Colby's anguish hardened her gaze toward her beloved friend.

"Fine." Ruth relented and took the shot herself. Then she poured a well whiskey for the sleaze bag.

"Thank you," Colby responded.

Just as Ruth put the shot in front of the murderer, the door opened again. The boys in blue finally made their appearance. Stinky Bum's nose prickled up and he knew instantly trouble found him. He took the shot down quickly before it got pulled from his grasp.

"Finally!" Colby yelled.

"Hey guys, thanks for coming," Ruth said casually. She wanted an army to come to the rescue but had to be satisfied with merely two. The amount of alcohol their tangy friend consumed insured a less aggressive arrest. He couldn't stand without toppling over. By rights, Ruth wondered if they might take her in too, for over serving. She motioned to the man at the end of the bar and the cops approached him cautiously.

"I guess you're here for me, huh?"

"It looks like it." Cop number one stated through his rather spectacular mustache.

"You tricked me good little lady. Not many can, but you surely did." He laughed at her and Ruth felt queasy. She could imagine him just shooting someone for no reason. He had an unreasonable air about him.

The cops pulled the man from the bar stool and he slid off easily. The stools were built into the floor so they didn't have to worry about the one he slouched upon clattering after him. They pushed him against the edge of the bar and started searching him. "Do you have any needles or sharp objects in your pockets, sir?" Cop number two, obviously the rookie judging from his clean shaven, mustache-free face, asked.

"I guess you'll just have to take a chance and see."

The cop started pulling out wallets from the guys pockets. The Haunters started to cheer - old Stinky Bum finally received his comeuppance. Relief flooded through Colby like an imaginary waterfall. "You don't look like a Helen," he stated, "Or a Jennifer, Charlie or William Farnsworth Jr."

"His name is Stinky Bum!" Colby shouted.

"Hush, I wanna listen," Matilda said.

A long whistle sounded when he got to the back of the guy's pants and pulled out a gun, cocked and ready to fire.

"What have we here?"

"That ain't mine."

"Ruth! Holy shit! I think that's the same gun!" Colby jumped up and down.

"Are you fucking kidding me?" Ruth asked.

"Excuse me Miss, maybe you should let us handle this," the officer hushed her.

"Sorry."

They emptied all the bum's pockets and laid his booty out on the bar. He had seven wallets, a wad of cash, the aforementioned gun, a harmonica and some playing cards.

"Some of that stuff is actually mine," he defended.

"We're counting on it." The officer pulled his hands behind him and cuffed him. The second officer led him through the boom boom crowd toward his squad car while the mustached one stayed behind to ask some questions.

"So you saw this guy stealing wallets?"

"Yeah, he's been here all night kind of annoying people too."

"Tell him about me!" Colby felt avenged already.

"Most people would have just kicked the guy out."

"I guess that would have been the smart thing to do." Ruth suddenly decided she liked mustaches. She averted her eyes from the snug fit of the officer's uniform, especially when he turned and displayed his perfect, taut buttocks.

"Hello, skip to the end please." Colby grew annoyed.

"Leave her alone; can't you see she's flirting?" Matilda said. "And he's a real looker too."

"Now is not the proper time for such behavior."

"How come when I say that, you just ignore me?" Bryce asked.

"That's different."

"It's really different. I don't see Ruth showing her boobies to the nice officer," Tiny Tommy said.

"Maybe she should try it." Colby crossed her arms against the onslaught.

"So do you work here a lot?" The officer flirted right back.

"Quite a bit."

"Always this late shift?"

"Usually."

"You know someone was killed here, bartender, working the late shift."

"Perfect segway," Colby said.

"Um Hmm." Ruth missed her cue and instead took the opportunity to stare longingly into Sergeant McDreamy's deep blue eyes."Hey! Can you just focus for one minute here?" Colby stood between Ruth and the Officer. "Remember me?"

"Oh right. Sorry." Ruth shook off the lust. "You know, the bartender got shot by a bum, a stinky bum. It probably wouldn't be such a weird coincidence if the same guy came back to the scene of the crime. You did say the gun was cocked and loaded." Ruth listened intently to her own argument and felt vulnerable all the sudden. She felt her knees give way. The officer caught her. "Oh my god, you don't think that he was gonna kill me too?"

"Well, it did appear that way." He didn't sugar coat it. No one ever learned a hard lesson about life with pretty answers.

Bryce snapped. "Ruth. You gotta get out of here. I can't protect you, like I should. You can't go like I did, or worse - like Colby!"

"Why am I worse?"

Bryce still remembered his parents' visit when they came in from Chicago to pick up his body. Ruth brought them into the restaurant to eat and talk and Bryce stood by the whole time. It tormented him for weeks. The upset he witnessed from both parents troubled him deeply. He regretted everything: leaving home, following a dream, dying. They might not survive a return to Jules Maes to claim another child's body.

"You've got quite a head on your shoulders," the officer said. "You thought quickly in the situation and had it under control. I admire that."

How could she tell him she had 5 Haunters who actually helped her, and if it had been up to her, she would have kicked the guy out hours ago. Answer: don't. She smiled what she hoped was a confident smile, ever thankful to the bar for hiding her shaky knees.

"Well, I've got your statement. I'm gonna take this guy in and see that justice is done."

She gave him the funniest look.

"What is he? One of the three Amigos? Where's your sombrero, idiot." Colby laughed.

"Too Cop-y?" He asked.

"Just a tad." Ruth ignored Colby, talk about a cock-block.

"I'll work on it." He smiled and extended a hand to her. "My name is Sam."

"It's nice to meet you." She shook his hand and knew he'd be back.

"Holy Shit! That was awesome!" Colby shouted when Sam left.

"Right? He was pretty cute, don't you think?"

"He was a handsome devil," Matilda agreed.

"I did like the look of that one," Cowboy Jerry nodded his head in agreement.

"What? No I mean busting the bad guy? Was I the only one paying attention to that part?"

"What do you think about mustaches?" Ruth asked Matilda.

"I think their nice, of course, in my day there were many more of them than you see now. They do tickle though." She winked at Ruth, which made her blush.

"Can we talk about Stinky Bum for a minute?" Colby couldn't believe that the flirtation took precedence over the arrest.

"I think we should talk about it too." Bryce's full attention was on Colby though, not Ruth. "How dare you put my sister into the line of fire like that! She could have been killed."

"She would have been in good company," bright side Colby stated.

"That's not funny."

"What if he left and never came back?" Colby did not want to be the bad guy in this situation.

"He came back once. He probably would have come back again." Tiny Tommy didn't want to be left out of this one. He liked Ruth too much to put her in jeopardy as well, but it was pretty awesome when the cops arrived.

"Well, for all we know, we prevented a few murders by catching him today. Come on you guys. I've been avenged!

Isn't that absolutely amazing?" Colby allowed peace to settle into her bones and her image fluttered from view a little bit.

"You're doing it," Tiny Tommy whispered. He didn't want to spoil the moment, but after three years, Colby finally disappeared a little.

"I know. I feel totally alive right now. I caught the bad guy! Man, it's awesome."

"No. I mean it. You're doing it!" Tiny Tommy clapped his hands in delight. Colby wasn't listening and no one else paid any attention to anything she did anyway, so Tommy celebrated for everyone.

"Do you think he's gonna come back?" Ruth asked.

"Stinky Bum? No way, he's staying in jail for sure."

"No, I mean Sam." Ruth gave Colby that *you're stupid* look, but even that didn't rain on her parade.

The room burst alive with the return of a marching band, every member in a state of disarray. Smeared clown make-up, missing articles of clothing and a complete inability to keep in tune with the swarms of musicians they strutted beside displayed the effects of countless libations. It stopped the conversation amongst the Haunters and Ruth. Hot Ass appeared from his secret hiding spot to help Ruth who rushed to control the musical rally. Cowboy Jerry and Matilda contemplated Ruth's love life further, and Bryce continued to cast evil looks at Colby, who in his mind, could be blamed for every bad thing that happened in Jules Maes.

Colby couldn't be bothered with any of it.

Roses smell great
Violets are stinkers
Looks like old Stinky Bum
Is going to the Clinker!

Colby laughed and circled the room floating through everyone one time and dove upstairs to be alone. She wanted to bask in the glory of success, and since no one else seemed intent on her victory, she thought she might as well just do it alone. She knew where the upstairs folk kept their booze and there was a shelf of it calling her name.

Selling the Store

"Thanks for coming you guys," John, the Bossman, said to the small crowd of his employees. He had called a special all-staff meeting that day.

Despite the earliness of the hour they all arrived on time and slightly cognizant. There was Hottie, Hot Carl and Hot Ass, Eye-baby, Creamy Dreamy and Chi-Chi's, who later became L-Jacks, Syrupy Sweet, El Hefe and Butters, Squeaky Miki, Papa Bear and Country Mike, J-Sin, Nate-Dog and Ruth. John, the Bossman feared that the people of Georgetown and Seattle might view him in the unkind vein of Sleazy Bar Owner, since most of the people who worked for him were pretty darn attractive. He never intended to hire them for that reason. They also all happened to be great workers with "take no shit" attitudes, which was the real reason they all worked for him. The "good to look at" was really just a nice bonus.

"You're probably all wondering what this is about, so I'll get right to it. I'm selling Jules Maes."

No one in the room understood right away. The lack of coffee and even greater lack of sleep only further intensified everyone's inability to grasp any real concepts at that point, so they all waited for him to explain before they gave way to any sort of emotional outburst that would only serve to waste precious energy.

"We've been tooling over the pros and cons of owning a business in this part of town and while the money we're making is getting better and better each year, the overhead is way too high. Not to mention the general lack of safety in the neighborhood."

"You mean because of Colby?" Eye-baby only met Colby once, but she always felt the sting of death in Jules Maes, a sort of restless unease, when she came into work after the incident.

"Yes, mostly that. But there have been other break-ins and hold-ups in the area that we need to be concerned about."

"So, I mean, you're just selling the place? What about us?" Squeaky Miki asked.

"I guess a nice way to say this is - you're all fired." John smiled half-heartedly.

"That's a nice way?" A light turned on for everyone in the room and a general feeling of discomfort settled over them.

"Fuck man, I could have slept in for this shit. Next time just call me and tell me over the phone." Country Mike got up and walked out, oddly relieved. He never really liked working down there anyway.

A few others rose and joined him out the door. They were too hung over to deal with the bad news and most of them suffered from fairly bad attitudes anyway, so John felt equally relieved at their exits.

"Who did you sell to?" Squeaky Miki thought she might be able to keep her job if the new owners were willing to hire some people on.

"Phil Lester."

"Phil Lester?" Ruth asked. "Isn't he the guy who tore down the ice house across the street?"

"Yeah, that's him." John averted his eyes from the remaining employees. "He bought the whole building."

Ruth's horrified expression pulled Colby, who'd been hovering in her favorite bar spot, over to listen. She hadn't heard a single word of the conversation up until that point. Despite her recent success at fading, she'd never been able to repeat the feat since then, which led her to believe that Tiny Tommy lied about it. No one else claimed to witness the miracle.

"He's not going to tear it down is he?" Ruth questioned further.

"Um... well, I don't really know." His nervous stuttering gave him away.

"Dammit John! He is? Isn't he?" Ruth had no intention of screaming her response, but it happened so fast she couldn't control the volume of her voice.

Everyone stopped their side conversations and listened. He looked around at everyone in the room and thought better of trying to lie. "Yeah. It looks like it."

"What's happening?" Colby hadn't really caught any of the argument.

"John sold the restaurant and the new owners are going to tear the building down." Ruth looked right at her and spoke without fear of anyone overhearing her. Anger fueled her response; otherwise she'd never risk such a blatant communication with Colby.

"Tear down? He can't fucking do that! We'll all disappear!" Colby went from zero to frantic in about a half a second.

"Relax, I'll figure this out." Everyone in the room had an eye on her now. "You know they can't leave, right?"

"Who can't leave?" John raised a single eyebrow toward the woman and her imaginary friend.

"The people who live here, that's who. They can't just pick up and leave."

"Well, I don't have anything to do with that, but I don't think he's just gonna kick everyone out tomorrow. Everyone will have time to formulate a plan before they have to leave, except you guys. Your last day is going to be next week."

"Next week!" The remaining staff cried in unison. "Thanks for the warning."

"Fuck dude, how am I gonna afford my new awesome Jeep payments?"

"This blows."

"Does anyone want to work my last shift?" Creamy Dreamy asked around, his impending unemployment holding no weight in his decision making process.

"I had planned on giving you all a nice little bonus, as a way to apologize for the sudden unemployment, but if you're not interested in working your last shift, maybe you're not interested in the bonus either," John staid.

"Just kidding, dude," Creamy quipped, but he caught Hottie's eye and implored her to pick up the shift with no words this time.

Later on that night, after the restaurant closed and Ruth finally had a chance to talk with all the Haunters about the impending disaster, she found it impossible to control her anger. She paced the floor intent on working out the problem, but with little success.

"He thinks he can just sell this place from right underneath you. That's bullshit!"

"Technically he can do whatever he wants; it's his restaurant and he is alive. If he knew we were here, he might not have done it." Colby always took John's side. He had been her favorite boss.

"This isn't about alive and dead. This is about the dead being *really dead*."

"We're all going bye-bye, for real." Milton actually found no reason to laugh or wiggle his penis.

"You saw what happened to the people across the street. That's what's going to happen to all of you." Ruth didn't sugar coat anything. She'd been pacing since the second she locked the door, but no answers presented themselves despite her ardent tread.

"We don't really know where they went." Colby tried to remain positive. "Maybe they went to a better place, like Heaven or something."

"Do you believe in Heaven?" Cowboy Jerry asked Colby.

"No, not really."

"What about hell?" Matilda looked a bit worried.

"Definitely," Colby stated irrevocably.

A group sigh reverberated through the Haunters and bounced through the room. With the exception of Tiny Tommy and maybe Bryce, few of the Haunters doubted their entry in to a glorious pearly gated Heaven. Most fear a well earned and fiery end.

"Well, shit. If I'm going to hell then I'm going to hell. It sure as shit beats this waiting around for something else." Colby spent marginal time in her life worrying about consequences, and she damned sure wasn't planning on wasting any of her half-life worrying about it either.

"What if it's awful?" Pearl wrung her hands together in worry. She was responsible for at least one woman's death, so she wouldn't be saved from a demonic fate.

"At least it'll be interesting. I mean how much worse can it be?"

"Having demons eat your insides out while you watch sounds interesting?" Pearl asked.

"Who told you that?"

"Only every preacher since I was three years old. They also mentioned some things about pain and torture, crying and screaming and the thought of eternal damnation is not a pretty one." Pearl worked herself into a very lady-like frenzy, mostly involving a lot of smoothing of fabric and hand fanning of her neckline.

"I guess that's why I never went to church," Matilda mumbled.

"This is serious. We have to do something about this. We can't stand by and let them destroy our home." Much as she despised their present situation, Pearl never rolled over and played dead. Her nature disagreed with that particular philosophy.

"I agree. We do need to do something, but what can we do?" Milton surprised everyone again with a calm demeanor. When he spoke lucidly, the group found it easy to overlook his obscene nudity. His penny-loafers continued to glisten in the low light.

"We need to figure out a way to keep the building from getting demolished." Ruth looked at her brother for the tenth time, each time she fought back tears. She didn't want to lose him again, not this way.

"I know! Why not just go up to that Lester guy and tell him all about the Haunters who live in the building and are in serious danger of dying, again, if he levels the place." Colby always thought honesty to be the best course of action.

"I hate to state the obvious, but you will lose all credibility if you use that tactic." Bryce shook his head and looked at Colby as if she were an idiot. He did it so often that Colby began thinking of it as a look of endearment, which made it so much sweeter.

"I know. But there must be a way." Ruth continued to pace.

"Well this here building is a historical landmark, ain't it?" Cowboy Jerry piped in.

"It has a lot of history."

"It's more than that. This here buildin' is the oldest survivin' buildin' in Georgetown. They built it in 1883 and that makes it historical." CJ puffed up with pride. He hit upon something and knew it.

"Of course!" Ruth exclaimed. "I can get the building labeled as a historical landmark and then they can't tear it down. Cowboy Jerry, you're brilliant! I wish I could kiss you!"

"Aw shucks." He patted the back of his neck as he always did when a lady paid him a compliment.

"And, I'll use all of you to drive my point home." The pacing thing finally started to pay off.

"I thought telling people about us would be a bad idea," Colby reminded Ruth.

"Not if I use all of your stories to remind everyone of just what this place means, historically, to Georgetown. I'm gonna need everyone's story, starting with you, Cowboy Jerry."

"Ya already know my story, heck, everyone knows my story." CJ wasn't one for repeating himself.

"I need more than just your story. I need to know how this place got started, you were here for that. And Matilda, I need to know all about the brothel. Maybe you and Pearl can both fill me in on John Pinnell. He's the most notorious man in Georgetown that ever came out of this building." Ruth looked eager to soak in some historical facts.

For the rest of the night, the ghosts told stories and Ruth listened. She wrote down the important bits, and formulated a plan, as best she could to try and win back the rights to Jules Maes Saloon. She needed to get the Georgetown gang to back her. Angry stories still buzzed around town concerning the destruction of the Ice House. After months of listening; she lost interest, but now with the condo craze poised to hit Jules Maes, she cared deeply.

Ruth sought them out at the All City Coffee, their unspoken club house. Many a tactic for many a revolution got its voice in the tiny shop. The air smelled of repressed hatred for The Man and Italian roasted espresso. You need only mention any sort of authoritative mediocrity attempting to invade the tiny haven of Georgetown to get the natives to strike up arms and destroy. Their strength lie there, almost solely, and Ruth depended on them for it.

"Lester is buying the town and we just can't let him." Ruth fingered her triple tall Americano. It burned her throat to drink it, but if you wanted to be taken seriously by the revolutionaries, you had to drink an Americano.

"He hasn't even started building the Ice House Condos yet, and already he's buying property across the street for more?" Dara practically spat. If anyone could be incited to start a riot in Georgetown, it was Dara. At 36, she tinkered around with power tools, made sculpture, drank too much, smoked like a fiend, and did all the other things that the "Bohemian's with a Death Wish" tended to do. She weighed in at just around 100lbs on her 5'6" frame, but stomped around in her steel toed boots as if she weighed 200. With the addition of just a bit more mass, she might have made a rather good bully since she wasn't fond of taking shit from anyone. Her claim to Georgetown fame lay in her rather vehement protest of the Ice House's demolition.

"It's such a shame. Why can't people just leave these old buildings alone?" Leslie wondered whimsically. Earth child, vegan, animal loving, tree hugger might be a few accurate descriptions of Leslie. Her hair frizzed as nature intended and her armpits stank equally as the good lord saw fit to make them stink. She harmed no creatures and took nothing that she couldn't replenish through hard work. Ruth liked her despite her pious views on just about everything. The vegan artists took the fun out of living life frivolously. Given the history of Georgetown, Ruth found it ironic they chose to settle in such a den of iniquity. On the first day of the Ice House Demolition, Leslie strewn flowers through the chain linked fence guarding the passers-by from the flying rubble. She wrote poetry to the building, telling the building how much it would be missed by the residents of Georgetow. Ruth disregarded her fears of Leslie's insanity. She needed everybody she could get.

Before she could rile too many Coffee Shop goers to her side, a most fortunate coincidence occurred. Phil Lester walked in.

"Don't look now, but the enemy has entered our lair." Dara narrowed her eyes in the direction of the doorway.

Ruth casually glanced over and spotted him. "I'm gonna talk to him." She walked right up to him without regard. "Phil?"

"Yes?" He didn't look good. He had big bags under his eyes and appeared as though he hadn't slept a wink the night before.

"I'm Ruth. I work over at Jules Maes."

"Ah." That was it, just *ah*.

Ruth was not discouraged by his lack of intelligible communication. All she really needed was for him to listen anyway. "I heard about what you're planning on doing to the building." She tried not to take on too much of a hard edge, but she thought she might just lose her temper if she didn't watch herself. Caffeine shot through her veins pushing hostility close to the surface like a Republican dignitary might on a trip to Iraq.

"Can this wait? I really need some coffee." He sighed. It was the sigh of a man on a bender. He smelled bittersweet, like his body worked all night to sweat out the whiskey he plowed down his throat. He pushed past her and walked up to the counter to order his coffee. "Triple

Americano," he ordered. Damn! He knew the secret to getting respect in Georgetown, too.

"Listen, I'm sorry to bother you, but I have a real problem with your plans for the building." Ruth wouldn't be ignored. He didn't say anything, just stood there looking like an old tired alcoholic. Ruth wanted to feel sorry for the guy, he was obviously hung over. But she had to maintain her hatred level if she wanted to win. "Mr. Lester, I implore you to reconsider. This building means too much to the town to just destroy it."

"It's a building." He turned around and faced her, steaming cup of java in his hands. His height gave him an unfair advantage. He appeared to be looking down his nose at her.

"It's not just a building, sir. It's rich with history. The stories that came out of that place are important and shouldn't be destroyed for something so common and cookie cutter." Ruth thought she made a pretty good argument.

"This is the exact same shit I heard when I wanted to tear down the Ice House. And it still means the same to me - nothing." He sipped his coffee and burned his tongue. He winced at the pain, though oddly pleased at being slightly more awake because of it. What was he talking about? He lost track five minutes prior. Why was this girl still in his way?

"I assure you, Jules Maes is nothing like the Ice House. First of all, that building was already condemned. You couldn't have saved it even if you wanted to."

"The building is ugly. It'll cost more to fix it up than to just tear it down. That's that. Good day." He brushed past her and walked out into the bright morning.

"Fuck." Ruth never felt more adamant about using that word before in her life.

"We'll get him." Dara came up behind her and laid a delicately strong hand on her shoulder. "Don't you worry."

WTF Do The Haunters Do Now?

"That's it huh?" Colby mused to her new awesome boyfriend. "Our time together has been so short, but powerful."

Bryce rolled his eyes for the 15th time that hour. He looked at his forced-girlfriend again and gritted his teeth. Her black hair hung in greasy tendrils framing her Picasso-esque face rather crudely. She hovered around awkwardly at times, holding her hands up toward her chest like a T-Rex; managing to hide the only thing worth looking at. The most common emotional response she elicited from Bryce was somewhere between horrified and confusion. Despite all that; he didn't exactly hate her. She had some almost charming traits about her, but for the most part she was still just as she had been the moment she died; a slovenly drunk, even without booze.

"God help me but I like you Colby." Bryce said in a sudden burst of camaraderie. She did have a great way of turning shitty situations into amusing anecdotes.

"That's a start." She smiled, genuinely, then decided to push her luck. "So, seriously, tell me what happened with you and Clementine." This statement elicited eye roll number sixteen. "You can't dodge this question forever. As your girlfriend, I have a right to know!"

"You're not my girlfriend."

"Did you sleep with her?" Colby's face crumbled a little at the question; not quite ready to face the truth if Bryce suddenly offered it.

"Yeah, that's it. I slept with her. We had sex all night long."

"I knew it." It was really more of a whisper that came out that time.

"Colby, don't be so stupid." A tingle of hope replaced the devastated expression on Colby's face, so Bryce squashed it. It was just his way. "Boy, if I could have though." A low whistle chopped through the air like a hatchet through Colby's heart.

"You think she's prettier than me, don't you?"

"Yeah."

"How can you be so obtuse?" The hurt in Colby's eyes masked her usual goofy expression.

"Do you even know what that word means?"

"No, but I heard it in a movie once."

"Well, ain't that sweet." Cowboy Jerry appeared into the conversation.

"Cowboy Jerry," Colby made no short work of verbally assaulting the newly appeared Haunter, "do you think I'm pretty?"

Cowboy Jerry took off his hat, scratched his receding hairline and promptly disappeared. He wanted no part of whatever the heck was going on at that moment.

"See!" Colby pointed to the emptiness.

Hours later, when Colby tired of barraging Bryce with questions of his love life and pondering the disappearance of Clementine; she gathered with the other Haunters. "Cowboy Jerry, do you think they'll be horses where we're going?" Colby asked.

"I don't reckon there will, but I also don't aim to be leavin' this here place any time soon. Don't worry, I'm double o positive that Ruthy is gonna figure this out for us."

"If anyone can, she can." Pearl looked on approvingly toward Bryce. She'd taken on a maternal role when it came to Ruth. And she thought it important to constantly reiterate her pride in Ruth to her brother, who she also felt was a handsome devil.

"Let's play a game." Colby sparked up suddenly.

"A game? Well shoot, I ain't played a game since I was a little tyke," CJ mused.

"What game was that?" Colby asked.

"Hide and Seek."

"Did they have that game 200 years ago?" Colby's eyes widened. Cowboy Jerry looked with disapproval but held his tongue.

"Aren't we a little too dead for such things?" Bryce asked with his usual biting sarcasm.

"Har, har." It was Colby's turn to roll her eyes. "Seriously though, let's play a game. Gather everyone around."

The other Haunters, vacant from sight but always listening, began to appear in the room at Colby's request. One thing Haunters were always on the lookout for was a way to waste some time.

"What are we going to play?" Matilda asked.

"Monopoly?" Colby joked. The blank stares of the Haunters caused Colby to once again question her comedic talents, but she pressed on anyway. "How about if we call this game *No Regrets*," Colby said for real. "Let's all talk about our biggest regrets in life."

"That's a good one," Dolores said.

"That's easy," Gerald said. "I regret eating that chicken!" The Haunters laughed heartily, but poor Gerald just felt really sad about it. Choking was the worst thing that ever happened to him.

"I don't mean in relation to your death. I mean in your life. What would you do over or take back if you could?"

The smile dropped from Gerald's face when he realized what Colby meant and a very sober Gerald stated, "I wasn't there when my Mama died. She called for me from her deathbed for days before the good lord finally took her." Colby didn't think it was a good time to recount Gerald's disbelief in the concept of Heaven as he stated earlier. People have different standards when it comes to their Mamas, so she let it go.

"Where were you?" Matilda prodded, gently.

"I was gambling with the family money."

"Ooo." Stewart's response prompted a quick rebuttal.

"You should talk! Your gambling got you killed. I was there, I saw the whole thing." Gerald didn't want to hold onto any guilt over his mama's death, but he did truly.

"It's true." In a rather gentlemanly fashion, Stewart acquiesced to his guilt.

"I did win, though, and I gave all the money to my Pa for the funeral and the household and such." Gerald's voice rose no higher than a whisper. "But I never forgave myself."

"Maybe it's time to forgive yourself," Colby hovered over right next to Gerald and laid a hand right around his shoulder in an attempt to comfort. "You can't hold onto this stuff forever. I'm sure your mama has already forgiven you."

"You're right," Gerald agreed, but needed to do some real heavy thinking before he might find it within himself to do any sort of forgiving.

"I know I am." Colby allowed the spirit of forgiveness to move through her, and she touched her hollow hand through Gerald's hollow heart, like a preacher might.

"What are you doing?" Gerald asked.

"You're welcome," she responded with reserved calm.

"I stole my best friend's girl." Bobby thought it might feel good to bring his own sins to the surface, but when all eyes turned toward him, he changed his mind entirely.

"Well, I'll be! Our nice boy cook was a rake." Matilda raised a single eyebrow toward the greasy spoon.

"It was kind of an accident, like love can be." He wasn't too keen on public speaking. "Anyways, she went right back to my best friend when I died. I guess they kind of comforted each other over the loss."

"Did you fight over her?" Matilda inquired further.

"We had an epic battle. It spilled over into the streets and we both came out of it bloody. He never did forgive me and when I died, things were still unsettled. I do regret losing his friendship over it. I should have just left her alone. I was jealous."

"Love'll make ya crazy," Cowboy Jerry agreed.

"I'm sure they forgave you." Colby reached toward Bobby with her magic hands.

"Will you stop doing that?" Bobby backed away fast.

"Mine was just the opposite," Milton chimed in. "I loved a girl, but I had to let her go."

"You had to?" Chelsea always sensed sadness in Milton, despite his perverse nature.

"I was from the poor side of town and she was from the wealthy. We came to care for each other but her people didn't approve. She wanted to run away with me, to stay with me forever, but I was too chicken shit to let her. Her father came to me with an offer of money to leave his daughter alone, and I took it." Milton slapped himself in the head at the memory. "Like a fool, I took it. I broke her heart, humiliated her publicly. I called her names and said bad things about her to all my friends, but all she ever did was love me. I deserve my fate." Milton disappeared.

The restaurant grew quiet for a moment. Milton didn't voice an opinion that differed from anyone else's. "Nice Game!" Milton shouted from the bathroom.

Silence resumed.

"Why don't you go and lay your hands on him?" Bryce opted.

Reluctant, but aware of her new power; Colby set off for the bathroom without hesitation. The Haunters strained their ears to hear the interplay, but only whispers sounded until Milton voice suddenly shattered the silence in a loud boom. "Hell and damnation!! I never thought I'd turn down a woman's hands, but you need to get out of my face and my bathroom now!"

Colby returned to eruptive laughter but tried not to let her friend's reactions distress her or her mission.

"My mama strangled me because I used to set fires," Tiny Tommy interrupted the irritating silence, and in so doing, provided the most shocking admission of the day.

"This one time I set a cat on fire and just watched it suffer and burn to death. Mama came in and put it out, then she put me out. She said I was the devil and I guess she might have been right."

"That's crazy." Chelsea felt sane for a minute.

"Who knows what I might have grown up to become. My guess is, Mama was right and I needed to be stopped."

"Are you sorry you did that stuff?" Colby felt no shame over being best friends with Satan, he was a funny bastard.

"Now that I understand what it was I did, hell yes I am. At the time, well, that's a different story. I was a child."

"What is it about people that make them do the most awful things?" Colby's piety was not lost on the others. She looked down at her magic hands, astonished at their sparkling clean appearance, translucent with raw healing power.

"Are you saying that you never did anything awful in your life?" Tiny Tommy's jaw dropped at her nerve.

"I'm like an angel right now!" She lifted her hands toward the ceiling. She didn't have a reason for the action, just theatrically it felt right.

"Hey look there's Bryce!" Tiny Tommy countered.

"What? Where?" A rather distracted Colby reached for the buttons of her blouse, ready to toss her breasts in his general direction. This induced more laughter at her expense. She pulled her mind back to the conversation at hand and offered some thoughts. "Of course I have done some awful things. I held up my end of stupidity just as high as anyone else on this planet, to be sure. But I never thought about how much it might hurt someone else. I never cared about anyone else until I died and started watching the Live Ones around us; the way they interact with each other is shameful. Nobody cares about anyone else these days." It was the first intelligent thing Colby said as a Haunter. She knew it to be true when the others nodded their heads in agreement. "I guess my regret is probably my eternal hatred for mankind," Colby said.

"We all have that here. Do you have a specific incidence?"

"I've had too many to remember." Mr. Jack Daniels purged her memory sometime in her early twenties.

"We're all pouring our hearts out here," Chelsea argued, though she had, as yet, to share anything.

"And this was your stupid idea," Tiny Tommy argued further.

"Skip to someone else for a minute, jeez." Colby stuck her fingers on her head to simulate a self-actualized *Vulcan Mind Melt* to try to extract some regretful past life scenarios.

"I was a thief." Pearl looked around with lowered eyes. She never thought she would utter those words aloud to a soul, either living or dead. She averted her eyes entirely from Matilda's; sure that anything she said would be viewed on with a gloating coolness.

"I used to pinch things. At first I took things from places like the Five and Dime and hotels. I couldn't help myself. I just felt a compulsion to steal."

"Everyone clips a thing or two from the Five and Dime, that's no regret either." Colby didn't have the slightest clue as to what a Five and Dime was, must have been a rare coin dealer or something.

But Pearl wasn't finished. "I had a dear friend when I was a teenager who lost her father to Gout, and he left her this pillbox. It was her most cherished possession. One day I just took it. She was beside herself and while she cried in my arms over the loss of it, I secretly had the pillbox in my pocket. I never gave it back. I could have just told her that I'd found it, easily given it back to her at any time. But I never did. Once I realized how easy it was to take, and then lie about it, I did it all the time, but now from friends and acquaintances. I took what they loved most in the world."

"What did you do with the stuff?" Bryce couldn't believe that the proper and Puritan Pearl actually had any regret at all, let alone a juicy tidbit like this.

"I destroyed most of it. I'd smash it with a hammer or put it on the train tracks and watch a train mush it into oblivion."

"Did you ever get caught?"

"Johnny Law always finds out," Colby quipped and laughed alone, again.

"Oh yes. That's the real reason I was living upstairs. They found out and disgraced me socially. The decent society folks shunned me and forced me to leave the city."

"That's about the best dose of irony I've ever heard." Matilda tried not to smile too hard.

"I deserved it," Pearl agreed. "I don't know what I would have done if someone took the only small piece of John I had left and destroyed it. I was as cruel to my friends as anyone could possibly be."

"It's nice to hear that you do have a human side," Matilda said. Pearl nodded toward the *almost* compliment.

"And your friends were kind of douche bags anyway." Colby added.

"What's a douche bag?" Pearl asked.

"It's something you use to clean out your vagina when it's dirty." Bryce laughed out loud, which Colby took as a green light to explain further. "It's actually quite an ingenious design really - " Bryce cleared his throat, loudly. "What?" Colby didn't know why every face in the room had bugged eyes and a grimace to match. "Oh! Speaking of cleaned out vaginas," Colby continued, triumphantly, "I thought of something. I had an abortion!"

"Good grief." Bryce lowered his head in the shame that Colby should have felt.

"Well, I did."

"Is it something you regret?" Bryce asked, knowing the answer already.

"Hell no! It was the best decision of my life. I was 23 and knocked up from a one night stand. Talk about stupid!"

"Doesn't count," Tiny Tommy pointed out.

"Really? But why? I was, like, responsible for someone's death."

"Honestly girl, you're thick as a woolen blanket." Cowboy Jerry almost felt sorry for her.

"Fine, I'll think of something else." Thinking was hard.

"Since we're all being so honest, I used to pee in things," Dolores said. The entire room gazed at the old woman as if she were a goddess: Dolores, the goddess of curing uncomfortable conversations.

"What kind of things?" Tiny Tommy used to pee in a lot of things as a child too, but it was a bit easier for him since he had an outy. He wasn't sure how he treated the image of a matronly woman copping a squat over, well, anything.

"Mostly the food and drinks I served," Dolores admitted.

"Oh, Dolores, you didn't." Matilda tried not to laugh. So far the game tickled her pink.

"Ew!"

"Gross!"

"Well that's just - I don't know what that is." CJ spat ineffectually.

"I felt perfectly justified in doing so, in the beginning. I was a black woman working in a white household."

"But you were always treated with respect," Matilda defended.

"Only by you, Ma'am. Most everyone else cared as little for me as they did for the floor coverings. I was called a lot of cruel names when you wasn't there, and treated awful bad, so I started taking my revenge."

"But, how did you do it?" Tiny Tommy simply couldn't let this one go by without further explanation.

"First I used to just go into the bathroom and fill a cup but it got to be hard to hide a cup full of hot piss. So I started doing it at home and bringing it with me everywhere. There was one day in particular when I can remember an awful bad chiding by some of the girls, so I went home and had the whole family piss in the jar. When I came to work the next day, I made up an awful sweet batch of my famous lemonade, making sure that everyone got some."

The room erupted in laughter.

"That was the best regret I've ever heard. I wish I had pissed in someone's drink when I worked here," Colby snorted. "You're an inspiration."

"I killed my horse." Cowboy Jerrys blurted his admission before he chickened out. Colby made a mental note to teach Cowboy Jerry about the importance of tact.

She also made a mental note to laugh at the irony of that lesson being taught by her. Further she made one more mental note to continue laughing about Dolores' admission, since it was the best thing she'd ever heard in her death.

"I pushed him too hard. I knew he couldn't make it, but I jest - " Cowboy Jerry's voice cracked. He began to ball like a small child who dropped his ice cream cone.

No one really knew what to do. In all their deaths, not one of the Haunters ever thought they would witness Cowboy Jerry break down. It tore them up inside, or it might have if their insides were made of something more substantial than air.

"I'm sorry. I didn't mean to get all sloppy." Of course, sloppy didn't mean much to a Haunter, but Colby didn't want to point that out just then.

"It's alright Cowboy Jerry. We all know how much you loved your horse." Matilda gave him a wink and a smile. She sure did like the old coot even if he did have a strange love for a horse.

"Well this is all terribly helpful." Bryce felt a bit awkward over CJ's emotional outburst.

"It is really helpful. I don't know how much longer I get to hang out with these people, and I haven't had much time to get to know anyone." Colby, of course, only meant Bryce. She barely knew her own boyfriend. In her head, she nominated herself *worst girlfriend ever.*

"We are not going to disappear," Bryce stated firmly. "Ruth will figure out a way."

"What if she doesn't?" Colby hated to be the bearer of bad tidings, but for the first time ever, she didn't oppose the idea of a serious reality check.

"You obviously don't know my sister."

"I understand what you're saying, but how is she going to combat the power of the Man? It's impossible."

"Nothing is impossible," Matilda argued. "Ruth found her brother after he'd been dead for six years. Now in my book, that makes her second in command to the lord God himself."

As if on cue, Ruth walked into the building. She'd been coming around a lot more often since John dropped the bomb about selling the place. She only had three days left before she had to turn her keys into the boss. She'd already cut a copy for herself and stowed it away.

"Hey guys!" She hoped she didn't look as stressed out as she felt, but she knew she probably wasn't fooling anyone. All the Haunters perked up. The already stellar build up of respect for Ruth only intensified with the understanding that their fate lay unequivocally in her hands. "What's going on? You all look so serious." Ruth thought she walked into a wake or something. "Look, I know things seem dire right now, but I'm doing everything I can."

"See," Bryce said, he might have been 10 years old and crossing his arms in a pseudo-tantrum state. Colby rolled her eyes for the second time that day.

"Actually, we were having kind of a Haunter's Pow Wow."

"That sounds interesting, what does that entail?" Ruth asked, grateful for a moment's rest from her constant thoughts of impending doom.

"We're discussing our biggest regrets in life."

"I know what mine is right now." Ruth gave a pitiful look. The failure of her attempts to save the building weighed heavy on her mind.

"I'm sure that this won't amount to your biggest regret," Pearl comforted.

"Oh sure, it's not like the fate of fifteen Haunters' after-lives are completely dependent on you. And if you fail, we'll all just disappear into a painful oblivion - that is if our ex-next door neighbors were right in their screams - and you will never see or hear from your brother again." All eyes turned toward Colby and though the set of hostile eyes settling on her limited to the number of fifteen, it felt like a lot more. "I'm just saying."

"She's right." Ruth had to keep everyone's fate at the forefront. It kept her motivated.

"I wonder what your life would have been like if you were half as honest with yourself as you are with everyone else." Bryce didn't like Colby's digs on his sister.

"What's that supposed to mean?"

"You're a drunk," Bryce blurted.

"I'll have you know I haven't had a drink in 2 years, 5 months and 7 days." She went on to mumble, "12 hours, 13 minutes."

"And why haven't you?" Bryce taunted her.

"Because I'm dead." They said it together; he sang it sarcastically which caused Colby to give him the stink eye.

"That's what I mean. You didn't quit, you were forced because you died. You still talk about it every day, think about it every day, hell, you still hover over top of the bottle every day just to pretend that you're still having a drink. If that's not a fucking regret, then I don't know what is."

"That was pretty harsh."

"Well? What do you expect? You don't take anything seriously. It's all a big fucking joke to you. Look around Colby; this is it, the end of the fucking line. You're dead! It doesn't get any more serious or permanent than this."

"We all deal with our afterlife in our own way. You hide away and stare at your rotting corpse, while the rest of us handle it our own way."

"It just so happens that my corpse has been gone for quite a while now."

"Quite a while, my ass! You know exactly how long it's been gone, to the day, just like me. So face it, boyfriend, we're exactly the same."

"God, you're infuriating! It's no wonder that guy killed you."

"You're being a complete dick," Ruth said. "What is wrong with you?"

"Nothing - it's her! She's driving me completely insane!" The grimace that decorated his face didn't lose its intensity with the lack of a lifelike, colorful flush.

"Earlier you said that you liked me." Colby tried not to look too deflated.

“I never said that.” The adamant horror in his expression fooled everyone but Colby.

“Really? Well, boyfriend, you say different things when we’re alone together than when we’re around other people. You don’t have to hide your affection for me.” She winked at him.

“I’m not hiding it because I don’t have any!”

“Are you bipolar? Is that it?” Colby experienced the spark of understanding again, which usually meant she was entirely wrong about something.

“I don’t see what coming from Alaska has to do with nothin’,” CJ mumbled.

“Am I the only one who is going mad because of her?” He looked around incredulously.

“Is there such a thing as Ghost Prozac?” Colby asked Pearl, who just gave her the old *smile and nod* response.

“You know what Bryce, I think you are the only one bothered by Colby anymore,” Matilda said. His tantrums were beginning to wear on everyone’s nerves.

“She don’t bother me none,” CJ said.

Colby nodded thanks to the two. Everyone else took their time deciding. By a show of hands and a few confused head nods, everyone agreed that Colby didn’t entirely suck. Bryce stood alone, in all his oafish asshole-ness.

“Oh Bryce, you’re so romantic.” Not to be deterred, Colby batted her eyes at him.

“Don’t you dare try to turn this around.”

“I see what you’re doing.” She smiled knowingly. “This is our first fight. I can’t wait for the makeup sex.”

“You’re going to have to wait *FOREVER!*” He couldn’t punctuate the word forever hard enough.

Not a single Haunter remained silent. Laughter shook the room like a runaway locomotive. The two may as well have been a couple married for fifty years.

“Did you used to treat your live girlfriends this way?”

“He didn’t have very many,” Ruth added.

“Yes, I did.” Bryce gave Ruth a look that reeked of unspoken raspberries and black and blue marks.

"You had them or you treated them like shit?" Dolores asked.

"Do I have to explain myself to everyone?" Bryce disliked the line of questioning; however, apart from disappearing completely, he doubted he could avoid them.

"Yes," Colby answered. "We're a family and that's what families do, or so I'm told."

"Tell them about Eliza." Ruth gave Bryce a knowing look.

"I don't really want to get into it." He began to fade away.

"Oh no you don't!" Pearl shouted at him. "You don't get away that easy, my young friend."

"Yeah, get back here." His behavior astonished Ruth. He never acted that way in life: he was a fighter.

"We all had to tell our dirty little secrets, that means you too."

"I never agreed to do it." The last thing he wished to share were the most intimate details of his life with thieves, gamblers and pissers.

"Fine, I'll tell them." Ruth wasn't afraid to air his dirty laundry.

"Shut up. It's not yours to tell." He dove through her to make a point, but it only made him look a little more pathetic.

"You better do it then, 'cause there's nothing you can do to make me shut up." She pinched the air roughly where his arm was, wishing with all her might that she could cause a bruise. She quelled her disappointment with the knowledge that if he was alive, she probably still wouldn't be able to bruise him.

"Fine. I dated a girl named Eliza and then I didn't. End of story."

"Hey! Good story," Gerald joked. "Somebody write that shit down and call Hollywoodland. We got us an Oscar winner."

"Uh, FYI Gerald, it's now called just Hollywood," Colby whispered, not wishing to stop Bryce from his story, but also not able to let such a blatant mistake go unchecked.

"Just Hollywood? What? Did they change the sign and everything?" He didn't believe her.

"Yeah." Colby nodded.

"Ruth?" Gerald only believed anything Colby said if Ruth agreed.

"I'm afraid so."

"Dang. That was a good one though." Gerald patted himself on the back anyway.

Colby saw Bryce try to fade away while the attention toward him waned. Feeling responsible for changing the subject, she stopped him. "Seriously, we're all friends here. What happened?" Colby softened her voice for the first time in her life (or death). Her interest in his story got the better of her.

Bryce sighed the biggest sigh of his existence. The last thing he wanted to do was rehash this bullshit. But the Haunters wanted to force it out of him like a fart in an elevator. So he clinched his butt cheeks and began the tale.

"I moved to Seattle to be with Eliza. Her family was from here and she had to return to attend her Grandmother's funeral. When she got here she decided to stay and help her Grandfather, since he was all alone and in need. So, boom, decision made, I followed her because I was in love."

"Love stinks," Pearl stated.

"Yes, it certainly does." Bryce began to feel the emotion of the situation creep up on him. He hadn't thought of this story, this woman, in so long he wondered if he had the capacity to do so and keep it together. He already felt choked up about it.

"So we were together and my music career started taking off. Things were great for a long time until she got pregnant."

"She was pregnant?" A small snippet of guilt settled over Ruth then.

"It was a pretty exciting time. I mean, we both knew it would be difficult. Neither of us had a job that paid too much, my music was barely enough to support me, let alone a pregnant girlfriend. So we had some tough decisions to make. She wanted to keep the baby and name it after her dead Grandmother, if it was a girl. I wasn't opposed to the idea, just scared."

"So you're like a DILF?" Colby asked.

"What's a DILF?" Bryce didn't really want to know but felt compelled to ask anyway.

"Daddy I'd like to fuck."

"Honestly Colby, you're disgusting."

"Why is that disgusting?" Colby meant that as a serious question, but for some reason everyone in the room merely carried on with the conversation without answering.

"Why didn't you ever tell Mom and Dad?" Ruth asked.

"I was going to. We decided to keep the baby. We were out celebrating and I got drunk, while she stayed sober, of course. She wanted to drive, but I insisted. I guess it was my male ego, but I just wouldn't let her. We didn't have far to go, but I guess, in retrospect, that didn't really matter."

He quieted for a minute, not really sure how to go on. This proved more difficult than he thought it might, or perhaps it was just as difficult as he always thought it might be, which is why he never wanted to tell it.

"What happened?" Ruth pressed.

"We crashed. She lost the baby."

"Bummer," Colby said.

"Is that when Mom and Dad came to see you?"

"Yeah, it was right about then. I was so messed up over it. I didn't really know how to deal with a parental visit at that point. I didn't mean to speak to them so harshly."

"Why didn't you just tell them what happened?"

Bryce and Ruth exchanged a knowing look.

"I don't do that."

Ruth shook her head at him, disappointed. "Why were you always so stubborn? They could have helped you.

We all could have helped you, but instead, I spent six years wondering where the hell you were."

"You can yell and scream at me now, but don't think I haven't regretted every day, every decision since that crash. It was the end for me."

Ruth took a minute to digest everything her brother said. She couldn't still be mad at him for dying. They were together now, sort of. She just needed to figure it all out.

"I'm sorry." She stood right in front of him with her head bowed like she did as a child in need of his help. "But you need to open up more, brother dear. Stop holding everything inside and talk to me, talk to anyone."

"I'll work on it, I promise."

"Oh, the promise of a dead guy. What's that worth?" Milton's haggard voice erupted from the bathroom. Everyone turned to the sound but no one responded. "I'll tell ya! Nothing! It ain't worth nothing!" Milton refused to let the silence bother him and answered his own question.

"Let's talk about the future." Ruth changed the subject, for as much help as the moments of melancholy afforded, they really needed to focus in on something a bit more constructive.

"Before we start, I just want to say that I am sorry for saying I was glad I had an abortion." Colby wanted to clear the air.

"Don't ask." Bryce quieted his sister before another hour long discussion concerning Colby's vagina commenced.

Georgetown Unites

Jules Maes buzzed with activity like never before. Customers and supporters filled every table along with posters, petitions and other general supportive items. An outsider looking in would consider the last day to be a successful one, but that couldn't be any further from the truth.

"Hey, I'll take a Manny's Pale."

"Fifteen." Ruth turned around and faced the man who spoke to her.

"What?"

"Fifteen." She repeated.

"I don't understand you." The man was confused.

"You are the fifteenth person to come up to me and order something from my back. Now by all means, you can continue talking to the back of my head and you may in fact receive some kind of response from my lower region since I'm a little gassy, but one thing you're not going to get is a beer. Got it?" Being Ruth's last day, she decided not to put up with any bullshit.

"Ha! In your face!" Colby laughed while she conjured up ways for Ruth to pee in the man's beer.

"Oh... sorry."

"Would you like to order something to my face, sir?"

"Beer?"

"Well, that sounds delightful." Ruth brightened at the notion. After the bulk of business subsided, Ruth began to make her rounds through the crowd. She needed to rally the troops if she planned to keep them interested enough to stay. John, the Bossman, wasn't around; he decided to take a mini-vacation. Ruth worried over the secrecy. Secrets rarely stay secret, especially when you're trying to keep a building from being torn down. Truthfully, John the Bossman knew exactly what Ruth planned, and he just let her go along with it. He sold the building, no take backs. Ruth became Phil's problem. He was ever so glad to get away from the chaos.

"How are things coming along?" Ruth asked Dara.

"Everything's looking good. We handed out all the flyers and we have about twenty copies of the petition being passed around."

"Petitions? Flyers? What good is that going to do?" Colby kept a close eye on Ruth.

"Every little bit helps." Ruth said, more to Colby than to Dara.

"Then what? Are we all going to sit around singing *Cum By ya*?" Ruth gave Colby a look. "I just want to know if I should start warming up now - pipes are a bit rusty," Colby muttered under her breath.

"I think you should address everyone, kind of get things going if you can," Dara nudged Ruth.

"Oh, well, maybe you should do it. I mean, I'm not much of a speech maker."

"Um... yeah, I'm not really allowed to give speeches in Georgetown any more."

"You're banned from speech making?"

"Ever since the riot, she ain't allowed," her partner, Joe, said. Joe, the old hippie, sported the balding long hair look that so many before him did. His clothes sagged along his bodyline and showed his sunken figure easily. Odd, old hairs poked from odd, old places while his ass continued to sink inward a millimeter at a time.

"Riot?" Ruth inquired.

"Sweet," Colby commented.

"You weren't here for the old Ice House talks, but basically that's when it happened."

"Yeah," Dara agreed. "Turned out a riot is the least effective way to help a cause.

"Okay, well, I guess I'll say something then." Panic filled her like Pabst Blue Ribbon might fill a pitcher, oozing fast and frothy. She turned away from Dara and took a couple deep, shaky breaths.

Colby recognized the panic and tried to calm her friend, marveling in the fact that she hadn't felt panic in years. "You'll be fine," She assured.

"Yeah, right," Ruth responded between gasps. She felt lightheaded.

"Start with this one:

> *Roses are blue*
> *Violets are red*
> *If we don't do something*
> *Them Haunter's all be dead... For real, yo.*

But you have to do the pause before you say the *for real* part. Like...for real, yo."

Ruth jumped up on a table before she could second guess her decision. She didn't know what to say; but thanks to Colby, she now knew what not to say. People noticed her up on the table and began to turn around and give her some attention.

"Turn down the music." Someone shouted from the back booths. The dirty melody of The Ramones, lost its triteness in silence. Colby breathed a sigh of relief, usually she could zone the music out, but there was something insidious about the Ramones. They dove inside her psyche and drove her mad with their repetitive riffs and insignificant sound.

Silence. But, not just silence, expectant silence. The worst kind of silence there is, especially if you are the person standing on the table, waiting to be heard.

"Don't screw up," Colby said.

"Hey, everyone...yeah...uh, how's it going?"

A few nodded here and there, but most just looked at her like she better wow them and right quick.

"Okay well, let's talk about the future." Didn't she use that line before?

"Say the poem! Roses are blue," Colby prompted.

"It seems that they want to shut us down." Ruth carried on in full ignorance of Colby's words. A few grumbles and no's followed the statement.

"Roses are blue - "

"And I say that's not going to happen." This time a few more shouts of approval followed the statement. Ruth began to feel the power of the live speech flow through her. She started to believe in her own ability as an orator and tried to harness the necessary energy.

"Sure, we have posters and petitions to sign, but where is that going to get us in the end?"

"Nowhere!" Someone shouted.

"That's right." Ruth pointed in the direction from where the voice came. "Nowhere, fast. I've sent in the paperwork to try to make this place a historical monument, and we still have to wait a week before we will hear back. One week. But I've just been informed that the new owners are planning to bypass our attempts by bulldozing the building before then." Grumbles and gripes roared through the crowd. "I say we beat them at their own game. They may be here to tear the place down, but they'll have to tear us down with it."

A great cry erupted from the restaurant and rolled off the tongue of the building in one long penetrating sound. Every person jumped to their feet, hands clapping with consent and joined in the unity of - well, unity. Colby stood by Ruth, impressed. From the look on Ruth's face, she felt the same surprise at the reaction.

"We are going to sit right in front of and around this building until those papers arrive." Ruth's voice struggled to be heard over the increasing volume of the crowd.

"What if the city doesn't let the building be proclaimed a historical monument?" Colby asked.

"Shut up, Colby!" Ruth's voice carried across the whole restaurant, loud and clear. And not only did she shut up Colby, but everyone else in the room as well.

"What did she say?" Someone whispered to someone else.

"I don't know."

"Who's Colby?"

"Did you just say 'shut up, Colby'?" Dara asked.

"Yes." Ruth reddened and thought fast. "You all remember Colby? Some of you were here when she was murdered." Ruth jumped off the table and headed to the front door. "It was right here." She pointed down to the spot where Colby's body lay. Then she wandered to a nearby stool. "And here is where we apprehended the murderer when he returned to the scene of the crime, two and a half years later."

"Who is she talking about?"

"I don't know."

"Colby? Colby? That name sounds familiar."

"She means Whiskey Tits."

"You should have a picture of Whiskey Tits up on your wall."

"That's just it!" Ruth raised her voice over the murmurs. "We have to remember. We can't let the history of this building be lost in the ruins like they were over at the Ice House. This building is too important to be destroyed."

She won the crowd again. With only the smallest modicum of persuasion, the crowd agreed to sit around the building until the papers proclaiming the place a historical monument arrived. They would work in shifts and do what they must to keep the place, or more to the point, the Haunters, alive (or dead). Ruth wished she could be honest with these people. Really what harm could it do to try and explain her true reasons to her new followers? She felt like she was using them for her own purpose and that was a horrid feeling. She didn't enjoy lying, even when it was for the greater good.

"Don't do it," Bryce whispered in her ear.

"What?" She raised an eyebrow at him.

"Oh well, I was just wondering," A woman gushed at her, answering her question as she thought it was directed at her. Ruth let her gush and instead listened to her brother.

“Don’t tell these people about us. They’ll think you’re crazy.” She gave him a look that said: well, aren’t I? “Trust me, we need their help now. Save that for another day.” Bryce disappeared leaving Ruth to figure out what the hell this rather short, round woman in front of her was babbling about.

The Rally of Georgetown

"My butt's asleep."

"I know." Ruth attempted to keep the sarcasm that rose in her voice at bay. She wasn't too sure how well she did.

"Seriously. Are you even paying attention to me?"

"I'm listening," Ruth answered.

"Geez, is that broad gonna shut up about her butt or what?" Colby shouted.

Ruth suppressed an outright laugh. For once she actually agreed with Colby. The girl beside her, she thought her name was Jenny or Janey or something else annoying, couldn't stop talking about her butt.

"It really hurts," J-something reiterated.

"Why don't you walk around for a little bit? Give it some air," Ruth suggested. It might have been the best thought she had all day: *giving a butt air.* She couldn't help but further think: *it's been a long day.*

"Bravo," Colby agreed.

"Can we do that?"

"Sure you can. You don't have to stay here all day. Move around, stretch your legs. Maybe cop a squat further down, around the other side of the building."

"But doesn't that ruin the whole idea of the sit-in?"

"No. You're fine. Just go ahead." Ruth stood up to stretch as if her example might lead the annoying girl to just disappear.

"Well, I mean, if you're sure." She seemed reluctant but made a move to walk away just the same.

Colby watched Ruth breathe in a sigh of relief. She wondered what it felt like to have lungs full of air again. Lately she'd been missing some of the more luxurious things involved in living: *drinking, breathing and drinking.* I wouldn't be opposed to killing someone for that feeling again, Colby thought, allowing the irony of her mind speak to flow through her. Dozens of workers walked through her body, attempting to break down the inside of the bar. Still a full day away from receiving any notice from the city as to the status of the building, things looked grim. Ruth seemed optimistic, but in the back of her mind, Colby wondered how genuine Ruth's optimism really was.

"Stop it!" Colby shouted at yet another worker as he strode heavily through her body.

"What's your stupid problem?" Ruth snapped. She'd been snapping all day.

"Nothing." Colby clammed up. She didn't like it when Ruth got annoyed.

"Can you just be quiet for, like, five minutes?" Ruth rubbed her eyes. She hadn't slept in two days and she looked exactly as if she hadn't slept in about four.

"Well, what fun is that?" Since none of the other Haunters possessed the ability to cross the doorway, that left it to Colby to keep them all informed. She took to ducking her head in every hour or so with updates. The previous evening, she made the mistake of trying to go inside for rest, but Bryce chastised her. He didn't want his sister left alone. Colby resisted the urge to remind him of how little help she might be.

"This isn't supposed to be fun, okay. This is serious."

"Why is it that *serious* is so boring."

Ruth looked around to see if anyone was watching her before she moved closer to Colby. Colby sensed trouble brewing. She knew that all the frustration that Ruth felt for the past couple weeks built up to a peak. Ripe to blow like Mt. St. Helen's, Colby tensed up in the close proximity and readied herself to take whatever abuse Ruth dished out.

"I guess saving your ass is pretty boring, huh?" Ruth got right up in Colby's face, nose to nose.

"Did I say boring? I meant really special and cool." Colby gave her a winning smile but it was no use.

"I'm busting my ass to save you guys in there and you can't give me even a little tiny bit of a *thank you*?" Ruth's face grew red.

"Thank you," Colby answered as directed, all the while thinking, *Here it comes!*

"Oh, like I believe that. You know, Colby, I haven't slept in days; I'm hungry and cranky and if you want to know the truth, my butt hurts too! And what am I doing this for? What? So you can sit there and make jokes? Are you having fun? Are you? 'Cause in my opinion this is the worst day of my life."

"Well, there's always tomorrow," Colby joked on. She noticed at least three sets of eyes staring out the window, none of which belonged to any living construction guy. She recognized Tiny Tommy, her mini-boyfriend, Bryce, her real boyfriend and Matilda. She wondered if the conversation translated well with verbal cues. She thought she might be looking like a complete douche right then. She was so busy staring with her peripherals at the Haunters in the window, she didn't notice Ruth begin to break down.

"It's just - I'm trying so hard." Her sobs stopped her voice. Colby knew the job of calming Ruthy down landed on her shoulders, and it scared the crap out of her. *Shit!*

Bryce tried to slam his hands against the window. Colby knew she had to do something to calm his little sister down.

"You're doing a really good job." Colby wondered why she always found herself in the center responsible zone when people lost their minds, first Tiny Tommy and now Ruth.

"No I'm not. I haven't done anything. All I've done is rally a bunch of fucking idiots to sit in front of an old building. A cute dog could have done that."

She spoke pretty loudly, in her sorrow. Colby saw a few heads turn in her direction, as if they overheard Ruth's mean words. Colby hoped they heard the desperate passion in her voice as well. She didn't mean what she said, obviously, she just needed to vent. Colby felt trapped suddenly. Ruth was outside her line of reference. She only really had a couple of feet outside the door to dwell in. She couldn't make any move toward her, to comfort her in any way without compromising her own well-being. Ruth knew that and purposefully stayed clear of Colby. Sometimes it felt good to just yell and scream.

"This is bullshit! It's all fucking bullshit!" Ruth yelled at anyone who would listen.

"Yeah," Colby agreed.

"We're not doing a fucking thing here. All we're doing is prolonging the inevitable. I was a fool!"

"Don't talk like that!" An older lady from a half a block away shouted encouragement toward Ruth. It was official; she could be heard from a half a block away.

The garbled dissent made its way around the building, past the girl with the butt that was asleep and to the ears of Dara. She stood quietly, trying not to draw too much attention to herself and made her way to Ruth.

"I've made a terrible mistake. I should have left my brother dead in my thoughts. I should have shunned my gift of sight and just become a little housewife in the middle of America somewhere. I could be the mother of two right now, with a dog and darn white picket fence but no! I had to come and do all this crap! I suck! I have no idea what I'm doing. Everyone is depending on me, and I'm going to ruin everything. I'm fat."

"You're not fat," Dara said.

"She's a little fat," a construction worker said as he passed through Colby and walked inside the building. This caused a ripple of sobs from Ruth, an irritating glance from Dara and Colby followed the guy in, flipping him off and proclaiming him the king of all douches.

"What's happening?" Bryce shouted at Colby but she didn't answer and simply wandered back outside to where the emotional action continued to unfold. To his merit, he did attempt to stop her; to his paucity, he looked rather ridiculous in trying, like a doggie paddling in sewage.

"Calm down." Dara put her hands firmly along Ruth's arms.

"I am calm," she said, amidst tears, slobber and hyperventilation-style sobs.

"Sure you are." Dara chuckled softly. She didn't want to antagonize Ruth. She'd dealt with erratic behavior before; after all, she dwelt in the Art world, a place renowned for its passionate outbursts.

"I just want to do well," Ruth admitted.

"I know. Sometimes, doing well means you have to let go of the reins. You have to let others take the burden for you."

"I don't need anyone to take the burden."

"Yes you do." Colby wasn't afraid to admit Ruth's weakness.

"Shut up!" Ruth shouted toward Colby.

"Okay, let's calm down." Dara hugged her close with strong sculptor's hands. Despite the overall manly touch of the woman's arms, it actually felt nice.

"You must think I'm completely insane," Ruth said directly into Dara's shoulder.

"Of course not, you're doing a great thing right now. It's bound to feel a little intimidating dealing with all this stuff."

"Do you want to know what I think?" Colby asked.

"No!" Ruth pulled away from Dara and wiped the tears from her eyes. She took a deep breath, willing it to take all the frustration away, but she knew that if she didn't get a nap in soon, no amount of heavy breathing would make a lick of difference.

"You can deny it all you want, but you are doing a great thing." Dara winked at her. "Chin up, my patriot!"

The moment of girlish hugging ended abruptly. Ruth thought Dara probably only allowed herself those types of displays once every decade or so. Ruth sat down in the entryway, and Colby nestled up beside her.

"It's gonna be okay." Colby tried to reassure her.

"What makes you say that?" Ruth looked at Colby with a dirty tear-stained face.

"What's the worst that could happen? I mean, honestly, we're already dead."

"That's comforting." Ruth smiled a little at the thought.

"Besides, what's the point in sticking around? They took all the booze." It was Colby's turn to sulk. She still dwelled on her anger over watching John pack the Jack Daniels away. To his credit, he did take a shot in her honor before he did so, the sentimental fool.

"I don't want anyone to disappear. I want you guys to stick around." She mused more to herself than Colby. "I feel like I know my brother more today than I ever did."

"You're sticking around for him? He's a stupid jerk and you know it."

"That's cruel words for your *supposed* boyfriend."

"We both know there is no way in hell we would ever date if either of us were alive."

"What if only one of you were alive?" Ruth giggled at her own sick humor.

"No, it probably wouldn't work then either. He sure wasn't a very pretty corpse once he started to decay - cute as a button as a dead guy though."

"Any way, why do you think he's a jerk?"

"He's just so dramatically melancholy. It's a total buzz kill. Do you think that guy has ever just chilled with a bunch of friends and got drunk while playing Twister?"

"I'm sure he's done that, but the question is, did he hate it with sarcastic wit the whole time?" Ruth completely understood what Colby was saying. The two women laughed together. "He's my brother; I have to love him no matter what his faults are."

"And he's my boyfriend, so I have to do the same thing, but that doesn't mean I won't point out his faults every chance I get."

"Why do you keep saying he's your boyfriend?" Ruth couldn't help but wonder.

"Duh! Because it's true?"

"Seriously, I mean it's a little creepy, don't you think?"

"I think it's very normal."

"It's completely unhealthy for you to be going around calling a ghost, whom you can never have any sort of real sexual relations with, your boyfriend."

"Is it all just about sex for you?"

"What? No. God! This isn't about me."

"Oh really? Well, when was the last time you had sex Miss Helpful Advice Giver?"

"That's none of your business."

"So it's been a while." Colby gave her a knowing look.

"I'm not gonna sleep with the first person I meet in the street okay."

"What about that cute cop? Whatever happened with him?"

"I haven't seen him."

"Did you look for him?"

"What am I supposed to do, stalk a cop? You're crazy."

A man with a chainsaw crossed her path right then and gave her an irritated look. "Why don't you get the fuck out of the way, sweetie?"

She reluctantly moved out of the way, but she followed his path inside to see where exactly he planned on taking that instrument of destruction. He was not alone in his pursuit. Four more large construction guys crossed her path with equally intimidating power tools.

"Find out what's happening in there." Ruth instructed Colby. She walked onto the sidewalk so the others might see her and rallied as many as she could to come toward the front door. She couldn't stop the construction guys from going into the front door, but she needed to do something quick. She had a terrible feeling.

Colby wandered into the building. Despite her attempt at a subtle entrance, three Haunters set on her the second her hallowed form crossed the threshold of their existence.

"What's happening out there?" Matilda asked.

"Why is Ruth so upset?" Tiny Tommy inquired.

"What the hell did you say to my sister to make her cry?" Bryce demanded.

"Everything is fine outside, what's going on in here?" Colby thought a little reverse psychology might work to her advantage.

"Everything is not fine. You tell me what's going on." Bryce got heated.

"Bryce, listen, if you're going to be my boyfriend you're going to have to learn how to relax and let women vent sometimes. She's been out there for two solid days without any sleep and not much food. She's tired and feels useless right now. If you were to go up to her and say 'boo' she would have burst into tears. Okay. Gawl. Now what's going on in here."

"What do you mean? Nothing's going on here." Bryce looked confused.

"What about those guys?" For the first time, Colby had a reason to look equally as confused.

Bryce turned and saw the guys for the first time. "Oh. Those guys? I don't know what they're doing here."

"Fat, lotta help you are." Colby turned to Matilda with expectant eyes.

"They just came in a few minutes ago. They've been carrying on about cutting something or other down, but I haven't figured out what they're talking about." Matilda turned into an undercover agent.

"I wouldn't worry about it." Tiny Tommy said.

"I think we might need to worry about this." Colby wondered at Tiny Tommy's flippant attitude. "This is actually kind of important."

"I know." He gave her his little boy irritated look. "I just mean that it's almost lunch time, and the taco truck just drove by. Trust me, these guys aren't gonna do anything until after lunch."

"You're brilliant!" Colby dove through him several times, which caused him to explode into boyish giggles. Besides the roar of a lion, the sounding of any bell no matter how big or small, and the triumphant squeak of a child with his first kazoo, Colby loved the sound of Tiny Tommy's laugh best.

As if on cue, the burly men dropped any heavy, important equipment and shuffled, single file to the door. They passed Ruth on the way and might have shoved her out of the way in their haste to make it to the truck, but she'd surrounded herself with quite a few more people. They walked by without incident.

"Keep watch!" Ruth waited for the construction guys to leave then dove inside to figure out what exactly was going on. "What exactly is going on?" She asked the Haunters.

"Uh..." Bryce stammered.

"Well..." Colby shrugged.

Matilda and Tiny Tommy had the decency to keep quiet all together.

"No one knows?" Ruth gaffed.

"It's not like they came in here and laid down the plan for us." Milton peeked his head out from the nearest wall.

"Well, they might have said something," Ruth countered. "How is it that half a dozen burly men come into this building with chainsaws and no one notices?"

"We saw them." Matilda's quizzical look toward Ruth did little to hide her irritation.

"Come on, give me something."

"Ruthy, you have to calm down," Bryce spoke in soothing tones.

"Calm down? Why does everyone keep telling me to calm down? I am calm. I'm as calm as I can be in the situation - whatever that is. If I didn't do everything around here, nothing would ever get done. I'm sick of it!"

Heads started turning in her direction outside. The protestors glared at her through dirty windows wondering many things: who she was talking to, why she thought no one was helping when clearly they were all outside helping, and why she was so attached to that building?

"In our defense, we literally can't do anything." Colby thought she was brilliant with this statement.

The scream that came out of Ruth's mouth rivaled the scream Colby unfurled to the dead world when she died. If the situation weren't so intense at that moment, Colby might have given credit where credit was due. But the agony in Ruth's scream conveyed a pain that ran much deeper than the current situation could ever hit upon. The scream stopped the traffic along Airport Way, kept the circling airplanes from landing at Boeing Field, and caused an accident on the 5 when a deer, upon hearing the high pitched sound, dove head first into oncoming traffic. Thankfully, no one was injured.

"If you say that one more time," Ruth growled.

"Which part? We can't do anything because we're dead?" Colby asked. Every Haunter winced as Ruth slapped the air around Colby silly. The protestors also watched with great concern as the loony woman inside swatted at the air.

"Everything okay?" Dara opened the door and shouted inside. She needed to quell any fear amongst those outside and assuage her own doubts about the sanity of her friend. Ruth waved toward the door. Dara took the hint, closed the door and gave her group the thumbs up. Ruth closed her eyes to compose herself for the fifth time that day. Outside, the crowd of protestors grew. They all waited for her to come out and tell them what to do. Inside, the crowd of Haunters waited also. Every single person in the small city of Georgetown, alive and dead, looked to her for direction. The intensity of pressure surrounding that moment gripped her like a vice. She needed to think, but the door swung open again and a gruff voice pulled her away from selfish thoughts.

"Ruth! They're coming back."

If a deep breath could cure all that ailed her, Ruth did her best to put the theory to the test. She closed her eyes, ears, mouth, toes, fingers, even her belly button just to try and suck in as much nutritional air as possible. She willed the cleansing tonic to give her clarity, purpose and direction. When she opened her eyes, she felt focused.

"Here they come." Bryce said, catching a glimpse of the workers as they rounded the corner.

"Like hell they do." Ruth burst out of the doorway with serious intent. The protestors sensed her mood change and matched it. Without a word, they banded arms together and blocked the workers from coming in.

"Why don't you and your band of dirty little grublets get the hell out of here?" One of the workers, who had no right calling anyone grubby by the look of him, shouted. Little pieces of undigested taco meat splayed out from the corners of his mouth when he spoke.

"Tell ya what, buddy," Ruth said, "you can get past me when you walk over my cold dead body!"

The man contemplated for a long minute and Ruth knew that if push came to shove, the protestors didn't stand a chance against these guys. Every one of them weighed as much as two protestors. Despite their burly bodies and angry demeanors, they came to work, not fight. They earned an hourly wage and if the protestors stopped them from work, they still earned that wage. Ruth knew these guys could care less about the politics of Georgetown, and they weren't likely to get angry at some people that were keeping them on the payroll a bit longer.

"Have it your way," the man finally answered. He stepped toward her, got up in her face with his barreled chest, and for a moment, she thought he would smash her right then. Everyone stood by watching and waiting to see what the guy might do. Ruth flinched as he reached across her and grabbed his coat which he left hanging on a nail outside the front door. He backed away from the crowd and reached into his coat pocket to retrieve his cell phone. The crowd roared in victory. Ruth joined them as soon as she cleared her throat of the remnants of her heart which had leapt up there when she thought the guy might clobber her.

They only needed one more day.

OMG, WTF and Other Clever Initials

A gentle shake roused her from excruciating non-sleep. Ruth looked up from her concrete bed in shocked confusion. She had been dreaming about rats riding triple-decker bicycles in cages.

"We need to talk," the voice said. She couldn't place the face. She awoke freezing and in unfamiliar territory. She didn't know why this man whispered to her and why her head nestled so uncomfortably upon someone else's foot.

"Let's go inside," he said in a firm voice. Obviously he had some coffee that morning already. He tried not to jangle the keys too loudly and wake the others. He preferred to keep the conversation between the two of them. Ruth shaded her eyes from the early morning grey that was Seattle weather and caught sight of the stained glass sign above the front stoop she slept on: *Jules Maes*. Right, of course - save the restaurant!

Ruth rose as quickly as she could, which really wasn't that fast at all and followed him inside. She rubbed the sleep from her eyes and tried to wake more completely, but without coffee it seemed a hopeless endeavor. She roused enough to recognize the man as Phil Lester, new owner of Jules Maes and enemy to all Georgetown.

"It seems the tables have turned," he laughed.

"What do you mean?" Lethargic suspicion drenched her question.

"The last time we spoke, I looked like shit."

"That bad, huh?" She couldn't muster the energy to argue with the man just yet.

She walked over to the mirror behind the bar and caught a glimpse of herself. She barely recognized the woman who stared back at her. Her dirty face looked weathered, gnarled, and above all, tired, so tired. She took a moment to entertain a waking fantasy about her bed, but only a moment. She looked around for any of the Haunters, but none materialized.

"I have something for you." Phil didn't sound happy.

"What is it?" Ruth asked, but when she saw the envelope he held in his hands, she knew. Under the grasp of his fingers, she barely made out the logo of the city of Seattle. They looked at each other for a while, both trying to gauge just what the other might be thinking. "Did you open it?" Ruth asked.

"I didn't have to. They sent me one as well."

"What's it say?" Doubt crept into her psyche.

"I'm sorry," Phil said.

"What? No!" She ran to him and tore the envelope out of his hand. She skimmed the letter until she got to the part where the city denied her. She'd already shed all the tears she could, screamed all the screams and felt every emotion. She had nothing left to give. She felt the cold hand of bittersweet relief grab hold of her and felt so guilty she thought she might vomit.

"So, that's it? You're just going to tear the place down?" She asked.

"That was the plan from the very beginning. I never hid that fact from anyone."

"How can you not even care a little bit?"

"I'm a business man. That's what I care about. Why do you care so much? I did a little checking on you Ruth. You've only lived here for a year or so, you're not even from this city. Why is it that this building means so much to you?"

"It means something to everyone."

"Yes, but you took it really personal and I want to know why that is."

"You took my job away from me, that's not personal enough for you?" She rolled her eyes at him

"That's just work. Work doesn't get people riled up like you are. If I could find just a few people out there with your passion working for me, I'd be able to tear down a building a week."

"You probably would too, without a thought or concern to the people that you harm in the interim."

"Who am I hurting? No one; it's just an empty building. It doesn't feel anything."

"You're destroying a legacy."

"Legacy doesn't lie in a building, alright? It's the stories that survive. Write a book or something." His flippant attitude irritated Ruth.

"Phil, please! I'm begging you not to tear this building down." She fell to her knees so fast; she didn't realize she'd done it.

"What are you doing?" Colby appeared from the backroom then.

"What are you doing?" Phil asked in unison.

Abandoned tears welled up in Ruth's eyes. "My brother is here," she whispered.

"Uh oh," Colby whispered back. She felt desperate for a bottle to sink into, but looking around she found none. Instead she nestled over a shiny thermos that she imagined one of the workers spiked with whiskey to get through his day.

"Your brother? Where?"

"Do you remember when we found the body upstairs, all those months ago?" Discomfort prompted her to rise and face the man before her on a more level playing field. A tiny screw poked out of her knee where it embedded itself during her prayer session.

"Yup."

"Well, that was my brother."

"Your brother died here?"

"He was murdered here."

"And so, you want me to keep the building in tact because you want to save the memory of your dead brother? I'm sure a lot of people died in this building. So what?"

"147 to be exact."

"147 people died in this building? How do you know that?"

"It's amazing the things one can learn on the internet." .Ruth smiled.

"You're not one of those hokey ghost hunters, are you?"

"No, I'm just a girl that misses her brother and this is my one real connection with him."

"I can appreciate that." Phil nodded his head in understanding. Ruth thought she saw a faint softening of his features, as if he might be pondering something of value. She looked to him with hope. "But, you realize, that doesn't make a fucking bit of difference, right?"

Defeat clouded her vision. The battle lost. "But... I'd hoped that..."

"I know. I'm sorry for all that you've probably gone through, but I'm not changing my mind over a memory. You have to move on with your life, Ruth."

"I'm fine. I can move on, but what about him?"

"What about him? He's dead."

"He's right, Ruthy, I am dead." Bryce appeared next to her.

"I'll tell you what," Phil said. "I'll make you a deal. I'll put off the demolition until tomorrow. You can stay here tonight and do what you need to; you know, to say goodbye or whatever."

She didn't know what to say. Disappointment consumed her like a forest fire. "That's very generous of you." She knew he was being kind but she ached at the thought of never seeing her transparent brother again.

"One condition though," Phil continued. "Get that riff raff off my property; they're stinking up the joint." She nodded toward him. "Lock up when you're done." He opened the front door and woke several people sleeping right inside the foyer.

After a few minutes of eye rubbing and confusion, they too became aware of the new brilliant morning and Ruth's absence.

"I'll be back," she told Colby and Bryce.

She spent the next half hour explaining the situation to her compatriots and politely asking them to leave. Surprisingly few people emoted outrage. After four days of diligent sitting and yelling, many of them were glad it was over. They all, of course, regretted the outcome.

Ruth came back inside after the last stragglers disappeared. Her swollen eyes glowed with emotion. She'd grown to love each of the Haunters, and the thought of never seeing them again devastated her.

A small group of Haunters stood by, waiting.

"Where is everyone?" Ruth asked.

"Oh, Ruth! It's extraordinary!" Pearl said with more enthusiasm than she might ever felt in her life or death.

"What?" A strange relief flowed through her when she realized she might have something besides impending doom to think about for the first time in several weeks.

"We're disappearing!"

"Disappearing? And that's a good thing?" Ruth thought Pearl might have finally lost her mind.

"It's wonderful," Matilda agreed.

"I don't understand."

"We're all finding our way to the other side, or alternate whatever - you know, where we're all supposed to be."

"Supposed to be?" Ruth simply couldn't follow.

"Well, we're not supposed to be here," Cowboy Jerry agreed. "It jest don't feel right. It's like I've been living a hundred years of agony."

"And then you came along and it was like we were all alive again," Milton said. "You were so fresh and young and youthful on the toilet."

"Milton!" Bryce chastised.

"What? She was." He mumbled back.

"Anyway, it was when the building got sold that we started to realize what we'd done," Bryce said.

"What did you do?" Ruth asked.

"We stole you from the living. We took away your life."

"We made you dead, jest like us." Cowboy Jerry's voice hollowed.

"We're dicks," Pearl said. Everyone turned and eyed her curiously.

"Truer words were never spoken," Matilda agreed.

"I'm here because I want to be," Ruth disagreed.

"You're hiding just like we are, and it's time for all of us to stop doing that." Bryce really meant it, Colby could tell.

"And so we have!" Pearl glowed.

"Tell me how it happened," Ruth said.

"It was all Colby," Pearl explained.

"Me? What did I do?" Colby asked. No one bothered to tell her anything about anyone moving on to another plane of existence. She wondered why they kept her out of the loop.

"Remember when you proposed that stupid game where everyone talked about their biggest regret?" Pearl asked.

"Yeah, you guys all hated that." Colby rolled her eyes at her fellow Haunters.

"Well, hate it or not, it was the key, just like you said."

"Wait, are you saying that I, Colby Marie Ryerson, was actually right about something?"

"Yes." Pearl grinned from ear to ear.

"I've gotta call my mother. She won't believe it." Colby didn't actually believe it herself.

"Chelsea was the first to go."

"Chelsea? But I thought she was crazy and shit." Bryce hadn't heard too much about the new disappearing phenomenon either. Both he and Colby were too intent on the protest to notice anything else.

"Crazy like a fox, apparently," Colby added.

"I was there when it happened. It was amazing." Pearl's face lit up in wonder.

"What happened?" Ruth felt numb with confusion. Why was this sounding like a dead version of *The Wizard of Oz: you had the power in you the whole time, Dorothy.*

"We started playing the game again."

"The game?"

"Yeah, the Biggest Regret game."

"I thought you guys hated that game."

"Just listen. We started playing and Chelsea began telling the story of her death. While she did, she forgave herself for all the dumb things she ever did. I watched as her form became more and more hollow. She became difficult to see. At first I thought she just grew tired of talking and started fading, like we all do... except you Colby."

"Really? A dig right now? That's just mean." Colby didn't appreciate the joke.

"There came this amazing light then," Pearl continued unabated. "I couldn't tell you where it came from. It wasn't like the traditional light from Heaven you might think of, it was kind of all over like, and then she glowed so brightly I couldn't see her anymore, and I heard her say 'don't be afraid' and 'goodbye'."

"So that's it? That's how it's supposed to happen?" Colby looked doubtful. "It can't be that easy."

"I'm sure it's different for everyone," Matilda stated.

"Who else is gone?" Bryce asked.

"Dolores."

"She was almost all the way gone anyway. We could barely see her anymore. She might have done it without Colby's dumb game," Bryce scoffed.

"Is it asking so much to give me a little support sometimes?" Colby scoffed back.

"What about Tiny Tommy, then?" Pearl blurted out. She ignored Matilda's attempts to stop her from saying it.

"Tiny Tommy?" Colby looked around for the first time noticing he wasn't there.

"Yeah." Matilda tried to ease the word out to calm Colby down. Already she saw a panicked look overtake her.

"What do you mean?" Hysteria slid around her head like the water flowed down a slip and slide.

"He disappeared last night," Cowboy Jerry said.

"No. He wouldn't do that without even saying goodbye." Colby dispelled the thought as impossible.

"I think it just kind of happened. He looked really happy," Pearl added.

"This is your fault!" Colby whirled around and confronted Bryce with an infuriated scream.

"What? Why is it my fault?"

"You told me to stay with Ruth. You wouldn't let me leave her side and now look! Tommy's gone. My Tommy is gone! How could you? How could you be so selfish?"

"How was I supposed to know?"

"How is it you didn't know what was happening? You were here, standing right here the whole time. It was happening around you!"

"So?"

"So? So? So, you let him disappear without telling me?"

"I didn't let him do anything. Don't turn this around to me." Bryce felt guilty over not noticing, but he refused to take the blame for something he couldn't control.

"I hate you. We are *so* broken up," Colby whispered to her now ex-boyfriend.

"It's not Bryce's fault," said Pearl.

"What about you?" Colby let her emotions take over. "What about any of you? Why didn't anyone tell me? That is the most heartless thing anyone's ever done to me - and that includes the guy who killed me." Colby rushed off, distraught.

"What's her problem?" Bryce exploded when he finally was able to speak up for himself.

"She just lost her best friend."

"She doesn't have to be such a bitch about it." Bryce's nonchalance put him in a bad light to everyone.

"Boy, you really are a selfish prick," Pearl said.

"I'm a prick? She's a bitch! We're just one big happy freakin' family!" He crossed his arms and prepared for any onslaught. None occurred since the rest of the Haunters were all too excited about the prospect of not disappearing in complete agony as their neighbors from the Ice House did. Bryce hadn't caught the fever yet and for the first time since his arrival in the Haunter's family, he was completely ignored.

"I'm ready to go." Pearl's smile could easily be mistaken for the brilliant light that opens the gate for the Haunters.

"Is it just that easy?" Ruth asked. "I wonder why no one figured it out before."

"Lots of people have disappeared over the years, but we never could figure out how it was done. I suspect the longer you're here, the harder it is," Matilda explained.

"We best go find Colby; I don't want to leave without saying goodbye." In Pearl's excitement, she forgot all anger and anxiety. Calm kindness guided her. As if best friends, she and Matilda took off in search of Colby. They followed the sound of heart wrenching sobs to Colby's form. Sorrow filled her form to such an extent that she looked as alive as Ruth. It flushed her hollowness into the most human state any of them ever saw. Neither woman knew how to approach Colby, so they both hung back and watched for a minute to strategize.

Colby worked herself up into an emotional tizzy, mumbling both loudly and incoherently. Laughing and crying simultaneously, she managed to flail her body around in anger, it didn't help. She focused in on a bottle that sat upon a shelf in the music hall, a Heineken bottle. With only a swig or two left of beer, it cast a meager shadow in the red-glowed room. The bottle sat on that shelf for days, a remnant of the death of the bar and thus the death of them all. She hated that bottle then. That ghastly green bottle mocked her and she wanted it dead. With all her might and energy she swiped at the bottle on the shelf but a funny thing happened. Instead of passing right through the thing as she had since the day she died, she made contact. Not only did she touch the thing, but it flew off the shelf and smashed into a hundred pieces, splashing left over beer and saliva swigs all over the floor. The room silenced and three pairs of rather large eyes stared with confusion and awe at the mess on the floor.

"How did you do that?" Matilda marveled.

Colby turned to the women and answered with a shrug. In her mind, at that time, she suddenly became a god.

So, This Is Goodbye

"You can say that all you want, but I still don't know how to do it." Bryce wasn't amused. He'd watched three other Haunters disappear and he still couldn't figure just what the heck they'd done. Everyone else seemed keen to understand, like a new dance step that just took a demonstration.

The afternoon passed by pleasantly enough. They might be at an afternoon barbeque rather than the last day any of them would ever see each other again. Not a hint of sadness crossed anyone's eyes. Bryce couldn't understand how all these people, who spent so much time together could feel nothing when it came down to leaving. Neither Colby, Matilda or Pearl reappeared. "I guess they must be having a real vagina-fest somewhere."

Ruth didn't laugh. "Come on," Bryce joked. "Lighten up. Why are you so uptight all the sudden?"

"You know what you did. Colby happens to be a very nice person, deep down."

"Very deep down - it's like a buried treasure, along with her virginity and sanity." He laughed at himself when the image of a broken old treasure chest came to mind, long emptied of its contents.

"That's completely uncalled for," Milton said. Bryce took a long look at the naked man in Penny Loafers and found himself without comment for the first time. Was he just schooled on proper etiquette by a naked ex-public masturbator? "If it weren't for Colby, we'd all be stuck here in screaming agony," Milton continued.

"See, she is a good person, deep down," Ruth reiterated.

"Will you stop saying that."

"What?"

"Deep down. It just makes me want to say mean things."

"Deep down, deep down, deep down - DEEP DOWN," Ruth chanted.

"Deep down!" Milton added.

"Shut up! Jeez, we should be a little bit more constructive and be talking about our escape plan. I need someone to explain it to me again."

"I'll show ya." Milton smiled.

"Milton? *You're* ready to go to?"

"I'd say just about - anything to get away from your bellyaching! That is, if Miss Ruth might do me one little favor before I go."

Ruth eyed him suspiciously. She knew what he was going to ask, and she didn't know if she had the stomach to say no, but the thought of it grossed her out.

"Before you ask me anything, I just want to go on record as saying that I think you are a good man Milton, and I am going to miss you."

"Well that's awful nice of ya." He tried to blush at her kind words. He looked down at his withered old penis and wished with all his heart that he had a little blood left.

"Ask away," Bryce tempted. He itched for a fight. All the emotions of the past few days weighed heavy on him, and Colby wasn't around to yell at, so he figured Milton was the next best thing.

"I guess I just want to have a little - kind of - hug." Milton stared at his shoes. Attempting to show his feelings in a non-disgusting manner proved difficult for the dead little pervert.

"A hug?" Ruth's shock registered clearly on her face.

"Well, yeah." He managed to look her in the eye somehow.

"Excuse me?" Confusion laced Bryce's nervous response. Why did a hug sound so sleazy?

"You're the one woman in my life – well, you know what I mean - my dead life here, that hasn't gone away. I mean, I know you're here because of him." He might have stabbed Bryce in the eye with the force of his point. "But you never neglected the rest of us either, and that's damned decent of you."

"I care for you all," Ruth agreed.

"I'm not exactly easy to care for. I mean, look at me." He waved down his body as if he needed to remind anyone of the silliness of his situation. Ruth could have sworn she saw those damned penny loafers gleaming in the afternoon light, like some darn ruby slippers.

"I think you're just fine." Waving him over with a smile, she opened her arms wide. The thought of hugging a naked reprobate, though never appealing, seemed perfectly appropriate. Without realizing, tears welled up in Ruth's eyes.

"Now look what you've done," Bryce said. "You made her cry."

Milton hovered in Ruth's arms and tried in earnest to feel something, anything, just one last time. He recalled all the things he missed in life: the smell of bacon cooking on a grill, the look of a woman when she truly felt loved, and pants. He really, really missed pants. He allowed himself to desire all those things again and then when he thought he might go crazy from the thought, he just let go. He wrapped himself into a tight ball inside Ruth. The slightness of her body made it impossible for him to completely disappear. And the more he thought about how much he didn't need all those physical things that he couldn't have, the lighter he felt until he glowed as bright as the others who left before him. Bryce watched in awe.

"Oh my," Ruth said her body took on an unearthly glow. She felt Milton stir inside her. Pearl, Matilda and Colby all came into the room then and watched from a distance. The more intense the light filtered around old Milton, the more Ruth felt his presence. The hug was no longer an empty gesture, but intensified into something that both of them actually felt. As Milton began to disappear with all the quiet dignity that a dead man deserves, he did what anyone might expect. He grabbed Ruth's ass.

"Yes!!" He shouted with glee as he departed.

"Milton," Ruth muttered.

"Nice one, Milt!" Colby shouted. Colby laughed out loud, and Milton looked up and waved to the ladies. He winked at Bryce and patted Ruth's behind one more time, then a brilliant flash blinded them all. When the light calmed, Milton was gone.

"He was a perv to the end," Ruth said.

"I'm gonna miss him, he had style," Colby admitted.

"We'll all see him again real soon, once we get to those pearly gates." Pearl believed wholeheartedly in a heavenly destination for them all.

"I ain't so sure that's where he's headed," Cowboy Jerry chimed in. He stood so quiet in the corner that everyone forgot he was there. He'd been trying to figure out how to leave like the others had, but watching didn't offer the insight he hoped it would.

"Yeah, I don't think they have ladies' rooms in Heaven."

"Honestly you two. People can change and they often do." Pearl's back straightened. It always did that when she tried to teach others a lesson about her view of the world. She had the straightest back Colby ever saw.

"Pearl's right. And I hope I do see him up there; his naked ass snuggling up to the angels singing on high is gonna be a hell of a sight." Bryce laughed. Colby joined in the laughter, despite her new detestation of her ex-boyfriend. The image was too sweet to abandon.

"I'm sure he has a robe by now," Pearl insisted.

"They give those out at the door, do they?" Pearl's knowledge of Heaven's processes fascinated Bryce.

"Well, I can't say for sure, but it's all proper up there. That much I know for certain." Pearl straightened up a bit more.

"How ever will I get along?" Matilda joked.

"Speaking of getting along - " Pearl nodded to Matilda.

"I guess it's about time for us too, isn't it?" Matilda agreed.

Ruth looked around the room at the remaining Haunters. "Is this all that's left?" She asked.

"I believe so." Matilda smiled at the small group, remembering all the experiences they shared. She looked at Cowboy Jerry and saw a genuine look of fear on his face. For the first time in his death, he needed some help.

"Cowboy Jerry, you wanna come along with us? There's strength in numbers." Pearl caught Matilda's line of sight and made the same realization.

"I reckon there is." He puffed up at Pearl's invitation. The three huddled together for a moment, intent on making the journey as quick as possible, but Ruth stopped them.

"Good-bye."

"You're gonna be alright, Miss Ruth." Cowboy Jerry looked on the girl as he would a daughter.

"You too, Cowboy Jerry. I'll miss you." Ruth kissed the air around his cheek.

"Shucks."

Matilda came up to Ruth next and gave her the beguiling smile she'd been known for in three counties. She might have pulled Ruth close to her bosom and squeezed her ass tight as she could, but the two weren't meant to have that moment. She nodded to her instead and curtsied. "You go out and find you a man, young lady. That's an order!"

"Alright, I'll do it." Ruth chuckled.

"But make sure he's nice - and respectable," Pearl clucked in, like an old mother hen.

"Make sure he has a nice big package," Matilda winked.

"Oh, yes!" Pearl agreed. "Flowers or chocolates, any of those packages are so lovely."

"Come on now, let's go." Matilda rolled her eyes at Pearl's innocence.

"Fine. Goodbye everyone." Pearl bowed slightly toward everyone individually. One thing her mama always taught her was to be polite.

"Bye." Bryce waved.

"Goodbye!" Ruth reiterated.

"See ya," a rather distracted Colby said. Bryce stared at her despite himself. She looked different.

Pearl came over to Colby and spoke in low tones, so the others couldn't hear. "Now don't get all caught up in your new tricks. Remember it's time to go," she warned.

"I know." Pearl gave her a stern look. "I know!" Colby repeated.

"Alright then. I'll see you in a minute." She gazed up, visually reminding her that Heaven waited. Matilda hoped their destination wasn't as lame as Pearl stated. Cowboy Jerry worried about who might be waiting for him, and Colby still severely doubted it was actually a "heaven-like" place they were destined for.

Pearl, Matilda and Cowboy Jerry grouped together and held hands, as best they could. They stood in silence for the first few minutes, pondering and trying to figure out their exit strategy.

"I forgive you for taking my husband away," Pearl said to Matilda.

"Thank you," Matilda replied with a devilish grin. "I forgive you for killing me."

"Oh good." The two women looked at Cowboy Jerry, who, in turn, looked confused.

"Uh... I fergive ya fer bein a dirty whore," he said to Matilda.

"And I forgive you for being a nasty old coot," she replied.

"Come on now - positive thoughts." Pearl chastised them as if they were children.

"Well Ma'am, I'm pos-I-tive she were a painted lady. Though the word lady don't really apply, do it?" Cowboy Jerry scoffed.

"And I'm positive that you are the most stubborn, lonely, and sad Cowboy I've ever known."

"How many cowboys ya known?"

"More than I can count."

"Whore."

"That's enough! Matilda, Cowboy Jerry; you two need to learn to get along or this isn't going to work." If Pearl could have taken them both by the ear lobe she would have given them a mark rendering pinch.

"Cowboy Jerry?" Matilda squinted one eye down into the perfect stink eye as she garnered the strength she needed to continue her thought. He looked at her expectantly and allowed himself to be ready for anything. "I love you!" She shouted with all the anger and sarcasm in her body.

"What?" His jaw fell around his belly button, no small leap for a man of his height.

"I love you. We've been together now for a long time and I've grown to cherish your friendship. I love you, I love you, I love you. So there."

"I love you too," Pearl added.

"Well.... Hell."

The glow started around the three and they felt the solidness of hands come together, which spurred them to say more nice things and really become one in the light.

"I reckon I have certain affections for ya, Miss Matilda... even though you're a nasty skank." Cowboy Jerry sounded sheepish.

"Wherever did you learn that word?" Matilda inquired.

Colby noticed their voices beginning to fade and the light grew more brilliant by the second. "It's working." She nudged Ruth. Ruth's attention waned from the exit and now she stared intensely at Colby for the duration of the light show.

"Where do you think?" The cowboy's fading eyes caught a hold of Colby's.

"Oh, I'm gonna have to reteach you some manners," Matilda chastised.

"Manners? You?" Pearl laughed at her friend in earnest. "Don't think for a second that I did not know what you were referring to just now when you suggested Miss Ruth look for a big package."

The rest of the conversation faded away as the Haunters disappeared fully into the light. No one spoke for a few minutes, until Colby, feeling the relentless stare of Ruth upon her finally said: "What? Jeez! You're freaking me out."

"I felt that." Ruth's eyes bugged out a bit.

"Good. Because you are, in fact, freaking me out. Bryce? Control your sister, will ya?" Colby floated over to her favorite spot on the now empty bar and hovered sadly.

"Colby!" Ruth practically ran after her. "Nudge me again."

"Nudge? What are you talking about?"

"I felt it. When you nudged me a minute ago, I felt your arm!"

"That's not funny Ruth," Bryce said with all the frustration he felt.

"I'm serious." Ruth's face took on the look of *serious as a heart attack*, her particular favorite type of serious.

Colby attempted to ignore the brother and sister duo but couldn't. The disappearance of her three Haunter friends left her without something else to focus upon.

"Just do it," Ruth said. Colby nudged her again and Bryce watched with awe as the two forms, Colby's dead one and his sister's o-so-live one, made contact.

"Holy shit!" he shouted.

"Yeah, holy shit is right." Ruth jumped up and down for a second at the revelation.

"Shit," Colby agreed, sort of.

"That was awesome."

"You finally did something awesome." Bryce's face spoke of an affection Colby knew wasn't really there. She suddenly took on the role of adorable puppy with a new trick, and she didn't like it.

"It's not awesome," Colby disagreed.

"It most certainly is." Ruth's excitement kept the negative vibe at bay. Her mind reeled over the meaning of it all.

"Can you teach me how to do it?"

"Well, if the way I came about having it is true, you should have been able to do it yourself years ago. I just got really sad and depressed and angry - that pretty much sums up your death, doesn't it?"

"Harsh." Bryce knew he deserved it; but it still hurt to hear.

"We gotta tell someone, do something," Ruth continued. She hadn't really listened to a word anyone said since she felt the nudge of a Haunter. Her skin still tingled in the spot Colby touched. Her mind continued reeling, but this time it didn't have anything to do with saving the building.

"Who are you gonna tell? What could you possibly do with this new found parlor trick?" Bryce never bothered to feel elated about anything longer than a few minutes.

"I know," Ruth brightened, "I'll call Faye."

"Who's Faye?"

"You remember, Faye, the tattooed psychic." Ruth grabbed her phone and walked outside the front door to make the call.

"So..." Bryce tried to keep up with the small talk.

Colby just stood there with her arms crossed against him. She wandered back over to the thermos, her new substitute for Jack Daniels. She sought its comfort with the understanding of its contents being nothing more than the dregs of six day old coffee. She tried to ease her chest over the top of it, but knocked it over instead. Bryce watched in fascination.

"Wow."

"This sucks." Colby looked defeated.

"Can't you control it?" Bryce asked.

"No, I can't control it. I don't even know what *IT* is." She sat down in a chair, for the first time in her death, she sat. It made her chuckle.

"You're sitting," Bryce whispered, fearful that calling out the action would make it disappear.

"I'm sitting," she said in disbelief. "Now this is awesome." She put her hands behind her head and leaned back into the chair. She put her feet up on the chair beside her and felt a smile tug at her lips for the first time all day.

Ruth walked back into the building excitedly, but she stopped short when she saw what Colby was doing.

"You're sitting," Ruth observed also.

"Comfortably," Colby agreed.

"Awesome."

Will the Real Ghost Hunter Please Come Forward?

The three spent the next half hour waiting for Faye and practicing those silly parlor tricks. Impending doom needed to wait for a while longer for the two remaining Haunters. They didn't notice Faye's arrival right away. She stood outside the door watching for a while before she made her presence known. She watched Ruth spring from one end of the bar to the other, talking and laughing and making things move without touching them.

"This looks fun." Faye decided against knocking and simply popped her head inside the door way finally. Her appearance seemed disheveled thanks to a sudden uptake of wind outside the door. Black hair covered her flushed face in wisps. Grey eyes swept the almost bare bar, taking in the scene before her. Saw dust, overturned tables and general clutter replaced the old world grandeur she remembered from so many months prior. She removed her coat and placed it on a peg that remained on one of the pillars. Her tattooed arms poked out from a sleeveless black dress begging to be noticed.

"Faye! You're here. Oh, this is so exciting!" Ruth overflowed with excited energy. Faye smiled at her aura which almost blinded her.

"I see." And she actually did.

"So, okay, one of the Haunters is doing the most amazing things."

"The spirits are?" Faye looked confused. She needed a minute to size up the situation. The amount of spiritual activity in the room intimidated her.

"They prefer the term, *Haunters.*" Ruth winked at Colby.

"Oh, well, that is new. I like it."

"She can stay." Colby smiled. Faye laughed, and Colby looked at her with confusion. Had she been heard?

"Someone in here likes me," Faye said.

"You can't see them?" Ruth asked.

"No. That's not really how Spirit manifests to me. I mostly hear things." Faye tuned her ears to the Haunters' sound, but stopped then and stared directly at Ruth with such intensity that Ruth felt a little uncomfortable. "But you can." Faye saw right through her. Her eyes said she knew everything and it both chilled and comforted. Ruth felt the burden of her secret lift from her shoulders. She thought she might be able to float away then, she felt light as air.

"Yes." Ruth's voice felt weak.

"Hmm... it's been a long time since you've had this gift, but you're tired of it," Faye continued.

"It can be pretty consuming."

"You don't want it," Faye agreed. "I had my time when it felt difficult too. But my Grandmother helps me through, she's my Spirit. Thank you, Spirit. I always thank her. She's my guide and it's very comforting. You have a relative too: a brother?"

Bryce's eyes widened. "Did you tell her that?" He asked Ruth.

"Oh, I see," Faye continued. "He's not the supportive type."

"I support," he responded with irritation.

"But you are full of emotion now," Faye turned her attention back to Ruth, "because they're all leaving. They found their path and they're leaving."

Cocking her head at the sharpest angle imaginable, she listened again. A penetrating eaves drop, so deep that she might comprehend the chirp of a single grasshopper in a giant meadow; like seriously intense.

"There's only two left." Faye's eyes opened in understanding.

"Maybe I should have brought you in when we were trying to save the building." Ruth realized suddenly.

"No one could have saved it," Faye sympathized.

Ruth frowned. She wondered if she'd asked Faye that question back when it mattered if it might have deterred her from trying.

"So your brother is still here... and his... girlfriend?"

"No!!" Bryce shouted.

"No... but it's someone who once held him in great affection. Someone with a *K* or a *Ka* sound... I'm not very good with names. Wow! I'm sensing some massive energy right here." Faye stood right in front of Colby.

Colby reached out and touched her on the face. She stroked it gently, with no malice, just a sort of idle curiosity. Faye took it well.

"That's Colby," Ruth said.

"Hello," Faye said to the air.

"She really can't see me?" Colby asked.

"Why would she?" Ruth questioned.

"I don't know. I can do live things now... I just thought maybe I was more visible."

"She's confused," Faye said.

"I think we all are. How is it that she can touch things? She never could before."

"I've heard of this happening. Anything can happen really. Spirit has all kinds of abilities that we can't understand."

"Haunters," Colby corrected.

"Ah, yes, sorry. Haunters. Thank you, Spirit," Faye apologized.

"So where does that leave us?" Ruth wondered.

"Us?" Faye looked at Ruth with confusion.

"Well, yeah. I mean what does it mean that Colby can do all this?"

"It doesn't mean anything. What I said before is still true. These people have to leave now. It's their time. So I guess what *you* have to do is... say goodbye."

"Wait. What?" Ruth didn't expect that at all.

"Ruth, honey." Faye searched her eyes and recognized a challenge. "Come here for a minute."

They sat in the two chairs that only ten minutes earlier, Colby lounged upon in comfort. Faye looked at the chair and smiled, feeling the Spirit signature on her butt cheeks.

"There is one certainty in this life," Faye started.

"Well, you can't say it's death, because look around. These people may be dead but they're still here, so what the fuck?"

"The certainty is that things end. True, we still feel and see the ones we love around us, but that doesn't mean they are really here. We have to let go of the things we can't have. Don't get me wrong, I firmly believe that we learn more about how to live our lives through talking with the dead, but you? Well, you're holding on tighter than anyone I've ever known and now it's starting to hold you back from living. I'm sure that your brother knows that and wants you to let go too."

"He doesn't," Colby said. "He's a selfish prick."

"Maybe not. But he needs to. Thank you, Spirit," Faye said in the direction she thought Bryce might be. As it turns out, she was exactly right.

"It's not that easy," Bryce countered.

"Yes it is," Faye responded. She turned to Ruth and said, "But, you can't be here."

"What do you mean?" Ruth asked.

"I can tell you right now that he's not going anywhere while you're still around. He's very attached to you... and this place."

Faye took a good look around again. Usually she spent a great deal of time grounding herself and finding the Spirits around her, but this place was so different. Though she knew there were only two, they had more presence than any she'd ever experienced before.

"Yeah, this is it." Faye heard something in the air speak to her. "It's definitely time for you to go."

"Are you talking to me or them?" Ruth was more confused than ever. She didn't know who to respond to any more.

"Everyone. Me. You. Just everyone." Faye shivered in the hot room, wiping away the goose pimples that formed. "Yep, that's what Spirit says. Thank you Spirit."

Ruth felt a sick panicked feeling settle over her. In all her haste to save the restaurant, she never allowed herself to think on failure and lose. She'd forgotten to prepare for this time to come.

"Come on," Faye stretched her hand out toward Ruth, "I'll help you."

"I can't just leave."

"Yes you can."

Bryce and Colby looked at the two women with confusion. On the one hand they didn't want Ruth to be left here all alone when they finally left, but also, her leaving before them made everything seem a bit too final.

"Don't leave me," Bryce whispered with more emotion than Colby thought him capable of. Ruth muffled her sobs into her hand.

"You can't stay. It's best this way," Faye said toward Bryce this time, sensing his resistance to letting his sister go.

Ruth let her sobs overcome her for a few minutes. She felt the calming effect that emotional outbursts sometimes allow. It swept through her long enough to expel the feelings she'd worn on her sleeve since the journey began and now, with them emptied, she thought she might finally be able to make a decision with sane rationality. Faye handed her a handkerchief. It glowed ghostly white in her hands and smelled like lilac. She noticed the embroidered blue rose on its corner and proceeded to swab her face off with it. A slightly freshened face, a heavy heart, and a deep sigh brought her around to face the situation head on, and she looked at her brother with new found strength.

"Don't do it," he pleaded.

"Bryce, I love you so much," she started.

"Please, don't," he continued.

"Faye's right. I have to go, so you can go."

"I'm afraid," he admitted.

"There's nothing to be afraid of," Faye assured him.

"Okay, that's annoying," Bryce said. Faye rolled her eyes at him.

"Colby will help you," Ruth promised.

"The hell I will."

"Colby." Ruth looked as though she wanted to send her to her room without dinner.

"Why should I help him? He's a jerk."

"Everyone deserves a second chance," Faye answered for her.

"Yeah, but do they deserve an eighth chance? Or ninth? Or tenth?"

"He's not that bad," Ruth defended.

The look on Colby's face spoke of her disbelief. To further annunciate her irritation with Bryce, she wandered over to a plastic cup long abandoned on the ground and hurled it through his form.

Faye laughed out loud. "I'm guessing that's a no?" she asked.

"Colby stop being such a baby. The sooner you two get going, the faster you'll see Tiny Tommy." Ruth couldn't understand why Colby was being so stubborn. It seemed simple enough.

"That's true," Colby whined.

"Are you ready?" Faye asked again.

"Yes, I'm ready," Ruth answered. She looked at Bryce who stopped verbally protesting and merely shook his head at her, pleading with his eyes instead. She sucked in her stomach and shook her head back, decision made.

"Goodbye Colby."

"Yeah, see ya." She waved half-heartedly.

Ruth didn't let it bother her, since she knew her real challenge would be her brother.

"Goodbye Bryce." Her voice did waiver, but she didn't allow her body to do the same. She continued on her path toward the door.

"Goodbye Ruth. I'll miss you." Bryce turned his back on his sister.

Ruth wanted to scream and shout and stay with her brother forever, but Faye led her out the door and around the building.

"Colby?" Bryce turned around to face her after a few minutes passed by in silence.

"What?" The curtness of her voice didn't affect him in his grief.

"Will you throw something for me?"

"Oh, I get it, now I'm just here to entertain you. Forget it."

"I'm really angry right now and all I want to do is pick up something really heavy and throw it as hard as I can. But I can't do that and you can."

"Oh."

She understood what he meant. A twinge of compassion ran through her and she looked around for something heavy. She found a hammer and threw it with all her might across the room, but it didn't quite satisfy the way she hoped. Bryce looked more defeated at the dull sounding thud. She looked for something more dramatic. This time she found a pile of thick nails. She took hold of them one by one and threw them like darts, right through Bryce's body. They stuck to the wall behind him in the pattern of a slightly crooked smiley face.

"Where did you learn to do that?"

"I used to play a little darts in my time." She shrugged her shoulders with humility.

"It looks like you were pretty good. Out of curiosity, what were you aiming for?" He noticed the darts landed a bit lower than he thought they would.

"You're balls."

"Did I really deserve seven darts to the balls?" He looked horrified. "Wait! Don't answer that."

Goodbye Already

"So?" Bryce asked.

"So?" Colby answered.

"Should we give it a try?"

"Are you trying to seduce me?" Colby flirted. Staying mad at Bryce was hard; she decided to let it go.

"I guess the darts worked; you're back to your old self."

"I'm not saying I want to get back together or anything, but I'd be willing to listen if you wanted to apologize for anything."

"Right. And what is it I'm supposed to be sorry for?" Bryce's sarcasm knew no bounds.

"Um, let's see... you treat me like I'm an idiot, you care more for yourself than anyone or anything else in this world, and you let my best friend disappear without telling me anything was even happening."

"Okay. May I respond?" He asked in a rather diplomatic manner.

"Please." She tried to be equally diplomatic in her manner.

"You are, I don't, and I didn't know."

Colby sighed deeply. Even now, with nothing to lose, he didn't offer an apology. What a waste of a perfectly legitimate crush.

"I should have picked the pervert," she mused aloud.

"What do you say?" He continued on without having heard her comment.

"About what?"

"Do you want to blow this place?" Bryce looked around the bar with contempt. He never wanted to leave a place more than at that moment.

"Oh, you mean right now?" Colby forgot that was the goal for the day.

"Yeah right now."

"Okay, sure." She hoped it didn't involve a lot of focus; she had no discipline when it came to such things. "What do we do?"

"I don't know. I thought you knew."

"I don't know."

"Oh great, I get stuck with you to figure this out." Bryce threw his hands up in defeat.

"You're the one that saw everyone disappear. What did they do?"

"Held hands, talked, focused and then poof... gone."

"Focused? Crap."

There they stood, staring at each other for over an hour and waiting for something to happen. It didn't.

"You're doing something wrong." Bryce began to lose patience after ten minutes By then he thought he might learn the nail trick and try it out on her.

"How do you know it's me?" If looks could call you an idiot, Bryce's look jeered much harsher terms her way. "Maybe we should be talking about the bad things we did, you know, like the game. Didn't someone say that the game was the key?" Colby asked.

"Oh yeah, that's right. They were all offering forgiveness to each other, I forgot," Bryce said.

"You forgot? We've been standing here for over an hour and you just now remembered the most important part of this whole thing? And I'm the idiot?"

"I forgive you for being annoying." Bryce smiled.

"I hate you."

"I forgive you for throwing nail darts at me."

"I still hate you, and by the way, you asked me to do that."

"I forgive Ruth for abandoning me... to you."

"It doesn't feel nice does it... being abandoned?" Colby spoke in a low voice.

"Now what are you talking about?"

"You know what I'm talking about."

"I know what I'm talking about."

"Well, that has nothing to do with what I'm talking about."

"For fucks sake, Colby... what the hell are you talking about?" Bryce's head started to swim, spin and twitter.

"Do I have to spell it out?"

"Apparently."

"C-l-e-m-something...." *Dammit, I suck at spelling,* Colby remembered.

"Clem? What is that?"

"Oh my darling, oh my darling, oh my darling?" She prompted in a voice that gave Bryce a headache.

"Clementine? " The answer rang flat, like Colby's croon.

"Bingo! Give the man a prize."

"What about her?"

"I want to know what happened."

"What happened with what?"

"Come on! I know something must have happened. You abandoned me all those years ago for that little floozy. I just want to know if it was worth it."

"Yes!" Bryce shouted unintentionally. "She was wonderful, bright, sexy, sweet and totally into me. So, yes, I'm sorry. I had a great time with her, okay?"

"If she was so freakin' perfect; then what happened to her?" Colby didn't think that she could feel any worse than she had a few hours ago when she discovered Tiny Tommy's disappearance, but she did.

"She disappeared. There was this intense light and weird sort of floating away thing - " Bryce cocked his head to one side as he relayed the story; suddenly realizing what he'd witnessed before.

"You are such a fucking idiot." Colby felt superior, really, really superior.

"Oh... right..." A note of understanding overtook Bryce's face. He refused to give Colby even a moment of satisfaction. The tiniest glimmer of smugness decorated her pudgy face and he wanted to squash it. He devoted every ounce of strength to getting the hell out of there and started to think on what needed to be done. Step one: forgiveness.

"I forgive myself for the accident," he mumbled.

"You should have done that a long time ago."

Colby's voice sounded squeaky, like that of a child. Bryce gave her a queer look in search of an explanation of the silly voice she used, only to catch her gaze down to a small child standing beside them.

"Hi Dad!" The squeaky voice continued. Bryce and Colby spent a few minutes doing double takes between each other and this new person that appeared out of nowhere. Neither of them knew exactly what to make of it.

"Are you calling me *Dad*?" Bryce finally asked.

"Yup." The boy smiled a familiar smile.

"And why are you doing that?"

"'Cause you're my Dad."

"I don't have any kids. I'm not a dad." Bryce spied the child with deep suspicion. He also spent a few minutes reviewing his sexual life and wondering if he'd broken a condom that he never found out about.

"You didn't actually have me. I'm the dead one from the accident," the boy explained.

"You're kind of big for a fetus," Colby remarked.

"Oh yeah, well, you see, that's the cool thing about dying when you're still in the womb. You get to choose whatever form you want. So, I picked this one. I don't know if you recognize me." He posed for his dad.

"Are you... me?" Bryce asked.

"No. God, the ego on this guy - I'm Marky Mark, when he was like 8, before he got that unfortunate cross-eyed look."

"Sweet." Colby tried to keep a firm hold of the situation instead of wondering if you could make an 8 year old your boyfriend when you're dead. With only three years on Tiny Tommy, this kid was super hot.

"Why are you here?" Colby asked.

"I'm here to help you."

"Hey, Bryce," Colby stated for the record, "Marky Mark, your dead son, is here to help us. Isn't that awesome."

"Shut up. This is not funny," Bryce said.

"Really, because I think it's fucking hilarious." Colby howled with laughter, which became contagious. Soon, Marky Mark started laughing along with her, leaving only Bryce to remain with a sour face.

"Your father has no sense of humor," Colby told the kid.

"Don't call me that," Bryce whined.

"See?"

"We have plenty of time to work on that." The kid put his hand through Bryce's and looked up at him with imploring eyes.

"So, what now?" Bryce felt his heartstrings tug a bit. It was a feeling he hadn't experienced in so long, he'd almost forgotten the power it had.

"We go." The answer was so simple that neither Colby nor Bryce probably could have thought of it themselves.

"Yeah, duh... we just go." Colby tried not to let any doubts cloud her sarcasm. Marky Mark shook his head at Colby in response to her negativity.

"Um... I'm sorry for killing you," Bryce said to the child, trying to rekindle the *forgiving spirit* they started earlier.

"That's not necessary anymore." Marky Mark smiled pitifully at his Dad.

"Well that's too bad," Colby stated. "It's pretty fun watching Bryce squirm through an apology."

Bryce gave Colby an off-handed look. The same look he always gave her and she'd grown to love. Verbally abusive and emotionally vacant men turned her on; it was a curse. "Why don't we have to do it?"

"I don't mean to toot my own horn, but I come straight from the source. I know the way back."

"Sweet! We get to take the express train!" Colby nodded her head with approval. She disliked work as a general rule.

"What do we do?"

"Each of you, grab a hand and we'll be on our way."

It suddenly occurred to Bryce that he could actually touch the boy. It'd been so long since he had contact with another that it jarred him. His son's grip felt warm and soothing; but the only thing that really mattered was that it *felt.* He chose not to dwell on the fact that the first touch he received since his death was the touch of his own dead son. He suddenly regretted his inability to let go of the past, else he might have found his son much sooner.

"Now, all you have to do is keep focused on your destination."

"Where is our destination? What's it like?" Colby couldn't wait to find out for herself.

"It's whatever you want it to be really. For me, there's a lot of puffy warm things."

"Ew, like the womb?" Colby shuttered to think of what a fetus might think of as Heaven: maxi-pads mattresses and blood clot pillows.

"Don't judge me," Marky Mark said. "What do you expect? I was a fucking fetus!"

"Well, apparently fetus's have a rather well-rounded vocabulary." Did that fetus just give her a look too? Like father, like fetus.

"Imagine what your perfect place might be and then just head to it. It's all rather simple."

"I wonder where Milton ended up?" Colby snickered.

"You're ruining this for me." Bryce spoke to her with closed eyes. The very image of Colby talking ruined his concentration, so he shut her out as best he could.

"Fine."

"Okay, no more talking." Marky Mark chastised them, as many others had before.

"Yeah shut up!" Bryce agreed.

"I was actually talking to both of you. Now, just imagine whatever you need to and then hold on tight." He didn't have much patience, for a fetus.

Colby took the hand as instructed, but her thoughts wavered almost immediately. How the hell was she supposed to know what her perfect place might be like? It might involve booze, oh, well who was she kidding? It would most certainly involve booze. Beyond that, who knew? She looked around the bar and felt sad that it was disappearing, for the first time. She really did like it there. If she weren't dead, she might stay there, on a bar stool, drinking her devils away, forever.

The light around them erupted into a blinding tunnel, the same tunnel they'd all been backing away from each time they saw it. She saw Marky Mark head toward it, up and away like a super hero. He pulled the two of them along with him.

Pretty strong for a little guy, Colby thought. But her mind turned back to the bar and the booze she still longed for. She watched Bryce and the boy continue on upward before she realized she had let go and remained behind. The light faded and the two Haunters motioned to her to follow before the light fully disappeared, but it was too late and all she could do was half-heartedly wave as they went on their way.

She hovered alone in Jules Maes.

"Crap!" She shouted into the ever darkening room. Did she detect an echo? Did her alcoholism really ruin her only chance at eternal peace? Were there any more nail darts around? She wandered around and collected every nail she could find and started playing darts. It kept her occupied through the night.

Reunion

Colby kicked the dirt around. It should have stained her foot red from the deep patina of the old brickwork, but she was still dead, so it had no effect. The joy of playing in the rubble hadn't worn on her yet, though weeks passed. She felt no fear or agony over the ever limited space she could spatially occupy. She just existed in a sort of bliss.

The construction guys lost interest in her after the first couple weeks of her taunting. She'd move their tools when they weren't looking or knock over their drinks. She'd steal their lunches and hide them away. Since the men were almost all Mexican workers, they'd come to regard her as *Lupe*. Frankly, Colby didn't care for the name. The men began to ignore her and now with the bulk of the building break down finished, only a skeleton crew remained to pick up the pieces.

Across the street at the old Rainier building that Colby remembered seeing torn down, the condos and office buildings gleamed new and bright. Undeterred by the noise of Boeing field or I-5 or Airport Way, the people came in droves for the cheap real estate. The face of Airport Way changed in a very short time. Phil Lester might be called a genius for quick building turn around. The neighbors didn't appear to be happy, but the businesses couldn't complain. With sales skyrocketing, Georgetown showed a profit it hadn't experienced since the time before Prohibition. Colby knew all this because the walls to the building no longer existed and now she heard everything that happened on the street. It amazed her how much business got done on the street, like the prostitution days of old.

"I guess I'll be gone soon," she said to the small pile of bones. Colby found that old rat corpse that rested between floors buried under some rubble and dug it out days prior. She carried it to a safe place and built a little shrine for her old friend. She named it Rudy. Rudy did not respond. He was the quiet type.

"I'm not really bothered by it, I guess." She shrugged her shoulders. Colby looked into Rudy's eye sockets for some understanding. She found some small black pebbles to place in the tiny holes and the effect made him seem a bit more friendly.

"Lupe!" Colby's head snapped around at the sound of her Mexican name. She'd moved some tools earlier in the day to a rather precarious spot, high up on the only remaining structure. It was no more than a shell of a wall, maybe six feet high. But she'd placed some rather expensive drills up there. She laughed as she watched the men try to grab it. Holding things from the clean-up crew comprised of a bunch of short guys, offered a lot of amusement - like watching midgets at a carnival.

"Good times," she chuckled.

"Don't you think that's a little immature?" The voice came from down by Rudy's head. Colby stared at her friend for a moment. She didn't know what was more shocking, the fact that her rat friend was speaking, the fact that her rat friend was speaking to her in a language that she could understand, or the fact that her rat friend did not enjoy her attempts at hide and seek humor with the living. It took Colby a few minutes to respond.

"No?"

"Well, your right! That was awesome! No wonder you're still down here." The voice sounded familiar to her. Colby let a glimmer of hope enter her heart.

"Tommy? Is that you?" Colby whispered.

A ghostly head popped out of the ground which she recognized immediately.

"Surprise!" Tiny Tommy smiled his shy smile. He looked into the pile of bones that his head hovered next to with suspicion. "Hello rat," he said.

"Tommy!! Oh my god! You came back!" She grabbed him by the head, lifted him from the ground and hugged him close.

"Easy. Watch the do." He giggled and hugged her back like they'd never hugged before, because they had, in fact, never done so.

"You're here, you're here, you're here!!" Colby chanted.

"What are you still doing here?" He halted her onslaught for a moment and pinned her down for some answers.

"I don't know. I just like it I guess."

"Don't you want to head up to where all the others are?"

"Do you really see any of them up there?"

"Yeah, Milton just had a BBQ yesterday. It was bomb."

"A barbeque? Milton? Naked, gross, perverted Milton hosted a barbeque in Heaven?" Colby stared intently at Tiny Tommy, waiting. It took about ten seconds for him to crack and the two just laughed together for a few minutes.

"That'd be funny though, right?"

"Yeah," Colby agreed clutching her side. "But just stay away from the wieners on the grill." More laughter.

"God, I missed you," Tiny Tommy said once he got his laughter under control.

"Me, too."

"What the hell? I've been waiting for you and you never came."

"I seem to remember someone leaving without me," Colby reminded him.

"Yeah, I'm sorry about that. But I sent Marky Mark down to help you. You didn't have to do anything, just hold on for the ride and you couldn't even do that."

"Are you judging me?"

"No, I'm just saying."

"'Cause it sounds like you're judging me."

"Well, I'm not."

"It just so happens that things are pretty cool down here for me right now, which you might have known if you'd waited long enough to say goodbye."

"Actually, I don't think that ever would have happened to you if I had said goodbye." His eyebrows rose to match her semi-hostile expression.

"How did you know?"

"I heard all about it, thank you very much."

"But still - it's pretty awesome."

"Show me."

Colby didn't hesitate to begin showing off. She showed him the old nail trick and how far she could throw things and how she could sit comfortably anywhere in the building, though it was much more comfortable when there had still been furniture. When the show ended, Tiny Tommy gave her a high-five. She eyed him curiously when he did so.

"You can do it too?" Colby didn't mean to sound disappointed.

"Yeah," he said. "Are you mad?"

"No, I mean, no. I just, you know, thought I was - "

"Special?"

"Kind of."

"Don't worry. Not everyone knows how to do the stuff we can do. So, it's still pretty cool."

He looked around at the dump left around the old spot that used to hold Jules Maes Saloon and shook his head.

"I can't believe it's all gone."

"I know. I've been here watching the whole time. It's pretty intense. The neighborhood kept protesting for a while."

"Did you see Ruth again?"

"She came by a couple times, but I just hid. I thought it might be too hard on her if she thought any of us were still here."

"That was decent of you." Tommy nodded his head in approval.

"I'm not always a shit head."

"That's not what I meant."

They sat together and stared at the piles of rubble for a while. It was a beautiful day, the sun shone bright despite the geography. The birds tried to chirp around them but were continually drowned out by the guttural sound of enormous engines speeding by only hundreds of feet above.

"Are you ready to leave all this?" Tommy motioned to the filth that surrounded them.

"What if I say no?" Colby asked.

"You want to stay here?"

"No, but I'm not really ready to go wherever it is we're supposed to. I really like it here on this plane, or whatever it is. I don't want to give up my gifts for some higher dull purpose. Is it really as much fun up there?"

"Well..." he started.

"Tommy, you're my friend, so I know you'll answer truthfully. Is the place on the other side of the tunnel anywhere near as fun?"

"No, it's not." Honesty felt good.

"Well, that's it then. I want to stay here." It was the simplest decision she'd ever made.

Tommy looked around again and wondered how it could remain so appealing to her, but he knew better than to argue. "If that's your decision and I can't change your mind, then I guess that's that." He gazed upward.

"Don't leave," she said. "Stay with me. It'll be so much fun."

"I don't want to stay right here."

"Okay, I understand that, but here's the thing. What if we could go somewhere else?"

"We can go somewhere else." He pointed upwards.

"No, I mean somewhere else, but here, like we are now."

"How is that possible?"

"We're different now. I've wandered outside the normal borders and found that the tunnel doesn't appear anymore. I think that I could go wherever I want now. I think I can just go. And if you can do all the things that I can, that means you can go, too." Colby's smile was wide and almost frightening.

"Really?"

“Um hum. Wanna come?” Colby held her hand out to her long lost friend and encouraged him to take it with her eyes. He looked at her for a long moment with indecision, but then the small crack of a smile appeared and she knew she had him. He grabbed her hand and the two twirled around in glee.

“Okay!”

They walked to the border and stood there for a long time, allowing the excitement of the moment to settle over them.

“Ready?” Colby asked.

“Ready.” Tommy said.

They each raised a foot, took a deep breath and stepped over the border and out into a new reality. Each step gave them more hope and it was right around the time they reached Lucille street, some three blocks away from Jules Maes that they began singing and laughing loud.

“Where are we going?” Tiny Tommy asked.

“Anywhere we want, Tommy. Anywhere we want.”

3530954

Made in the USA